THE SECRET SCROLLS

BOOK ONE

THE TRUTH SEEKERS

CALEB AND KATIE GARRAWAY

REMNANT

The Secret of the Lost Scrolls

Remnant Publishing
Copyright 2017 Caleb & Katie Garraway
ISBN: 0-9914963-8-8

REMNANT MINISTRIES
215 S. Marion Avenue
Washington, IA 52353

Remnant Ministries is a ministry sent out of the Marion Avenue Baptist Church. It is our passion that God would use our ministry to reignite a sacred fire in the hearts of His people to do their part in reaching this generation before it is too late. We believe that from the youngest to the oldest, it is our time to do our part in reaching our generation! God has not called us to be comfortable or complacent, but to be courageously committed. **Remnant Ministries** is God and Country in nature with a strong three-fold thrust: Redemption to the lost, Revival to the church, and Restoration to the country.

www.remnantministriesonline.com
calebgarraway@gmail.com
917.412.0059

Scripture quotations are from the Authorized King James Version.

PROLOGUE

Rome, Italy
_64 AD_

T he hot night air swarmed around the two hooded, cloaked figures as they kept to the shadows of the nearby stone structures. The full moon was high in the sky, but smoke and sparks billowed up, covering its luminescent light. Fire rampaged through the streets, catching building after building as if it were alive and seeking out its next meal. The fire started small at first but grew, and panic ensued. People rushed screaming from their houses, struggling to hold onto what few belongings they could carry. The flames had taken over nearly half the city by now and would devour it all by morning if not contained.

But the fire was not the only danger that night.

A decree went out, proclaimed from every street corner by the Roman commanders. Nero had ordered the arrest of all Christians, blaming them for the blaze. Roman soldiers shouted as they broke down front doors, scrambling to find the ones responsible.

The two hidden figures pressed their backs into the wall, letting the darkness conceal them as another squad of Romans strode by with their swords clanking by their sides, dragging men and women behind them. They screamed for mercy, but the soldiers were deaf to the sound. They marched on, faces set with their task, feeling no sympathy for those they hunted down.

One of the cloaked men, trembling from the cries, surged forward as if to help, but the other hastily pulled him back before he stepped out of the shadows, shaking his head. Once the Romans passed, they raced out into the street, ducking down another alleyway, and threw back their hoods, struggling to catch their breaths.

"We could have saved them, Stephanas!"

"No, we cannot risk being caught ourselves. God will help them, Timotheus. We are needed *elsewhere* tonight if we are to be successful in our mission. Come, we have little time." He drew his hood back over his head and checked the way was clear before he ran out into the street again.

Timotheus sadly agreed and followed his friend. The burlap bag on his back bounced with every step, a constant reminder of what they risked on this night. There was so much at stake if they were caught now. If they did not make it out later with what they would be carrying, he knew what the penalty would be and his heart beat even harder beneath his breast.

The sharp barking of dogs stilled their steps, and Stephanas shoved them into a nearby barn filled with livestock. They ducked in a pen with the sheep and waited.

"The dogs have found something. See what is in there!" a soldier yelled.

The door creaked open and Timotheus scrunched his eyes shut, waiting to be discovered amongst the stench of sheep and cows, cowering in the filth. They could hear the dog lightly growling and sniffing methodically. After a moment of silence, the beast whimpered as its master yanked on its chain.

"Just livestock. Keep moving!" The door shut and both men breathed out in relief.

"God surely is with us this night," Timotheus whispered.

"Yes, my friend. The Lord has led us this far; He will not fail us now."

The comrades snuck out the rear of the barn and ran toward a great stone building that stood guard over the entrance to the city aqueducts running below the streets. After they slipped quietly inside, the fire creeping ever closer to their location, Stephanas brought out a hand-drawn map of the underground system. He held it up to a nearby torch. He knew the underground passageways of this city better than most, having once been a military man himself. Each of the Empire's main cities had a network of aqueducts and sewers below its streets. Few knew these led to more important parts of the city, including the prison cells.

"Grab the light. We have little time and a long way to run!"

Timotheus stayed right on his heels as they found the stairs leading down and disappeared into the dark, dank tunnels. The stench was horrific, but Timotheus ignored it. His heart raced as fast as his shuffling feet. Closer, so close to their goal, and yet doubts plagued his mind. There was a great possibility they would be caught and even be killed. He gulped hard and pushed forward, unwilling to speak his doubts aloud. Shouts echoed down to them from above, but they pressed on, winding through the tunnels until Stephanas made a sharp right turn. The sound of dripping water faded away, replaced by utter silence. Fear gripped his chest, but Timotheus whispered a prayer for strength to see this through to the end.

"We are here!" Stephanas softly announced as they reached a wooden hatch in the stonework's ceiling. "Douse the light." Timotheus threw the torch back down the tunnel and it dimmed, skittering across the stones.

Stephanas placed a finger to his lips and gently lifted up the trapdoor. Through the crack, the men saw the warden of the prison sitting at a rickety table, his back to them. Shouts called out for aid and he complained loudly, grabbing his sword and whip as he made for the door.

"Can they not do anything right?" he muttered, passing so near the door on his way out, Timotheus feared they would surely be caught. But the warden moved on and once his steps faded away, they slipped through the door, hurrying to the table.

Timotheus kept watch while Stephanas flipped through the logbook, searching the scribble for a name, one name in particular. He placed his finger on the page with a smile of triumph. "There, this way!"

The men raced down a corridor, their sandals slapping hard on the stones beneath their feet. Men's faces appeared at the bars, some reaching out to these two strangers in the dimness, but they could not slow down, they could not stop. The fire would only rage for so long and they needed that time to escape.

When they turned a corner, Stephanas slowed and held out his arm to stop Timotheus.

"Guards up ahead," he whispered on a breath and they crept back down the corridor.

"What do we do?" Timotheus asked and chanced a glance. "They are coming this way."

"We do what we must, but no more." Stephanas looked down and found a rock the size of his hand. "As quietly as possible."

Timotheus nodded and readied himself for the attack. His heart pounded and his hands shook, but when the guards turned the corner, he leapt into action. Stephanas knocked the one in the head while Timotheus wrapped his arm around the other's neck, cutting off his air. He followed the man to the floor and waited for him to close his eyes and stop moving. Trembling, he climbed to his feet with the help of Stephanas, staring wide-eyed at what they had done.

"They are alive, but if we do not move, *we* will not be. Come!"

They continued down the corridor and finally came to a stop outside a cell in the very back. The flame light of torches in their sconces cast dancing shadows all over the walls. Stephanas placed his hands around the rough, wrought-iron bars and lowered his head in respect as he said, "Paul, we have come for you."

The man in the cell turned around and stared confused at the two disciples. "Do my eyes deceive me? What are you doing here?" Paul asked in surprise, as he reached through the bars to clasp hands with Stephanas and Timotheus.

The three men had been on many different paths together, leading them throughout the known world to spread the Word of God. Timotheus became as a son to Paul and though he was glad to see him, fear clutched at Paul's heart for this young man putting himself at risk. Stephanas stood firm and strong, always the soldier. He was once a very different man, a jailer of Philippi, but now Paul considered him family. His eyes darted behind them, but they remained alone.

"You should not have come," Paul told them. "You risk too much."

"We will risk everything for what we must protect," Stephanas argued. "We cannot breach this cell, not with so little time, but we can keep them safe for you."

Paul hung his head. "If they catch you, you will find yourselves here with me. Is that what you want?"

"You have endangered your life for the same cause, have you not?" Stephanas pointed out. "Old friend, please, we must keep those texts safe. You know this. We will not be caught, I promise you."

"You cannot predict the future, my friend," Paul chided with a gentle smile.

"No, but I have faith, as you have taught me to have. God will protect us. Please." He stretched out his hands.

Paul hesitated, but Timotheus stepped forward, reaching through the bars and resting his forehead against Paul's the best he could. "You have been as a father to me, aided me when I needed it. Lifted me up and showed me the way," he whispered. "For once, let me aid you. Let us do this, I beg of you."

A sigh slipped from his lips and Paul nodded, reluctance in his eyes. "Very well."

He turned from the bars and rushed to a darkened corner of the cell. He moved aside the rough mat on the floor which served as a bed and pried up a loose stone from the ground. Stephanas murmured to Timotheus to take the documents; he was going to stand watch. Those two guards would not stay passed out for long.

When Paul turned back to the bars, he carried in his hands animal skin scrolls filled with precious writing. "These three books, they *must* reach safety," Paul instructed as Timotheus opened the burlap sack from his back. "Protect them at all costs. The church of God needs them preserved. There is nothing more precious..."

"Yes," Timotheus calmly assured him and sealed up the bag. "Yes, I understand. We *will* succeed."

Paul held Timotheus' face in his hand and looked him in the eye. "Whatever happens, remember God is with you. Be safe, my son. And you as well, Stephanas," he said as the other man strode back to the cell. "You watch your back."

"If death comes for me, it will not be at my back," Stephanas growled and clasped Paul's arm. "May God be with you always, my friend."

"And you. Now go, quickly. If the Romans do not catch you, this raging fire may."

"A fire being blamed on us," Stephanas snapped angrily. "Nero. Any excuse to attack Christians."

"Do not tarry. You must leave," Paul urged. "Nero's day will come."

Timotheus slung the burlap sack over his body diagonally and felt a sharp pang in his heart as they backed away from the cell, but they could not stay. Stephanas was right; breaking Paul from his cell would take too long and the warden who held the only key was no longer in the prison. Paul remained at the bars until they reached the end of the corridor and the two men lost sight of their friend, locked away in this horrid place.

"You have them?" Stephanas asked.

"Yes, they are secure," Timotheus tapped the fastened strap across his chest. "Can you find us a way out of here?"

Stephanas nodded firmly. "Stay beside me, my brother. Our escape may not be as easy as our path in!"

They neared the two guards still unconscious on the floor, and Timotheus held his breath as they tiptoed around them. Once clear, they rushed down the corridor to retreat back through the hatch that led them into the tunnels. They were halfway there when a loud grunt sounded behind them.

"Halt! Stop them!" one of the guards groggily shouted, staggering to his feet and reaching for his sword. The prisoners began to jeer and chant, their hands beating the bars of their cells, eager to witness bloodshed.

"Run!" Stephanas yelled and they broke into a sprint, but the sound of a loud clanging bell drew more surprised shouting and the mad rush of steps as guards headed straight for them. Timotheus looked down the hall to see one of the guards pulling hard on a hemp rope attached to a bell. He turned to rush back that direction and stop the harsh ringing, but Stephanas grabbed hold of his cloak and tugged him down another corridor.

"It is too late! We go out the front!"

"We will be caught!" Timotheus argued as they ran.

"No, no, we will not. Go!" He shoved the younger man forward and covered their backs as Timotheus raced for the entrance to the prison. He burst through two metal doors, unlocked thankfully, and ran right into a courtyard. There were no guards, yet, but they would be upon them soon enough.

Behind him, Stephanas shut the doors and picked up a spear from a rack nearby, sliding it through the handles. "Hurry! That will not hold long."

Bodies bashed the doors from the other side and Timotheus jumped. Shouts for them to stop or face the consequences reached his ears, but Stephanas grabbed him again, pulling him across the courtyard to a readied chariot that the Romans used for patrols. They were too busy with the fire to pay attention to the alarm bell ringing from the prison, yet. Timotheus jumped in and flicked the reins as Stephanas hurried to open the gate. Once through, he jumped into the chariot and they raced away from the prison. The doors burst open a moment later and it was not long before Timotheus heard the thundering hooves and creaking wheels of more chariots giving chase.

"Head for the gates!" Stephanas ordered as he picked up the bow and the leather case of arrows left in the chariot. He fitted an arrow to the bowstring and waited.

Timotheus heard the guards yelling, but dared not take his eyes from his path. People filled the streets still, rushing to escape the fire, the Roman soldiers doing little to stop it or calm the masses.

Stephanas ignored the shouts and cries of those in need throughout the city. He closed his eyes, breathing in deeply and when he opened them again, his focus centered on the two chariots giving chase behind them. He drew back on the bow and loosed his first arrow. The shot hit one of the guards in the chariot and he fell off the back. He notched a second arrow and braced his feet as the chariot made a sharp right turn down another street.

"Stephanas!" Timotheus shouted, panicked.

They had turned down a street with a gate ahead. Romans hurried to close it, but Stephanas switched his aim and fired two quick shots past Timotheus' shoulder. The soldiers fell back with grunts of pain, arrows jutting from their chests between their armor plates, and the horses burst through the gate, not yet closed all the way. The chariot leaned to the side, threatening to spill them out, but Stephanas moved his body to the opposite side and it righted. Flames reached out, threatening to consume them as they drove down a street where the fire hungrily ate away at all in its path. The heat was incredible, making it hard to breath or see as sweat dripped down their faces.

Timotheus urged the horses on faster as arrows rained down on them from above. The Romans had taken up the chase, jumping from one rooftop to the next, shouting orders to stop them. Stephanas ducked low as an arrow came within a breath of his face. He drew back, aiming behind them to knock out those approaching much too closely for comfort. His fingers nimble, he loosed arrow after arrow on the men chasing them from above and behind. He struck the driver of a chariot still pursuing them and it careened out of control, smashing into a building. A second one following it barely made it around the crash, the man holding the reins pushing his horses on harder and faster.

Stephanas looked down and saw he was running low on arrows. *My next few shots will have to count.* The Romans kept pace with them overhead, but soon they would run out of rooftops and be forced to the ground. Wiping the sweat from his eyes, he pulled back on the bowstring, timing his shot just right when suddenly he felt a searing burst of pain. He looked down at the arrow that had just stricken him in the chest. Staggering from the hit, he grimaced in pain, but he could not fail Timotheus. *Not now.* He drew back, yelling with the pain overwhelming his body, and fired.

The arrow hit home in the chest of the second driver and the chariot failed to turn in time. The second man in it screamed as they crashed into one of the burning buildings lining the street. Stephanas sagged behind Timotheus, staring at the arrow sticking out of the right side of his chest.

"Timotheus," he rasped.

"Brother!" Timotheus yelled in a panic, but drove the chariot onward, heading down another street and away from the Romans. When they were out of sight, he pulled the horses to a stop, quickly unhooked them so they could flee the flames, and reached for Stephanas.

"You will make it," Timotheus said firmly as he gently hoisted his friend to his feet. "You *must* make it."

"If God wills, then so be it," he muttered, leaning on the younger man. "Break off the shaft."

"I cannot!"

"We will not be able to avoid detection if I am walking through the city streets with an arrow protruding from my chest," he stormed. "Break it, quickly."

Timotheus gripped the shaft of the arrow as Stephanas gritted his teeth. His stern face showed no sign of fear as his friend took a deep breath to try and calm his shaking hand. With one hard twist of his wrist, he snapped the shaft as close to Stephanas' body as he could. The man only made a minimal grunt of pain, but blood seeped from the wound. He reached around, but the point had not pierced through his back.

"We cannot leave this arrow in you for long, my friend," he warned, tossing the broken wood aside.

"Nothing can be done here. We must move, quickly. They will discover the chariot soon enough," Stephanas panted, still hearing shouts echoing in the distance among the crackle of flames.

Timotheus shoved his brown hair from his face and glanced up and down the street. "Which way? I have been turned around."

"Take us to the screaming voices."

"You wish to join the mob? We will be trampled!"

"No, we will disappear. Listen to me, Timotheus. We do not have time to debate this. We will not be safe until we escape the city."

Stephanas hung his head. *Oh God, I ask for strength.* When he straightened, he sensed a rush of urgency flow through his body. "Get us to the crowd first. We must disappear before we are caught and all of this is for nothing. If we move away from the fire and the crowd, the guards will spot us too easily."

Timotheus drew their hoods over their heads and, holding up Stephanas, began moving through the wreckage of the streets. He looked up, walking toward the flames and the cries for help. A few turns later and they came upon the main road. Roman soldiers corralled everyone together, funneling them toward the exit of the city.

"We may yet make it, my friend," he whispered to Stephanas.

"No, no, we will not. Stop!"

Up ahead, a guard from the prison was out of breath as he bent over, his visage twisted with rage. They watched his lips hastily move, barking out orders, as he waved his arm over the crowd of people who rushed to evacuate the city.

"They search for us," Stephanas warned. "We cannot leave this way."

Timotheus lifted his head, searching for a way out when he recognized the buildings on the next street. Pulling Stephanas with him, he slipped from the crowd now being checked by the Roman soldiers, and ducked down another street and another, winding through the back alleys of the city.

Each step took them farther from the burning flames and the Romans.

"Where do you lead us?" Stephanas asked, but his voice was weak.

"To safety, I hope," he replied. "The home of Amplias. I visited him with Paul some time ago. He lives near here."

"Do you trust him, even now?"

"Paul trusted him, and I trust Paul. We have no choice. We need to escape this city and he may be the only one who can help us."

Stephanas' legs gave out and Timotheus had to take more of his weight. When he glanced under his friend's hood, blood dotted his lips and his breathing was more labored than before, his skin pale and sickly.

Dear God, let him live. I cannot do this on my own, he prayed, moving as quickly as he could toward the house of one he hoped was still a friend.

When they reached the stone home on a much quieter street not yet being searched by the soldiers, Timotheus knocked on the door, doing his best to keep the sound muffled. "Amplias! Please, we are friends," he called quickly through the door. "Amplias!"

The door opened and Timotheus did not wait for an invitation before he dragged himself and Stephanas through. "Close it, hurry!" he said, throwing off his hood.

"Timotheus?" the white-haired man was startled, quickly shutting and latching the door. "What are you doing here? What has happened to this man?"

Stephanas sucked in a breath, but it rattled in his lungs. Blood covered his chest and when he coughed into his hand, his palm was filled with a dark crimson. "I am not long for this world, brethren. We must finish…what we started."

"You! They are after you," Amplias whispered, horrified. "Those guards shouting in the streets. You endanger me and my family by coming here!"

"We had no choice," Timotheus begged. "Please, Amplias, we need to escape the city." He quickly brought around the burlap sack that was strapped to his chest and opened it up to reveal its precious contents.

The old man looked down, immediately recognizing what they carried, and then glanced back up from one to the other. His gaze lingered on Stephanas. Amplias knew this injured man was not going to survive, but the younger one, he must escape. *I cannot fail them,* he pondered to himself; *I cannot fail my God.* He understood that their smuggled possessions were worth dying for.

"Come. I may know of a way, but it is dangerous," he informed them.

"Any path we take now is dangerous," Stephanas whispered as Amplias and Timotheus supported him between their bodies. He groaned in agony, but forced his eyes to remain open as they moved through the house and out to the courtyard in the back. Amplias set Timotheus to readying one of the horses, hooking it up to a merchant cart. Stephanas grabbed hold of Amplias' robe and pulled him close. "He must escape," he whispered. "He must. He carries with him the three books. They must make it out of this city. Swear to me."

Amplias covered Stephanas' hand with his own, nodding firmly. "Yes, my brother. I will do my best, but I can only get you both so far."

"Not me," he whispered, so Timotheus would not hear. "Timotheus. Only him. I will not last the night, but I will ensure his escape however I must."

Amplias' face darkened with sadness as he rested his hands on the man's shoulders. "Then I pray God is with you this night, friend. You have sacrificed much for us all. Come, we do not have much time. If the soldiers reach our street before we can get out, they will discover you."

Timotheus rejoined them, announcing that the cart was ready. He and Amplias assisted Stephanas in climbing into the back, each movement painfully jarring the arrow stuck in his body. Once he and Timotheus were up, Amplias covered them with hay and a heavy wool blanket.

"Do not make a sound," he warned, tucking the blanket around them.

The cart started to move a few moments later and Timotheus squinted, trying to peer through the fabric and hay, but could see nothing but the distant orange glow of the fire-lit darkness. He could not even smell anything for the strong scent of the hay surrounding them. Stephanas shifted and clamped down hard on his cheek to stop from screaming out in pain. His blood was warm against his body, making his cloak and shirt sticky with it. He closed his eyes, but when his mind drifted, he forced them wide open and listened to the creak of the cart, the roll of the wheels against the cobblestone, the subtle breathing of the young man next to him, and the neighing of the horse.

Through the hay, Timotheus reached out a hand and found his friend's. They could not speak, but Stephanas sensed Timotheus willing his strength into him. He knew, however, it was much too late for that. Stephanas had seen much of death and dying in his days before meeting Paul. He knew better than most when the end was near.

The cart eventually came to a stop in an even quieter part of the city. If Stephanas closed his eyes, he could imagine there was no fire rampaging through the city, no rush of people trying to escape the flames, and no Roman soldiers using it as an excuse to persecute the Christians.

"We are here," Amplias whispered, pulling off the wool blanket. "I do not believe we were spotted, but there are always patrols near here."

"Where are we?" Timotheus asked, sitting up and quickly climbing down from the cart.

"In the back of the former house of Aquila and Priscilla," he told them, looking around. "Where the church secretly meets. Very few know of its location."

They helped Stephanas from the cart and he fell into Timotheus, struggling to stand. Amplias gave him a worried gaze, but Stephanas shook his head and the old man sighed.

"This way," he beckoned. They walked from the courtyard behind the house to a room tucked away, one used for storage. Crates and jugs were stacked and shelved around them, freshly dusted. Amplias moved toward a rug in the center of the floor when shouts and barking of dogs suddenly pierced through the silence of the night.

"Check the houses! They came this way!" a man ordered. "Find them. Find them!!"

"A patrol," Amplias whispered, horrified. "How is it possible they saw us?"

"No matter," Stephanas said and pushed off Timotheus. "Show him the way out. Quickly!" Timotheus started to speak, but Amplias dragged him to the rug on the floor. He flipped it over, revealing a trapdoor set into the ground beneath it.

"Take this map," Amplias said, drawing it out of his robes. "It will lead you through the catacombs and take you outside the city walls. Do not lose your way down there, do you understand me?"

"Amplias, you must leave," Stephanas warned. "Forget your cart. Just run, quickly."

"May God be with you both," the elderly man whispered and without another word, hurried from the storage room and out another slim door behind the courtyard, slipping away into the shadows of the night.

Timotheus stared into the depths of the catacombs. "There are stairs," he told Stephanas.

"Find a torch." As the younger man dug through the storage shed to find anything he could use, Stephanas peered out of the doorway. The soldiers were close, very close now. He shrugged out of his cloak, tossing it aside in a bloody and ruined heap, revealing the short sword he had sheathed at his hip.

Firelight flickered to life behind him and he glanced heavenward for a moment before ducking back inside. "Lead the way," he ordered Timotheus. "I am right behind you."

Hefting the torch high with one hand and gripping the map in his other, Timotheus climbed down the shaky wooden steps and into the catacombs. No one would know of this trapdoor unless they had been here before. It was not an original entrance into the crypts. Timotheus would be safe.

Stephanas had to keep him safe.

"God go with you, my brother," he softly called down to Timotheus. "Remember what you do, you do for the good of us all!"

"Stephanas?" The young man whirled around; his eyes widened in disbelief before Stephanas shut the trap door and latched it. He pounded his fists against the door, but Stephanas refused to open it again. "*No!* We go together! I will not leave you behind! Open the door, I beg of you! Open this door!"

Cringing from the pain nearly unbearable now, Stephanas knelt at the door and said, "No, my friend. You must go. And may God grant you safety!"

He ignored Timotheus' yelling, replaced the rug and for good measure, shoved several crates around it the best he could. Praying his friend would take heed of his words and leave the city, Stephanas exited the storage room and left through the courtyard as a patrol of soldiers made ready to storm the house. They had not seen him yet, creeping out of the darkness. He drew his sword and dragged the point along the street, drawing their attention now.

"You have come for me!" he yelled. "Here I am."

"You dare draw a blade in the presence of the Emperor's men?" one of the soldiers yelled.

"I dare to do many things," Stephanas replied.

The soldiers moved down the street, away from the house, to surround him. The street was not very wide. Fighting them all would be difficult. If he had not already been wounded, he might have had a chance. Now, all that mattered was ensuring enough time for Timotheus to escape. As the soldiers finished circling in around him, banging their swords against their large shields, Stephanas closed his eyes, soaking up the moment. He lifted his sword to his lips, kissed the blade, and murmured, "*Father, into Thy hands I commend my spirit.*"

"Quit your praying, Christian," one of the soldiers scoffed. "No god will save you now."

Stephanas opened his eyes and smiled. "Nor you, my friend," he whispered and with a battle cry, he charged into the open arms of death.

CHAPTER I

London
Present Day

A dinging sound echoed through the airplane cabin and Drew Howard opened his eyes. He yawned, stretching the best he could without annoying the other passengers around him. He fingered through his short dark brown hair and checked his reflection briefly in the back of his cell phone case. His bright, blue eyes stared at him and he grinned crookedly.

"Seriously? We came here to spend spring break with Uncle James. I don't think he cares what your hair looks like!" his sister, Kaci, teased from beside him.

"Hey, we're in England. You never know who we might run into."

"Oh yes, we must look our best in case we bump into the Queen," she joked in her best British accent, still scribbling away in her beloved journal. She stopped a moment to roll her green eyes at him before gazing back at the pages before her.

Drew mouthed her words, mocking her, and she nudged him with her elbow. He knew many of his friends didn't get along with their sisters, but he and Kaci were basically twins.

Only one year separating them, they'd been close all their lives, partly because of their proximity in age but mostly because of their late father. Though he led a busy life, he had always spent as much time as he could with them, taking them to do exciting activities like zip-lining, spelunking, diving, and rock-climbing. He taught them how to be adventurous and trust in each other. Drew might never admit it aloud, but his little sister was his support system as he was hers.

The seatbelt light flashed again and the flight attendants took their seats.

"If I can have everyone's attention," the pilot's cheery, accented voice said over the intercom, "we will be landing shortly. Please be sure your seatbelts are securely fastened. Welcome to London."

"London," Kaci sighed excitedly. "Can't believe this is our first time here."

"Uncle James is busy, you know that."

"Yeah, just like dad often was," she said, frowning. "I miss him."

Drew squeezed her hand. "Me, too, but you know what Mom says. He's with us, always with us."

She smiled and nodded firmly at his words. Life had been hard since their dad died, for them and their mom. She was a busy lawyer, and when they lost their dad, it hit her just as hard. She buried herself in her work these days. One night, she broke down in front of her kids, fearing she was becoming a terrible mom. It was the first time they'd seen her this vulnerable since their dad had tragically passed, and they'd hugged it out like the close family they were. She told them it would take time for all of them to adjust. That was part of the reason she sent them to England to spend some time with their

Uncle James, her brother, and hopefully get to experience some adventure like the old days.

"You think she's really going to be alright without us?" Kaci asked worriedly, curling her long golden brown hair around her finger nervously. "She sometimes forgets to eat."

"Mrs. Thompson said she would look in on her." Drew gripped the arms of his seat as the plane descended. No matter how many times he flew, landing was always the worst part for him. He always had to look out the window to brace himself when the wheels were about to touch down on the tarmac. Kaci gently laid her hand on his forearm, and soon enough, they were taxing toward the sprawling airport.

"Thanks," he grinned sheepishly at her.

"Anytime, bro," she winked at him and then glanced out the window as well, eyes bright. "Hello, England!"

"What do you think we're going to do the whole time?" Drew asked as they waited to pull up to their terminal and disembark. "I hope Uncle James doesn't drag us around to museums every day."

"Mom said he had some fun activities planned for us."

"Yeah, like teaching you how to drive so she doesn't have to."

Kaci blanched. "No way, not here. They drive on the other side of the road. I can't do that!"

"I probably couldn't either, to be honest with you." He had earned his license a month ago and Kaci had her learner's permit. Their mom wasn't the best driver in the world, but it fell to her to teach her two kids. They both nearly gave her heart attacks every time.

"Maybe he has a pool?" Kaci asked hopefully.

Drew shrugged. "I guess we'll find out."

They unbuckled and exited the plane in the long line of other passengers. Once they were off the plane, they followed the stream of people to the baggage claim and waited for their suitcases. Kaci quickly spotted hers, a large bright orange one with a tropical floral print. Drew's was their dad's old duffel from his Army Ranger days. Luggage in hand, they moved through the airport and out to the main lobby.

"There he is!" Kaci exclaimed, pointing to a man holding up a sign. "D and K Monster Team," she read. "He's never going to let that go, is he?" she mumbled.

Drew burst out laughing. "Probably not." When they were little, they would act like monsters and try to terrorize the adults at family functions. Instead of scolding them as some of the other adults did, Uncle James would join in, usually giving them ideas based on stories of legends he heard in his travels. "Come on!"

They politely moved through the swarm of people, as a tall man with tortoiseshell glasses waved at them, brown hair with grey starting at the temples showing beneath his favorite ivy cap. He beamed at his niece and nephew as they burst through the crowd and hugged him.

"No, this can't be Kaci and Drew!" he laughed in his deep, accented voice. "You've changed a lot since last I saw you!"

"Hey, Uncle James!" Kaci said, bouncing in her canvas sneakers.

"Miss us?" Drew asked.

"Did I miss you? Now what kind of question is that?" He ruffled Drew's hair and kissed Kaci on top of the head. "I can't believe how big you both are! What does your mum feed you in the States, eh?"

James Alexander had not seen his niece and nephew for five years and in that time, they both shot up in height and were no longer the little kids he remembered. These were teenagers.

"We missed you at dad's funeral," Drew said, as he hugged his uncle.

"I wish I could have been there, buddy," he gave the boy's shoulders a squeeze. "I was on a dig in South Africa and could not get away. My prayers were with you, though," the man smiled.

"It's okay, Uncle James. We're just glad to get to spend time with you now!" Kaci said excitedly.

He draped one arm around each of their shoulders and led them out of the airport down the bustling sidewalk toward the old truck he'd had as long as the kids could remember. Uncle James lived far outside the city and a truck, he always told them, was a much more practical vehicle for the land he owned in the quiet, green English countryside.

"How was the flight?" he asked after their luggage was stowed in the bed and they climbed in the front seat.

"Not so bad. Drew slept through most of it," Kaci said.

"That's the smart way to pass the time," Uncle James agreed. "And your mum? How is she holding up?"

Drew and Kaci exchanged a worried glance. "She's hanging in there," Drew admitted.

"It's been rough for her, though. She's been keeping busy, taking on some pretty big cases," Kaci added.

James sighed and spoke under his breath, "Oh Susan, I told you not to work too hard."

"No, it's good for her," Drew insisted. "She needs it. We understand."

"You two are amazing kids, you know that?" he told them with a warm smile. "Now, I thought today you would like to look around Cambridge with me? Afterwards, we'll go out for some good old-fashioned fish and chips. I know of the best place. And then eventually we'll head back to the house, okay?"

The kids nodded excitedly, ready for their London adventure to begin.

◊ ◊ ◊

"I'm beat. I forgot how much energy you young people have," James said, taking off his ivy cap and swinging the front door open wide to let them all inside. "Welcome to my home."

Kaci gasped in surprise and Drew nodded in appreciation of the old mansion, all stone on the outside and immaculately carved woodwork on the inside. Their uncle told them to pick out whatever bedrooms they wanted and chuckled as they raced upstairs, bags in tow. He worried at first when his sister had called, saying she wanted him to take the kids for a couple of weeks. He spoke with her at length about it, but in the end he'd given in. She was doing a good job of hiding her emotions from her kids, but it was getting harder. Some time alone would let her grieve and spend some quality time with the Lord for the comfort and healing she needed.

James wished he'd been there more for her, but worse still, wished he had gone with David, his brother-in-law, when he said he was going off to that new dig. James accompanied him at times, his linguistical genius coming in handy at archeological digs. David was an engineer, but he worked on excavating dig sites, finding new ways to get around unburied structures and statues while doing minimal damage to them. He was good at his job, but one day he just disappeared. The crew he was with said he died in a terrible accident, but no body was ever recovered.

"Mr. Alexander, I trust your niece and nephew are settling in well?" Simmons, his butler and friend, asked as he approached from the right wing of the home. The old man walked spryly for his age with the step of an old-fashioned maître d'; he beamed up the stairs at the sound of laughter. "Ah. Nothing quite like the laughter of excited children, is there, sir?"

"They do seem glad to be here."

"Simmons!" Kaci yelled, bolting down the stairs. "We've heard a lot about you!"

"All good things, I hope," he chuckled. "And how old might you children be?"

"I'm 15 and Drew's 16. I have my learner's permit," Kaci proudly announced.

"Good Heavens, save us all," he joked. "You going to have your uncle teach you how to drive?"

Kaci and James shook their heads at the same time and they all burst out laughing. A phone rang down the hall and Simmons excused himself to go answer it as Drew was coming down the steps.

"Nice pool, Uncle James."

He grinned. "Feel free to use it at your leisure. You two can go anywhere you like in the house."

"Mr. Alexander? Call for you!" Simmons spoke from the hall.

"I'll take it in the study," he replied, winking at his niece and nephew. "Want to see your uncle's office?" As he turned to head into the next room, they followed close behind. Their excited murmurings relieved him. They had the same curiosity and love for knowledge as he and their dad had shared. David, an American, had come to England for university and became fast friends with James, a couple years his senior.

Eventually, David and Susan had fallen in love and moved back to the states soon after they were married, now almost 20 years ago. The two mens' love for adventure and the pursuit of knowledge had bonded them as brothers back then and lasted to this day. James sighed sadly and then picked up the phone while the kids explored his office.

Kaci nudged Drew, pointing to the wall of photographs from all over the globe. Most were of ancient ruins, deserts, dig sites, jungles. So many places, Kaci couldn't even begin to imagine where he'd gone to take such amazing pictures. He'd explored almost the whole world over and she longed to do the same, as did her brother. It had always been their dream to join their dad on one of his digs.

But then he was gone. Sadly, she realized the dream had died with him.

She ran her fingers over the old leather-bound books filling the wall of shelves, some of the titles in languages she didn't recognize. She came to an entire row of Bibles, old and new, along with commentaries and Old Testaments in Hebrew and New Testaments in Greek.

Drew was engrossed in a map hanging from the opposite wall, tracing his fingers along the strings attached to pins, placed there by his uncle. He recognized a few markings scribbled on the large map, hovering around a particular focal point in South America. He called his sister over.

"Those symbols are from World War II, aren't they?" he whispered, giving her a strange look.

Her brow furrowed slightly. "Yes...and it also looks like he wrote the word *'Paititi'* with a question mark over here," she tapped her finger at another spot circled on the map in the same continent.

"Hmmm. Wonder what that could mean?"

Drew turned his ear when Alexander's voice turned deeper and he spoke quickly. When he turned around, his uncle was jotting notes on a pad of paper, nodding.

"Who was that, Uncle James?" Drew asked after the man returned the antique phone to its cradle.

"That, my boy, was the start of a new adventure," he mused, looking down at his notes. "I know you both wanted to spend your spring break relaxing by the pool and being lazy." He moved around to the front of his desk, sitting on the edge.

"Unfortunately," he peered at them over the top rim of his glasses, slowly letting a lopsided grin spread across his face, "I may need your assistance."

Kaci and Drew shared a glance then nodded. "What is it?" she asked.

"That was a friend who works with the archeology department at Cambridge. From what I gathered through his excited chatter, they just discovered a half dozen or so second century sarcophagi underneath the ruins of an old cathedral." He paused for dramatic effect, grinning widely when both kids leaned in. "They came across something unique inside one of them, and they want my help understanding what it is they've found. Interested?"

Kaci jumped up and down as Drew rubbed his hands together. "I'm so in," he said.

"Good. Keep your bags packed, my monsters. We are going to Spain first thing in the morning."

He turned around to gather papers off his desk and turned back to see them high-fiving and cheering silently behind him. When they noticed him watching, all three burst out laughing.

Yes, this is going to be good for all of us, James decided. He would call his sister in the morning and then be off to Spain. His mind raced the remainder of the evening with what his friend said they had discovered. He hardly dared believe it, but he wouldn't know until he saw them with his own eyes.

CHAPTER II

Alexander breathed in the fresh air and let out a deep sigh of relief. He grinned to himself. After so many years of traveling to different sites around the world, he would have thought his dislike of airplanes would have disappeared, but it was alive and well. The cramped spaces and the lack of fresh air still bothered him. Having his niece and nephew along with him this time made the flight more tolerable than usual at least.

He spent the hours of the flight filling them in on what he knew of the church they were going to see. They were always so inquisitive, Kaci and Drew, just as their father had been. Alexander frowned until a hand suddenly grabbed his arm.

"Uncle James?" Kaci asked. "You ok?"

"Yes, perfectly fine," he assured her with a grin.

Santiago, his old college friend who had called him about the find, was to meet them at the airport. As they exited the terminal, Alexander used his great height to peer over the crowd before him. "Do you remember what I said about the church we're going to today?" he asked as he quickly led the three of them through the masses of travelers.

He glanced behind him when neither of them responded and chuckled to see their eyes wide and filled with amazement and wonder at the structures around them. Old stone buildings with impeccable Romanesque architecture surrounded them.

"Earth to monsters?" he teased and Drew laughed.

"Sorry. Right, the church," he said. "It was built over the foundations of one of the first churches."

"Established by..." Alexander hinted. "Kaci?"

"By the Apostle Paul on his fifth missionary journey, according to history, right?"

Alexander waved over his head when he spied his friend. "Yes, you are correct! Now I would like you both to meet a very good chum of mine, Santiago Azul." He made it past the last few people before him and clasped hands with his large amiable friend.

"Alexander! This is what it takes for you to visit me, my friend?" Santiago said as he shook Alexander's hand heartily. "What has it been now? Five years?" He scratched his head, covered in dark curly hair.

"Six, sadly," Alexander sighed. "I do wish I could've visited sooner."

Santiago waved away his comment. "You are a busy man, much like myself." He spied Kaci and Drew behind Alexander and offered them a bow with a flourish of his hand. "And these must be your monsters I've heard so much about."

Kaci offered him her hand and he politely kissed the back of it. He started to do the same to Drew, but then burst out laughing and shook it. Drew joined him after the look of confusion left his face.

"Come friends. My car is waiting just there."

Santiago led them down the street bustling with cars and taxis, people rushing every which way. Kaci and Drew spun in circles, chatting excitedly about their new surroundings. Their dad had been to Spain a few times and brought back pictures, but he never got the chance to bring them there himself. Alexander hoped there would be time for his friend to give them a decent tour of Seville before they had to fly back to the UK.

Once they were piled in his SUV, Santiago drove them through the busy city streets toward a part still mostly dominated by older buildings, many in the process of being renovated.

"The cathedral was in the middle of being torn down, oddly enough," Santiago explained, driving with one hand and weaving in and out of cars so fast it had Alexander gripping the door handle. His niece and nephew laughed silently behind him, having the time of their lives. "Quite providential, otherwise we may never have made this discovery."

"What exactly is so exciting about these sarcophagi that you wouldn't tell me about over the phone?" Alexander asked, gritting his teeth as they took a turn rather quickly.

Santiago laughed cheerfully. "Ah, my friend, always so impatient."

"I am not impatient. Merely curious as to what has the great Santiago so fascinated."

"You know," he said, leaning over the center console even as he drove, "patience is a virtue."

"Says the man speeding through the streets," Alexander replied, no longer able to contain himself, and his friend laughed even louder. The professor had to laugh with him, the sound infectious, but then they took another sharp turn making the tires slightly squeal and he was back to praying quietly under his breath.

Santiago made another turn and then another before he finally slowed and they pulled up outside a large cathedral dating back hundreds of centuries. "When they were working," he explained as he turned off the vehicle and Kaci and Drew peered between the front seats, "a large piece of machinery toppled over. Wham!" he yelled, slamming his palms together and making them all jump. Alexander grumbled while the kids laughed behind their hands. "Fell right through the wall of the cellar."

"What was on the other side?" Drew asked anxiously.

"Ah, my young friend, mystery was on the other side. A spiral brick staircase and at the bottom," he said, lowering his voice to an eerie pitch, "a tomb of the dead."

"Sweet," Drew breathed and Kaci nodded right along with him.

"If you two have nightmares later, you can blame Santiago," Alexander teased and climbed out of the vehicle. He stretched his tall frame, leaning back to take in the full majesty of the cathedral standing tall and proud before them, despite its obvious aging over the years.

Out of the three spires stretching toward the heavens, only the far left one remained intact. The other two had crumbled and fallen inside the cathedral. The stone was weathered and chipped around the corners, while many of the immaculate stain glass windows were missing pieces, a few gone altogether. The colors were brilliant in the early afternoon sunshine and Alexander couldn't wait to step inside and see the bright colors reflecting along the walls.

"It's beautiful," Kaci said in awe.

"Wait until you see the inside," Santiago informed them. "She may be rough around the edges, but this old building has quite a few stories to tell."

They followed Santiago up the broken and uneven stone steps leading to two large doors. They were wooden, carved with intricate details and wrought iron pieces inlaid along the designs. Santiago pushed them open and they creaked eerily on their old hinges, rust flakes falling to the ground as the group moved past him and inside. Kaci and Drew hurried in, spinning in circles to capture every detail of the interior.

From the stale air they breathed, it was clear the cathedral had been abandoned. A strange smell hung about, not a bad smell but old, and the dust tickled Kaci's nose. She rubbed away a sneeze, pacing farther inside. The stained-glass images showed various scenes from the Bible, but they weren't even the best part. More intricate stone carvings surrounded them on all sides, angels and demons, saints, and some of the most beautiful crosses she had ever laid eyes on. She moved forward, not watching where she was walking, and Drew caught her arm.

"Careful," he whispered.

Broken pews were scattered around and she'd nearly run right into one. Old songbooks littered the ground and each step they took sent more plumes of dust into the air.

"It's so quiet," she said to Drew.

He nodded frowning. "Like a weird quiet, too." He reached out a hand as if to touch the strange muffled silence filling the room, but someone's clapping hands startled them both. With a yelp, they jumped and turned to see Santiago beaming and Alexander laughing.

"Ready to see the best part? The team from Cambridge is downstairs. Come, come," Santiago urged and hurried through the cathedral. He disappeared through a skinny doorway to the right of where an old stone altar stood, covered in layers of dust and dirt. His steps echoed loudly as he clambered down a set of stairs. "This was the old cellar," he explained when they joined him in the dimly lit room. "And you can clearly see where the machinery hit the wall."

Alexander walked over, running his hands along the stones and peering into the spiral staircase that had been hidden for centuries. "Fascinating."

"Quite, but that is only the staircase. I'm certain what you're looking for is farther in."

Excited at what he was called here to see, Alexander passed through the giant hole in the wall and carefully made his way down and around the ancient spiral staircase. An old rope was attached to the right side to use as a makeshift handrail, and he held on tight. Slipping and breaking his neck was not part of his plans for the day. Santiago had told him over the phone the Cambridge archaeology team had been invited and was already processing the tomb, which begged the question of what they found that Santiago would think would require Alexander's expertise.

At the bottom of the stairs they came to a small room and a single exit leading off. "A tunnel?" he asked surprised as Santiago and the kids joined him. "How did they find this?"

"Air," Santiago explained. "The team cleared out the few pieces of old artwork stashed here and about, but there was a strange gust of air they could not find the source of." He walked to the opening and pointed to an old sconce on the wall. "Secret passage. This part of the wall slid away. It became stuck halfway and they had to break it down so they could get through."

"But the mechanism worked for the most part? After all these years?"

"Interesting, is it not?" Santiago chuckled and took the lead again. "We are nearly there, friends, nearly there."

"This leads to the tomb?" Drew asked, his words bouncing off the stone tunnel around them.

The musty air was damp and dank. Kaci ran her hand along the wall, but pulled it back when ice-cold water met her fingertips. "Are we beneath water?"

"We are in fact very close to a river, yes," Santiago replied. "The crypt itself has a small stream running through its center, two drains, one at either end. We assume it was built this way to prevent it from flooding."

It grew brighter as they neared the end of the tunnel and Alexander blinked against the bright spotlights set up near the exit of the tunnel and surrounding the crypt. He tilted his head back to see the painted walls, faded over time, but extremely well preserved. The murals were hard to make out, but several faces stared back at him, leading up to the vaulted ceiling above. Kaci and Drew followed him and he grinned to hear their excited whispering.

"This is all extremely beautiful," Alexander told Santiago as his friend stepped up beside him.

"You have yet to see the best part." He nodded toward the team of men and women working around seven large stone tombs built into the floor of the crypt. "These are not just any dead men."

"Who would be buried here?"

Santiago leaned in closer as he whispered, "Church leaders from the second century perhaps?"

Alexander's jaw dropped as he shook his head. "You're not serious."

"Look for yourself."

Alexander glanced at his niece and nephew, watching him closely, and then hurried to the first sarcophagus. Each one had been pried open and the archaeological team paused their work as they watched the well-known professor peer into the first one. Bones stared back at him, any clothing worn by the man broken down and lying at the bottom of the sarcophagus. Alexander's fingers closed over the edge as the musty air filtering out of the tiny space hit his nose. The bones were in amazing condition, including the skull that seemed to smile back at him.

"Are they all like this?" he asked and waved for Kaci and Drew to join him.

"Six of them," Santiago explained, walking around the other side of the sarcophagus.

"Wow," Drew whispered. "It looks almost perfect."

"And dead," Kaci added with a shudder. "Very dead." She leaned over the edge as Drew reached around behind her back and when she was a little closer, he grabbed her arm and yelled. She squealed and jumped, smacking him on the arm as he cackled. She was laughing, too and Alexander rolled his eyes.

"Am I going to have to worry about you two?" he asked with a half-smile as Santiago grinned.

"No, Uncle James," Kaci muttered and shoved her brother playfully again.

"You said six," Alexander said, getting back to why he was brought here. "But you said there were seven found."

Santiago nodded. He stepped aside and Alexander spied the sarcophagus set up on a pedestal above the rest. Carvings were etched into the stone, but they were hard to make out. The plain stone lid was set to the side, no markings or indications of any kind to explain who this man was and why he was set above the others. He saw the table set up to the right of the platform and noted the papyrus laid out on it. Alexander frowned. As he leaned over to see into this sarcophagus, his frown deepened.

"He was mummified?" he asked surprised.

"Yes," a man stepped forward and held out his hand. "Antonio Vargas. I'm in charge of supervising this project. It is a pleasure to meet you, Professor. I have heard much about you."

Alexander shook the man's hand, but he was so focused on the mummified corpse, nodding was all he managed to do. "You've removed most of the wrappings already?"

"We have."

"Mummified? I thought only Egyptians mummified their dead?" Kaci asked.

Alexander peered at the bodies and the few bits of scraps covering the skeleton still. "This is a different kind of mummification, a poor man's way. Do you know what this is?" he asked and pointed to a scrap of papyrus on the body.

Drew and Kaci moved closer to examine it, but both shook their heads.

"Instead of linen, they would use discarded papyrus. Think of it as using old newspaper instead of fancy tissue paper," he explained. "It was essentially made into a paper mache of sorts and wrapped around the corpse. If they took the time to do this, that means whoever was laid to rest here was of great importance to these other six men, or at least that is what I would assume."

Santiago's smile only grew wider. "The team has spent all yesterday and this morning removing the wrappings, piece by piece, using soap and water."

"And?" Alexander urged.

"Look for yourself."

The team stood close by the table as Alexander made his way there next, not wanting to leave this curious mummified body yet, but still being drawn in by the scraps. He looked at each piece laid out before him, ready to tell his friend there was nothing special about them, but then he looked closer and his eyes narrowed. He set his glasses atop his head and leaned over the table, squinting at one of the pieces.

"Are those...those are words," he whispered.

"That they are," Santiago agreed. "On every piece. Words, and a few have whole sentences. The team has been working at piecing them together, but unfortunately, none of us is familiar with this ancient form of Latin. I hoped you would have a way to help us read these better?"

Alexander reached out for a pair of latex gloves from a box nearby and gingerly picked a piece up. "My kit, it's in the vehicle. If you don't mind?" He glanced at Antonio.

"Please, by all means. We are as curious as you are to understand this incredible find." He graciously asked one of the junior team members to hurry to Santiago's car and retrieve Alexander's kit. After she was told where it was in his suitcase, she hurried away, Santiago's keys jingling in her hand. "What do you believe it could be?" Antonio leaned in.

"Religious text of some kind?" Alexander mused.

Kaci and Drew stood on either side of him as he set the first piece down and examined another. "It's hardly legible," Kaci murmured. "Just gray smudges. How are you going to read it?"

"Carefully," he replied. "Very, very carefully."

As it did with every new find, Alexander's heart pounded in his chest and though he did not show it, he was giddy with what the team here uncovered. If these men were church leaders, these could very well be bits of Scripture written on the papyrus, but he had never seen such a thing outside of ancient Egypt and the surrounding region. They were in Spain. His interest was beyond piqued and when the woman returned with his kit, he instructed Drew on what to do.

"Open the kit," he said and Drew set it on a clear space on the table, unzipping the black canvas binder-like case. "There is a small container of white colored paste and that brush there. Open the paste for me, please, and set it down."

Drew did as asked and handed Alexander the brush. Once the papyrus was back on the table, he ever so gently brushed the paste across the surface. The room held a collective breath, as did Alexander. One wrong move, and he could destroy this potentially valuable piece of history.

"Will it work?" Kaci whispered.

"I would like to say it is guaranteed," Alexander replied, "however, there is a chance it will fail. Fingers crossed that it won't."

Antonio mumbled under his breath and Alexander was certain the man was praying. Santiago's hands were clasped behind his back and he stared intently at the papyrus as did the rest of the team. Once the entire scrap was lightly covered, Alexander set the brush down and waited, watching the time on his wristwatch.

"What is it doing?" Drew asked.

"Right now, the paste is reacting with the ink, soaking into it. If it works, it will convert the ink into a clear, invisible substance that we will be able to see with a little extra help."

As the time drew closer, he told Drew to pull out the small handheld UV light from his kit.

"And the answer is…" His voice trailed off as he flipped the switch on the light and moved it over the papyrus.

"It worked!" Antonio announced excitedly. "It worked!" He gibbered in Spanish and Alexander let out a sigh of relief. "Please, can you do them all?"

Alexander turned off the light and handed it back to Drew. "It will take time, but yes." He asked a few of the team members if they could help him while Santiago offered to take Kaci and Drew around the crypt so they could explore it further.

Kaci and Drew walked to the other six sarcophagi, peering inside to check out the decrepit bones and the decaying clothes that remained. "Did they hide this crypt on purpose?" she asked.

"We are unsure," Santiago replied. "It is possible, but until we know more, it is hard to say why or how these men came to be down here. We know from the lids of the six sarcophagi that they were church leaders, but there are no names carved on any stone."

"And the faces?" Drew leaned back so he could examine the murals again. "Why decorate the walls like this?"

"The cathedral above was built over the foundations of another one. It is possible this was not blocked off originally or meant to be hidden. Those of faith may have visited this often, as we would go to a cemetery to visit a loved one's grave," Santiago said, admiring the murals with a smile. "Such intricate artwork is amazing for that century. It would have taken a very long time to paint so much detail."

"And now it's all faded away," Kaci said sadly. "Will you try to restore it?"

"After this find, all I know for certain is this cathedral and everything beneath it can no longer be destroyed for a strip mall," Santiago said with a laugh. "They may try to restore it, or they may salvage what they can and transport it to a museum."

Kaci and Drew walked around the crypt, hopping over the canal with a trickle of water steadily flowing down the center. They wondered about where it led and if there were any other tunnels stretching out from this room. Their musings kept them occupied for the following hour, as they made up stories of who these men were and why they were buried in such an intricate tomb. Each tale became more elaborate than the next. They were in the midst of creating a story where each of these men was a part of a clandestine Christian group within the underground church when Alexander lifted his hand over his head.

"We have them, or at least most of them," he announced and the kids, along with Santiago, hurried to rejoin him. "It will take several more hours to do every scrap, but for now, I think we have enough to begin our investigation."

"What do they say?" Drew asked.

"It's certainly an interesting combination of texts," Alexander said, motioning to the way they sorted the papyrus. "These pieces hold references to Homer and Aristotle's works, but then these over here, these are extremely interesting. They contain religious texts of church history, parts of books I've never heard of."

"Surely, you're joking," Santiago said laughing, but stopped when Alexander shook his head. "You have not heard of them? How is that possible?"

He tapped his fingers on the table, staring intently at the pieces. "We have tremendous amounts of testimonies between 30 and 70 A.D., but then it's as if everyone involved in the church suddenly vanished. The church flourished, but there are no texts, no writings of any kind, at least none that we have found. No actual written histories of those missing years." He smiled softly as he added, "I've always called those the 'lost years.' There are rumors of course, of stories being passed by word of mouth from one generation to the next, but no one found any writings to prove said rumors...until now."

Santiago and Antonio glanced from the papyrus to Alexander and back again.

"How do you know this for certain?" Santiago asked.

"Always the skeptic," Alexander teased. "But that's good. Some of these lines, they're found within the volumes of the 'Ecclesiastical History' by Eusebius of Caesarea. His words were the only ones we had and we assumed they were not very widespread since they were the only ones we found. These writings, they tell of Thaddeus preaching the Gospel in Edessa and other journeys of the apostles. It seems they confirm that the stories passed down through the generations were indeed true!" Alexander wanted more time with these pieces so he could fully dissect each word and understand what these writings were doing wrapped around this dead man's body. "You have certainly found something, my friend."

Santiago beamed. "I told you, did I not?"

"There are more layers on the body," Antonio said. "Shall we remove them next?"

Kaci and Drew watched from the sidelines, not wanting to get in the way and content with watching the process of the team and their uncle working at removing the next layer of papyrus. Kaci wondered what their dad had done when he helped with digs and sites and wished more than anything they had been able to watch him at work, just once. His passion for history rivaled their uncle's and made her even more resolved about what she wanted to do with her life.

"That could be us one day," she told Drew quietly.

"You want to hang around dead bodies for a living?" he asked with a surprised look.

"Maybe not bodies, but digging up the past? Discovering lost pieces of history? Doing what Dad did. You don't think we could do it?"

"I think we could definitely do it," he told her. "I just wish Dad was alive to do it with us."

"Me too." She fiddled with the hem of her shirt. "Do you ever think about the chance that he's not dead? That maybe they were wrong and he's out there somewhere, trying to get home?"

Drew shrugged and Kaci wanted to kick herself for bringing up their dad. The loss was hard for her, but she knew it was twice as hard for Drew. He looked up to their father and wanted to be just like him. They'd been so close and then when he didn't come home, she thought it would break her brother.

"I dream all the time about him walking in the front door," he admitted. "But we can't move on with our lives if we keep holding onto the past. What do you think Dad would want us to do?"

"Move on with our lives," Kaci sighed. "And not let Mom work too hard."

"We'll work on that one when we get back home."

She nodded in agreement and they fell silent, watching the team work meticulously around the dead body. Kaci was wondering how many more layers were left to find when Alexander held up his hand.

"Wait. Wait, what is that?"

Kaci and Drew moved closer, standing on their toes trying to see.

"That is not papyrus," Santiago whispered. "Animal skin?"

"Wrapped around the chest cavity," Alexander said as he reached in and carefully pulled the tanned piece of material out of the sarcophagus. Santiago reached out and held up the other end and together, the men moved it to a spot on the table, hastily cleared away by the team. They laid it flat and carefully pressed down the edges. "There's writing on this, as well!"

"That close to the heart, they hoped to keep it safe," Santiago said. "What do you think it says?"

Alexander's eyes narrowed as he leaned over the table, picking at the edge of the skin. "There's something here."

As everyone watched with bated breath, Alexander separated a piece of parchment from the animal skin. Santiago moved around the table, holding down the skin as Alexander separated one from the other. He flipped it over and frowned at the gray smudges.

"Drew?"

His nephew hurried over to open the paste again and hand the soft brush to his uncle. Alexander repeated the process he used on the papyrus, and counted down the minutes for the ancient ink to soak up the paste. When enough time passed, he asked Drew to turn on the UV light and hold it over the parchment.

Alexander's eyes moved over the ancient text as he began to share with the rest of the room what was written. "Let me word this in our modern vernacular; here's a fairly accurate translation: *'I, Mikhos, am the son of Symeon, who was a preacher boy of Timotheus. After Timotheus perished at the hands of the pagans, I witnessed my father and his brethren bury our pastor, along with three sacred parchments, smuggled...out during the...great fire in...Rome.'*" He lifted his head at the words and met the wide eyes of his niece and nephew. "Great fire in Rome?" Kaci asked.

"I remember learning about that in school. Happened in 64 A.D." Drew said with his eyes locked onto the parchment. The message from the past seemed to leap off of the page at him. He smiled as some of the archeologists raised their brow toward him in curiosity. "Sorry, ancient history is kind of a thing of mine."

Alexander nodded and Santiago waved for him to continue. "Right, let's see. *'To preserve the truth within, these scrolls were hidden from the heretical hands of the Gnostics who are described in the writings of the second volume of the Commentaries of Irenaeus. Lest the location...the location of our fallen leader...'"* he paused, mouthing over a few words to ensure he translated them accurately and could correctly make out the writing, "Sorry. Hang on...okay. *'Lest the location of our fallen leader and the precious...possessions that lie with him be lost forever, my companions and I have devised a path...'"* He paused and then finished with awe in his voice, *"'illuminated by the Holy Spirit for the ones He deems worthy.'"*

Alexander's heart was in his throat as his pulse raced. It couldn't be, but these words before him, they couldn't be a lie, could they?

"What does the rest say?" Antonio asked.

"'This journey is for the dedicated believer, not the faint of heart. If God wills, may His chosen ones be successful.'"

Drew moved the UV light lower. "There's a symbol there, Uncle James, and a signature."

"You're right. A torch with a lit flame...possibly stamped with a signet ring?" he mused, sliding it so Santiago could see it as well.

"You can't possibly think this means what I think it means," Santiago whispered as if scared to even get his hopes up. "Alexander?"

"The location of the tomb of Timothy," he whispered.

"One of the great mysteries of the early church," Santiago said in awe.

A team member spoke up. "No one has ever found anything concrete regarding it's whereabouts, have they?"

"Until now," Antonio remarked.

"If this is referring to the tomb of Timothy...these parchments mentioned, what are they?" Drew asked. "Why are they so important?"

Alexander glanced at his nephew as he said, "The first thing that comes to my mind for some reason is: *'The cloke that I left at Troas with Carpus, when thou comest, bring with thee, and the books, but especially the parchments.'*"

Kaci and Drew exchanged a confused look, but it was Santiago who said, "II Timothy 4:13. Written by the Apostle Paul. You think...you think Timothy was buried with his writings? These parchments...they could be Paul's?"

Alexander's mind raced with the possibilities, trying to fully grasp what was happening. "I don't know, but this note mentions the Great Fire of Rome. Like Drew mentioned, that occurred in 64.A.D., the same year it is believed 2 Timothy was written."

"What was the Great Fire again?" Kaci asked.

"Drew? Do you remember?" Alexander said, turning to his nephew.

He squinted in thought. "I remember learning that Nero set a fire," he started slowly, "to clear out part of the city so he could build bigger and grander buildings, but he blamed it on the Christians because he wanted more reason to persecute them. The fire burned for six days, destroying entire blocks of buildings and killing thousands of people."

"Correct," Alexander smiled. "There is a chance Paul himself was imprisoned in the city at this time."

"And someone snuck the parchments out of the city to keep them safe," Santiago finished. "Do you understand what this means? What these words say? There is a path to find the lost words of Paul!"

Alexander quickly lifted a hand to halt his friend's train of thought. "Not *lost* words, no. All of Paul's inspired writings are in the Bible already. And I believe that these are more than mere correspondence he wrote with pastor friends. They *have* to be something of great significance." Alexander gestured down to the old parchment, "Notice that Mikhos called them *'sacred'* and *'truth'*; only the Word of God are those two things. Also, the very fact that someone would risk his life to smuggle them out during the treacherous Rome Fire indicates to me that they are of far greater worth and value than just a common letter."

The eyes of everyone around Alexander widened as he spoke in a reverential tone, the realization of what he was suggesting hitting him as well. "My friends, I believe that these scrolls could very possibly be second copies – exact duplicates – of New Testament manuscripts. Possibly in the original author's hand! Imagine finding something so rare," Alexander spoke under his breath in awe. "And the implications it could cause for the modern day church."

"Where do we start?" Drew asked, his eyes bright with curiosity and a sense of adventure Alexander was used to seeing in his own reflection. Kaci's enthusiasm mirrored her brother's, and he realized he made the right decision in bringing them along for this trip.

"Clues," Alexander told him. "We need clues." He reread the parchment as one of the junior archeologists jotted the words down and then asked for her to slowly recite them back to everyone. He closed his eyes, listening to the words, tilting his head ever so slightly as he hung upon every syllable.

"I, Mikhos, am the son of Symeon, who was a preacher boy of Timotheus. After Timotheus perished at the hands of the pagans, I witnessed my father and his brethren bury our pastor, along with three sacred parchments, smuggled out during the great fire in Rome. To preserve the truth within, these scrolls were hidden from the heretical hands of the Gnostics who are described in the writings of the second volume of the Commentaries of Irenaeus. Lest the location of our fallen leader and the precious possessions that lie with him be lost forever, my companions and I have devised a path illuminated by the Holy Spirit for the ones He deems worthy. This journey is for the dedicated believer, not the faint of heart. If God wills, may His chosen ones be successful."

He opened his eyes and softly stated, "Irenaeus."

Santiago's head bobbed and said, "He was an early church leader in the second century. Probably a contemporary of this man here," pointing to the mummified corpse.

"But why is Irenaeus mentioned?" Drew asked.

Kaci nodded. "Yeah, kind of random, don't you think, Uncle James?"

"Well, the mention of Irenaeus could be nothing. Or it could have been placed in this message for a reason. His remaining works were archived in the rare and ancient section of the vast Alexandrian libraries. His original commentaries are still intact there," Alexander informed her. "Perhaps, the clue that could set us on the right path is there as well."

Kaci and Drew grinned widely, but it was the latter that said, "Why are we still here then? Off to Alexandria!"

The professor couldn't argue. "Off to Alexandria," he repeated. "And our quest begins."

CHAPTER III

D rew and Kaci spent another few hours down in the crypt as their uncle helped clear up any more translations needed so the team could continue their work there. When they finally climbed the spiral staircase back to the cathedral, Kaci and Drew were babbling nonstop about getting to go to another country with their uncle. He reminded them they should call their mother and let her know what was going on.

"No!" they said together and he arched a brow, smirking at them.

"And why not? She knows we're in Spain," he pointed out.

"Yeah, but this is Egypt and it's a little farther away," Kaci mumbled.

"She might get too worried about us and what if she asks you to take us back home?" Drew added. "Then you'd have to put this quest on hold and you might lose the trail."

"Exactly, and you need us to go with you," Kaci insisted proudly.

"Is that right?"

"Well yeah," Drew said, laughing. "What other monsters do you know?"

Alexander's brow furrowed as he removed his glasses to clean the lenses with his shirt. "I have to tell your mum where we're going," he argued, and when they started to protest, he raised a finger. "But I will leave out the part about our discovery. For now."

They hugged him and he embraced them back as a deep rumble of thunder was heard outside, shaking the ground beneath their feet. Lightning flashed outside the windows and rain dripped down the walls and from the holes in the ceiling.

"You three wait here," Santiago told them as he drew up the hood on his jacket. "I'll bring the car around."

"It's just water," Kaci argued, but another bright flash followed by a sharp crack of thunder made her jump. Santiago winked and set off into the storm to bring up the vehicle. "I'm not scared of storms," Kaci mumbled under her breath.

"Of course not," Drew agreed and she shoved him slightly. "What? There's no shame in it."

"Don't tease your sister," Alexander said and draped an arm over Kaci's shoulders. "I never liked storms as a kid, either."

She didn't say anything, but jerked her head to look up into the night when another crack of thunder struck close by. She crossed her arms tightly together to keep herself from involuntarily shivering.

Alexander had thought the weather report forecasted clear and sunny skies all day. Somewhere in the back of his mind, a warning voice rang out with a sense of foreboding that he was getting in over his head. It was ridiculous, of course. What was the harm in tracking down lost scrolls and parchments used by the Apostle Paul? It would be the discovery of a lifetime. *This is only a storm,* he reasoned to himself.

A car horn honked and they pushed out the front doors of the cathedral, racing to jump into the SUV. Alexander apologized to his friend for getting the seats wet, but Santiago shook his soaking wet hair in reply, dousing them all again.

"Not to worry! It's only water. Now, to the hotel! You three are going to need your sleep."

"Sleep and three tickets out of here as soon as we can get them."

They had reservations at the Hotel Posada del Lucero, a historic 16th century building off the beaten path. The university always obliged Alexander when traveling and he requested a place with a little historic value. Luxury hotels were fine for other tourists, but he wasn't here to see the sights and relax. He was here to work. The rain poured down around them as Santiago weaved expertly through traffic. Alexander was gazing absently in the rearview mirror when a black sedan cut over suddenly behind Santiago. He frowned, hating how irresponsible drivers could be in bad weather. Santiago changed lanes up ahead and the black sedan drifted over as well, a car behind, but still with them.

Alexander turned around, ignoring the curious glances of his niece and nephew, and stared keenly out the rear of the SUV. "Santiago, change lanes."

"What for?"

"Uncle James?" Drew asked, but Alexander didn't reply to his nephew's confused look.

"Just do it, please."

Santiago switched lanes. Alexander held his breath and waited. The black sedan disappeared from his sight as they slowly passed a couple of cars. He was about to turn around, telling himself he was simply being paranoid as a result of too many intense hours in the crypt; but then, the car was there, sliding over a few vehicles behind them now.

"Do it again."

"I trust you will explain why you're making me drive like an erratic old woman," Santiago pointed out as he switched lanes again.

The black sedan seamlessly pulled over again, craftily blending in with traffic. Alexander turned back to face the front. "We're being followed."

"What? Who would follow us?" Santiago glared into his rearview mirror.

"I don't know."

"Uncle James, what's wrong?" Drew asked again.

"Nothing, yet. Sit tight," he told them and nodded to Santiago. "Can you lose them?"

Santiago flashed a wry grin and barked a laugh. "Who are you driving with?"

He sped up and passed three cars in seconds, then shifted over to the right lane. He zipped along, increasing his speed, and turned right at the next intersection. Alexander grabbed hold of the door handle as Santiago took the turn quickly and he feared they would spin out, but they didn't even squeal the tires. He made another left and then a right, but the black sedan hung on. It sped up so it was on their tail now, and Santiago murmured prayers in Spanish under his breath.

"Hang on," he muttered and cut across another lane.

He hit the accelerator and they were driving within view of the Guadalquivir River. Alexander turned around to stare out the back window as the black sedan gained on them.

"Still there."

"Thank you for that update, my friend. Just give me one...more...moment," Santiago grunted.

At the next intersection, the light was turning yellow, but he gunned it and Alexander yelled for the kids to hold on. The light turned red and Santiago barreled passed several vehicles making ready to cross the intersection. They all yelled as cars slammed on their brakes, honking their horns, but then they were through and he made another two rights, circling back into the city.

"Are they still there now?"

Alexander turned around, but didn't see the black sedan. "No, no, they're gone…" He trailed off when a set of headlights bobbed into view from another side street. "How in the world did they manage to…I think they have your doppelganger driving."

"Oh no, my friend. There is only one Santiago Azul, and he does not take kindly to being followed!"

Alexander's knuckles were white from holding onto the edge of his seat as Santiago made a sharp left turn and then a right and another left. They wound up driving down a skinny alley the SUV should not have been able to fit in. Worried his niece and nephew were scared, he turned around to check on them, but though there was fear in their eyes, they were smiling from the thrill of the chase. Alexander envied their youth and lack of understanding about just how serious their situation could become in a matter of moments.

Santiago made another sharp right and the tires squealed. He fishtailed and the kids yelled as they crashed into one another in the backseat. Suddenly, they found themselves in a parking garage.

"Santiago?" Alexander frowned.

"Trust me," he replied and drove lower and lower underground.

The light was dim, but a far back corner of the garage was hardly lit. Santiago sped toward that corner, spun the car around and expertly parked in seconds. He shut off the engine and lights and told everyone to duck down. They were off the main drive of the garage and unless the people following saw them go this direction, they shouldn't find them.

After a few minutes of utter silence, minus the occasional rumble of thunder, Santiago and Alexander poked their heads up, peering out the windows.

"You think they're gone?" Santiago asked.

"I don't see anyone. Who would follow us?" Alexander asked worriedly. "Who even knows I'm here, or why I'm here?"

"As far as I know, the only team contacted was from Cambridge."

"Uncle James? What's going on?" Kaci asked this time.

"I think someone doesn't want us to follow this path we may have discovered," he answered truthfully. They were old enough to be abreast of the situation and he never enjoyed hiding the truth from kids. Honesty was always better than a white lie, or a sugarcoated version of what was really happening.

Kaci bit her lip nervously, but Drew put his hand on her arm. "But they're gone, right?"

"Yes, they're gone, but I fear you should not stay at the hotel the university booked for you," Santiago warned them as he started the car and drove quickly out of the parking garage.

"And where do you propose we do stay?"

Santiago winked and turned onto the road leading out of the city, north towards the countryside. "When was the last time you saw Mama Selina? I'm sure she has missed you, her sweet Alexander."

"Years. The last time, she threw a rolling pin at me."

"If I recall you insulted her breakfast," Santiago explained as Kaci and Drew laughed in the backseat.

"I did not insult it. I merely stated the differences between her version of a traditional English breakfast and what the English actually eat," he muttered, feeling as if he was a little kid all over again about to be scolded. "You think she'll have room?"

"Mama Selina always has room for those who need it."

"Where does she live?" Drew asked, leaning forward between the front seats.

"A few hours north of the city, out in the countryside. She owns a quaint bed and breakfast in some of the most beautiful rolling hills and farmland. She will be thrilled to meet you both." Santiago smiled at the sibling's reflections in his rearview mirror.

"Why don't you two try and get some rest?" Alexander suggested. "It's been a long day."

Kaci thought she was too wired to sleep, but with the rumbling of thunder and the steady motion of the car, she closed her eyes and drifted away. She dreamt of the crypt and finding the dead bodies, but they were up and moving around. She ran away, right into a crazy storm and the dead bodies were now in a car chasing them through the city. Kaci kept running and running, but they were only getting closer. Someone called her name and she thought it was her dad. She called back, but no sound came out of her mouth.

"Kaci! Wake up."

Two hands grabbed her shoulders and she jumped.

"Easy," Drew said, laughing. "We're here."

She blinked and rubbed her eyes. "I was having this crazy dream."

"I noticed. I couldn't sleep."

"Are you worried about being chased?" she asked after realizing they were alone in the SUV.

"Honestly? A little, but we can't let Uncle James do this alone, can we?"

Kaci thought of their dad and how he never came back home. What would happen if they left Uncle James and he never came home again either? "No, no, we can't. I'm just scared I guess. Who would be after him?"

"I don't know. We'll keep our eyes open, watch his back for him."

Kaci nodded firmly and he climbed out. She hopped out behind him and Alexander waved them over to where he and Santiago stood speaking to someone they couldn't see yet. When they approached, Alexander stepped aside and a short, plump woman with weathered skin, a warm smile, and greying black hair pulled back in a bun stepped forward.

"Kaci, Drew, this is Mama Selina," Alexander said, introducing them. "She has been a God-send for me and Santiago on more than one occasion."

Kaci held out her hand for the older woman to shake, but she hugged her instead, squeezing so hard Kaci couldn't breathe. Though she looked homely and unassuming, Mama Selina was an independently wealthy widow who had a vested interest in archeology. As Kaci looked through the opened front door over her head, the decorations within her beautiful home reflected her taste for artifacts.

"Finally, he introduces me to his little monsters! Not so little any more though, eh?" she announced with a heavy accent as she set Kaci back on her feet and did the same with Drew, even picking him up off his feet to his surprise. "Oh, you two look famished! Inside, inside. I have plenty of dinner to go around!"

Alexander laughed as she wrapped her arms around their shoulders and guided them into her rustic two-story cottage. Vines grew up along the outside walls and warm light filtered out through the windows. The structure appeared old and when they stepped inside, it was so cozy Kaci had the strangest sensation that she was home. Mama Selina guided them straight into a large kitchen with tile floors and a brick oven along the back wall. Food was already spread out on the wooden kitchen table and she plopped them down on a bench.

"Dig in," she instructed firmly. "If you are spending time with Santiago and Alexander, you will need all the strength you can get."

"What's that supposed to mean?" Alexander asked as he ducked through the low doorframe.

"It means trouble follows you two," she said, holding a rolling pin in her hand and eyeing them through tiny slits. "And here you are dragging your niece and nephew into a mess. Why?"

"We asked him to," Drew answered.

"He's our uncle. Where he goes, we go," Kaci agreed.

Mama Selina's frown deepened and she waved the rolling pin at Alexander. "If you get them into danger, this will not be the only thing I throw at your head. Now eat, all of you, and tell me what sort of trouble you've dug up this time."

◊ ◊ ◊

Across the Mediterranean Sea, a man moved through the shadows as night fell over the city. He moved quickly, not wishing to be seen by anyone, ducking his head low until he came to the doorway of an old stone building most believed abandoned. He knocked hard on the door, pounding with his fist. A slat near the top opened and two eyes peered down at him. He whispered roughly before the door was opened wide and he was allowed inside.

Once off the street and in the flickering torchlight filling the landing, the man was handed a heavy, dark blue cloak with red running in a stripe down the back. After the man was cloaked, he drew the hood over his head and accepted the torch handed to him by the guard at the door.

He turned toward the stone steps leading down into the bowels of the earth. The tunnel led beneath a structure many visited as a tourist destination, not knowing what rested beneath their feet. More torches lined the path and sentries stood every twenty yards, a safeguard in case they were ever discovered. The man hurried along, the cloak billowing out behind him. He passed several other entrances to different parts of their lair. The network of tunnels had grown over the centuries and now encompassed miles of land under the ruins of the Temple of Diana in Ephesus. The tunnel sloped downward and soon the man came to another set of stairs, wider and much higher than the first. He hesitated at the bottom, but it didn't matter how long he waited. He brought news from Spain and their leader needed to be updated of the situation. Gripping the torch firmly in his hand, he hurried up the stone stairs, his steps echoing through the vast cavern.

It was here, in the heart of the earth beneath the temple of their beloved Diana, that the Demeon brotherhood was formed thousands of years ago. Sealing their bond with a blood oath, they dedicated their lives to their leader, Demetrius, the sworn enemy of the Apostle Paul. Their purpose was to try and stop the spread of the newly-birthed church comprised of followers of the supposed Messiah. They were never successful. Through the centuries, the Demeons tried various tactics, the most recent being infiltration, searching for a way to bring Christianity down from within.

As the cloaked messenger neared the top, he took a moment to watch the torchlight glint off the ornate brass archways, four in all, leading into the main cavern of the Demeon's lair. Red and blue banners hung over each one, bearing the symbol of Diana. Stretching from each archway was a marbled path, forty yards in length, leading to a central elevated platform reserved for their leader, Kadir. The man stepped through the center archway and a guard took the torch from him, setting it in an open sconce on the wall behind him.

Lining each path were Roman-styled braziers with flames that cast ominous shadows on the sleek marble. The cloaked man hurried along and reached the end of the path where it attached to the central platform. Six Roman columns marked the entrance into the sacred place. Beyond was a dais with a throne surrounded by marble busts of various servants of the Demeons throughout the centuries resting on ornate pedestals. He had always disliked the statues. Their faces scowled down at him and he swore their eyes watched him with dark intent. In the very center of the space was an altar, but none of these details registered with the man. He'd seen it all before.

What concerned him was the figure sitting on the golden throne, absently running his fingers along the arm of the chair as he leaned to the right. One of his advisors whispered to him.

This man, their leader, Kadir, was not one to be trifled with. He wore a crimson-colored cloak, but his hood was thrown back revealing the mark of the goddess tattooed on his bald head. Years before, the left side of his face had been burned, leaving a small portion of his cheek missing. A thick strand of hardened scar tissue ran from his upper jaw over the gap, connecting with the left side of his bottom lip. The luminescent light overhead, which focused on the large symbol of Diana above his throne, made his head shine. Kadir's eyes focused on him, and the man sank to one knee immediately, head bowed.

"Hold," Kadir said, his voice coarse as he held up his hand. The man speaking to him fell silent and fluidly stepped to the side, also lowering his head.

"Reveal yourself," Kadir commanded and the messenger slowly drew back his hood. "Ah, yes. Arius, you have news for me."

Arius nodded, but kept his gaze on the marble below his feet. "I do come with word, my lord."

"And? Please share it with me before I grow old and wither away." He teased, but there was an edge to his words.

Arius dared raise his head, but lowered it again when the gazes of the two advisors flanking Kadir landed on his. Those men frightened him almost more than Kadir. They were abnormally tall and cloaked in dark blue velvet cloth. Though their hoods were up, their stark, albino faces shown clearly along with their piercing red eyes. Their hands were folded within their large sleeves as they waited without a sound for Arius to continue.

"I have news from Spain, about our friends."

Kadir let his right leg fall from where it rested on his left and sat up straighter. "I trust our friends are now in good company? Tell me, when will they arrive?"

Arius cringed. "I am afraid we do not have them, my lord. They lost our men in the city and have…have vanished from our sights."

Kadir's hands gripped the arms of his throne. "Is that so?" he asked in a low calm voice.

Arius bowed lower. "It is. The men went to the hotel, but the professor and his team never arrived. They are no longer in Seville and we fear we do not know where they are headed next."

Kadir stood and Arius flinched, hunkering down even lower. The albinos didn't move as Kadir paced down from his dais, circling the altar and Arius. He clasped his hands behind his back, his steps heavy on the marble floor. For a short moment, Arius thought Kadir wouldn't blame him for the failure of their men in the field, but then a hand reached down and grabbed the front of his robes. He hoisted Arius up and shook him hard, muscles bulging as he seethed.

"We have eyes and ears everywhere. If this Professor James Alexander finds what he seeks, it will destroy our cause! The parchments of Paul are no longer a myth, and we *must* find them. We *must* erase them from time. Do you understand me?" He threw Arius, and he slid across the platform. Kadir's hands clenched at his sides as he stalked closer. "Find him! Find where he is going and stop him, whatever the cost."

Arius nodded, scrambling backward. "I understand, my lord. I will contact our spies, see what we can find."

"If you fail me again, Arius," Kadir gritted his teeth, "it will be the last thing you do."

"I will find them, my lord. I swear it."

Kadir nodded and stalked back to his throne. Arius found his feet and stood, waiting to be dismissed to carry out his next move. *I must immediately contact Carlos Bontega to see if he has any more leads.* This man was his source in Spain who had informed him of Alexander's find. He served as foreman of the crew most archeology departments used on their digs in Western Europe. Conveniently, he was on the Demeon's payroll so the brotherhood could stay current on any discoveries being made in that part of the world. Bontega was subtle in helping things related to the church mysteriously disappear or remain undiscovered while a dig was being conducted. Unfortunately, since Alexander has been so persistent with his work that night, Bontega didn't have a chance to discard anything essential. *Maybe he has a picture of the professor and his children.* Arius smiled. *Yes, we can hack into the government's system and run facial recognition through all their traffic cams.* It would take some time, but it could be a solid lead. Kadir's voice boomed through the cavern, snapping him out of his concentration.

"Humanity is always being tested, my friends. Conflict and war is the crucible in which we evolve. Every battle makes us stronger and the one we face now is no different. Those who fall will be forgotten, but those who rise, they will be remembered forever. We, my brothers, we will be remembered."

Arius reverently bowed his head and Kadir waved his hand dismissively. He hurried out of the cavern leaving Kadir alone with his two most trusted advisors.

"Do you believe it to be true?" the one on the right said, his voice whispery.

"I believe our time for sticking to the shadows is coming to an end," Kadir said, sitting back down. "For too long we have sulked and crept in the darkness. Fighting battles the rest of the world knows nothing about."

"The rest of the world is not ready," the man on the left argued.

"Why not? How much longer until we show our true potential? If they find these lost documents, if they locate them…we could lose all the ground we've gained."

He scratched at the scar on his face and the tissue running from his cheek to his mouth. The skin was puckered and pulled from the old burn wound. Most days, he forgot it was there, unless he spoke with his men. Most were smart and pretended not to see it, but there were those few who stared a few seconds too long.

They never did so again.

"We only preach caution, as we have done from the beginning."

"Heed our warnings, Kadir. If you push too hard too fast, you risk crumbling your infrastructure. Your men will leave you if they sense weakness, if they sense you are not as strong as you claim."

"I have the goddess Diana on my side," he argued firmly. "I need nothing else."

"For some that is enough, but there have been rumors that you are not the leader promised."

Kadir nodded slowly. "And who is making such claims?"

"Men who for the moment, remain loyal to you."

"What are you both saying?" he asked impatiently.

"As we said, we only caution you on your next actions. Remember our end game, Kadir, remember that it will not come swiftly if you are not smart. If you are not careful."

Kadir was tired of being careful and tired of waiting. He had been patient for years, striking quietly at the church and its teachings, breaking down its defenses bit by bit, revealing to the world the weakness and frailty within. He glanced over his shoulder, but the two men were gone, slunk back to their chamber behind the throne. Good. Kadir was in no mood to argue with them. They were so old. Part of him wished they would die and leave him be, but no one knew how old they truly were. Some said they were blessed by the goddess. Others, that they were cursed, doomed to wander the earth as pale as the moon so they would be burned by the sun.

Alone on the elevated platform, Kadir pondered his next move. If their information was good, this professor was on the verge of making an incredible discovery that would benefit the Christian world yet again. Kadir had to stop him. These first century Biblical scrolls had been lost for centuries and Kadir intended to keep them lost, at least to the rest of the world. If the brotherhood found them, had control of them, they could keep them hidden and continue to blind the church to the truth.

He paced around the platform, his cloak swirling out behind him. He stopped before the altar, breathing in the incense burning in the bowl and taking in the flicker of the four lit candles in honor of their goddess. He leaned on the marble altar, staring intently into the fire, praying quietly about what to do.

I seek a sign, he thought, closing his eyes. *Tell me what you desire of me. Tell me you seek vengeance and I will make it happen. I will bring them down for what they have done to you.*

A chilled gust of air washed over his neck and Kadir opened his eyes, watching the candles flicker. One suddenly went out and he bowed his head, whispering the chant of their brotherhood.

"We are the Demeons, worshippers of the great goddess Diana, followers of her prophet, and our leader from ancient times." He bowed his head again, kissed the altar, and left the platform behind to ensure Arius found this professor James Alexander. Perhaps there was a way to bring this man into the fold and show him the truth.

If not, then he would be another fallen soldier in the fight for humanity.

◊ ◊ ◊

Alexander closed the door quietly, smiling to see Kaci and Drew sound asleep. He walked down the hall and rejoined Santiago and Mama Selina in the living room of her bed and breakfast, a fire roaring in the hearth.

"They are asleep?" Santiago asked.

"Yes, thankfully." He plopped down in a chair and thanked Mama Selina for the cup of hot tea she handed him. "Do you have any ideas who is after us? Who would even know about this besides that team?"

Santiago shook his head. "All I know is that if you are to get to Alexandria, you can't fly internationally and risk being caught."

Mama Selina whispered something under her breath, but Alexander didn't catch it.

"What's on your mind, Mama?"

She pursed her lips as she glanced from him to Santiago. "With the number of archeologists that I have financed over the years, I have heard rumors. Rumors of men, men who are against the church. They are dangerous."

"Who are they?"

"I don't know, but I do not like that you are being followed. Stay here, please. Or fly home."

Alexander held her hand and smiled warmly. "I'll be fine, Mama. We lost them today."

"Today yes, but what of tomorrow? Or the next day?"

"I have a friend who may be able to help us out," Santiago chimed in.

"You and your friends worry me," Mama scolded. Alexander chuckled as Santiago shrugged. "When will you boys stop? You are in your fifties now and still you find trouble."

"You're only as old as you feel," Santiago argued as Alexander turned to him.

"Who's this friend?" he asked.

"A pilot and it just so happens he owes me a favor." The Spaniard pulled out his cell and his thumb slid across the screen. "He has a plane, and I'm sure he will be willing to fly you all to Alexandria tomorrow."

"Just like that? What kind of favor does he owe you?"

Santiago's eyes glimmered with mischief. "Nothing for you to worry about."

"And he's trustworthy, your friend?" Alexander asked, trying not to let his worry show.

"I would trust him with my life, and so I would trust him with yours. Do you really think I would put your family at risk? They have lost enough already," Santiago said sadly, staring into his mug. "Their father, did they ever find the body?"

Alexander stiffened and his gaze was drawn to the fire. "No, nothing. He just disappeared."

"And they're certain he's dead?"

"I haven't heard anything since and I don't want to get the kids hopes up by telling them there's a chance he's alive. It's better for them if they can find a way to move on," he said, though he didn't quite believe it himself. His brother-in-law had been one of his closest friends. Losing him was hard on everyone.

Mama Selina stood, then patted him on the shoulder. "I will prepare breakfast for you in the morning. I know there is no use in trying to stop you. I will give you some cash to help you on your journey. Get some rest, both of you." She kissed them both on the cheek before shuffling down the hall to her bedroom.

The men stayed before the warmth of the fire, chatting quietly well into the night. They steered clear of the day's events and the danger Alexander felt they might be walking into. He simply caught up with an old friend, laughing and reminiscing over some of their past experiences. Before they finally went to bed that night, they prayed together that all would be well.

Alexander knew finding these scrolls wouldn't be easy, if they even still existed. *So many potential variables*, he thought. How many clues would there be? Could scrolls survive all these centuries? Would they run into a dead end? And who was pursuing them? He rubbed his eyes as he lay back on the soft pillow and luxurious silk sheets. He felt his fears melt away as he gave them to the Lord and faith filled his heart. His mind drifted peacefully, and in a matter of moments, his tired body relaxed in much needed sleep.

CHAPTER IV

Alexander woke his niece and nephew early. They grumbled at first until he told them Mama Selina had cooked them a sumptuous breakfast to get them going. He hid his concerns about how today would go and said he would meet them downstairs in the kitchen. Santiago was speaking quietly with someone on his cell when he walked in. Alexander already contacted a man he knew in Alexandria to meet them at the airport. Although his colleague was out of the country, he assured Alexander he would send another man who could be trusted.

Mama Selina poured him a cup of her famous coffee and he breathed it in, letting the strong aroma give him a kick and tear him away from his thoughts of what should theoretically happen after they landed in Egypt.

"My pilot friend will be ready to go as soon as we get there," Santiago said, tucking his cell away.

"Did you happen to tell him of the danger we could possibly face? He needs to be on guard." Alexander asked quietly so Mama Selina wouldn't hear. But he should've known better.

"There you go again," she muttered angrily through her thick accent. "You are here and then gone and I have to stay here wondering what kind of trouble lurks on your tail. What am I to do with you boys?"

"Uncle James being scolded," Drew teased as he and Kaci appeared in the doorway.

"Wait 'til we tell Mom," Kaci added.

Alexander gave them both a wry smile. "Very funny. Sit down and eat your fill. We'll be leaving in a few minutes and we're going to have to condense your luggage, so only take what you absolutely need," he instructed. "From here on out, we're most likely going to be moving pretty quickly."

He watched them eat, checking for any signs of feara or uneasiness, but they chatted excitedly with each other about finally getting to Egypt and seeing Alexandria. They were certainly not afraid, but Alexander couldn't decide if he was happy about how much they took after him, or worried they would one day find themselves in the same sort of peril he did on a frequent basis.

"Do not look so serious," Mama Selina said from beside him. "I know I fuss over you like I would my own son. But they are strong. I can tell."

"Yes, they get that from their late father," he said. "Part of me says to leave them behind, but a much stronger voice is telling me they're a part of this. They have to be with me on this adventure."

"I wish I could tell you which one is right, but when have you ever ignored your gut?" she asked with a wink. "If you believe God is telling you that they will help, that this is good for you and them, then bring them. Have some faith."

He smiled softly. "That's usually my line."

"Usually, just not today."

Once breakfast was finished, Drew and Kaci followed Santiago back to his SUV so they could go through their luggage and whittle their items down to a backpack each. Alexander wondered how long it would take them, but after ten minutes, they held out the suitcases filled with items they were leaving behind with Mama Selina.

"That was fast. Are you sure you have what you will need?" he asked.

Drew and Kaci looked eager to be on their way. "Yep! Adventure is waiting."

"Undergarments? Toothbrush?" their uncle prodded.

"Toothbrush? Oh...whoops!" Drew shrugged and glanced at his sister. "I'll just borrow yours."

"Over my dead body!" She stared, horrified at him and pretended to gag.

Drew ran and grabbed his toothbrush, stuffing it into a side pocket of his knapsack. "Okay, *now* we're ready!"

Kaci slung her bag over her shoulder. "Let's go!"

They said their thanks and goodbyes to Mama Selina and Santiago drove them through the countryside, headed eastward toward the out-of-the-way airstrip where the pilot said he would meet them. The conversation remained light on the drive, Drew and Kaci asking endless questions about Alexander and Santiago's adventures that led them to meeting Mama Selina in the first place. When they arrived at the airstrip, there was a small charter plane waiting for them. The man standing by it threw his arm over his dark head of hair, waving at Santiago.

"I'm going to speak with him and then we should be good for take-off," Santiago said as they exited the vehicle. "Oh, and Alexander, I'm coming with you, my friend."

"Are you sure? This trip could get crazy."

"Eh, we've experienced worse, have we not? Besides, someone has to watch out for the three of you." Santiago chuckled as he walked away, answering yet another call on his cell phone. Alexander couldn't make out the conversation, but noticed his friend seemed on edge. The Spaniard was always putting up a brave front, but probably was as apprehensive on the inside as Alexander.

As Santiago hung up, he motioned for the rest of the group to grab their belongings from the SUV and follow him to the small charter plane. The pilot was Egyptian, named Ahmad. He was a short man with a thick mustache, sporting sandals and a light untucked short-sleeved shirt. He hastily greeted them all with handshakes and assured them that flying into Alexandria would be no trouble at all. He gestured widely to his aircraft, beckoning for them to board the plane while he took their few belongings and loaded them.

"What about your SUV?" Alexander asked Santiago.

"I have someone collecting it soon. That's who was on the phone."

Alexander noticed Santiago's eyes were darting back and forth nervously; he placed a reassuring hand on his friend's shoulder. "We'll be fine. Relax."

Santiago seemed to calm down, his features becoming more composed as he settled into his seat. The plane's engines were loud, but not unbearable and they could still hear each other talk as the pilot drove them down the runway and then lifted off into the sky. Alexander clutched at the armrests, not releasing his white-knuckled grip until they leveled out and were flying steady. Ahmad came on the intercom overhead, clearing his throat to speak in the most professional English voice that he could.

"This es your captain specking. We haf a forecast of clear skies ofer the Mediterranean. We vill be touching down in a few hours in Alexandria's local tine of three o'clock. Sit back now and 'joy this flight."

The two young people snickered at Ahmad's glorious attempt at English pronunciation.

"Hey, he did his best," Drew commented with a big grin. "'A' for effort?"

Kaci nodded and then turned to Alexander, tapping him on the shoulder. "Uncle James, you alright?"

"You know, I don't particularly enjoy flying and this is a rather small plane," he remarked.

"Well then. What about this clue we found? Do you think it will lead us to the scrolls?" she asked, and Alexander smiled in relief at the distraction his niece offered.

"Honestly, we are taking a shot into the dark with this. Mikhos was cryptic in the epitaph he left behind...but I am really sensing that there is some significance in starting our search with the commentaries of Irenaeus." He rubbed the stubble on his jaw. "He mentioned that they had '*devised a path illuminated by the Holy Spirit*' and that it was a '*journey.*' That indicates there will most likely be several clues to follow. We will certainly need to pray for God's wisdom and guidance if we are going to ever discover these scrolls."

"Do you really think that these parchments are actual books of the Bible or just some of Paul's own personal writings?" Drew asked.

The professor shifted in his seat and leaned forward, "The more I mull over what Mikhos said and some of the wording he used, the more convinced I am that they are books of the Bible. If we are able to find them, it would be the *greatest* discovery of Biblical texts in all time."

Kaci and Drew looked at each other and nodded eagerly. Alexander continued, feeding off of their energy now and forgetting that he was on a small aircraft. "These manuscripts could possibly be original texts, but they're most likely handwritten copies from the actual originals. Either way, here is the significance. I believe they will ultimately prove that the King James Version is the correct and only form of the English Bible that has not been corrupted over the centuries."

He smiled as he removed the small Bible he always carried with him from the leather pouch at his hip. "By the way, did you know that we are direct descendants from one of the scholars who worked on one of the committees that translated the King James Version of the Bible in the 1600's?"

"*What?*" Kaci exclaimed. "No, no one told us."

"Well, we are."

"Is that why you're so into linguistics?" Drew asked.

"One of the many reasons, yes. It's *amazing* how God gave us His Word." He thumbed through the worn pages of the Bible he had kept for many years by his side, accompanying him on every adventure and getting him through some very rough times. He realized that this was a perfect moment to teach his niece and nephew an important truth about the Word of God.

He opened to II Timothy 3 and laid it on the table, pointing his finger to a specific passage. "The Bible says here in verses 16 and 17 that '*All scripture is given by inspiration of God, and is profitable for doctrine, for reproof, for correction, for instruction in righteousness: That the man of God may be perfect, thoroughly furnished unto all good works.*' The word inspiration even means '*God-breathed,*'" he explained. "Essentially all Scripture was given by the very mouth and breath of God, through man. Every single word."

Drew and Kaci leaned in closer as he spoke. Santiago smiled softly and leaned back in his seat closing his eyes. He'd told Alexander once that his professor voice could be very soothing. He'd even dozed off once during one of Alexander's lectures, years ago at Cambridge.

"But the Bible was written by a lot of different people," Drew said.

"Yes, over a period of fifteen hundred years, forty specially chosen men from all different walks of life were used as instruments so God's Words could be given life. Given a chance to spread."

"What did all these men do? How did they get their writings to mesh so well with each other?" Kaci asked, frowning.

Alexander flipped through the pages, running his fingers over the words. "Some were farmers, others ex-slaves, priests, tax collectors, even a cupbearer," he smiled. "And that is the most amazing aspect of it. Despite the contrasts in their lives and being separated by sometimes hundreds of years, their writings all fit together like a masterful puzzle. Each man, no matter who he was or where he came from, was inspired by God to write down all He wanted mankind to know."

"But none of the writings really sound exactly the same," Drew pointed out. "I've read the Bible through a couple of times, and they all sound different."

"Exactly, and that's the point," Alexander said excitedly. "God used these men, but he used their voices, their individual styles to influence the writings. There are many that argue these men were placed in a trance and the next day found pages and pages of written words before them with no recollection of how it happened. But God didn't flow into His men and use them simply to write words down. They weren't puppets on strings or programmed robots. He wanted there to be a uniqueness within the telling of His Word, but still have the words come together as a whole." He turned to II Peter 1:21 and quoted: "*'For the prophecy came not in old time by the will of man: but holy men of God spake as they were moved by the Holy Ghost.'* Just as a ship is moved and carried by the wind across the sea, God breathed His Word through His men, using their voice, their hands, and inspired them to write."

Drew and Kaci nodded along with his words, but Alexander saw subtle hints of confusion still.

"Think of it like instruments instead," he said. "If we all played three different instruments, but played the same song, do we not sound different, but have the same melody coming from each of us?"

Kaci caught on. "And there's one central theme within the Bible, like the same melody," She smiled. "I get it!"

"And what is the central theme?" Alexander asked.

Drew exchanged a look and smile with his sister before he answered, "Jesus Christ. He's the main theme, right? He's the One Who came to bring salvation to mankind."

"Very good. I'm going to make proper scholars of you two yet," Alexander said proudly. "Every time a sacrifice was described in Exodus, Leviticus, or Numbers, they pointed to the sacrifice that Christ would make. Psalms praised a Prince of Peace and the prophecies spoke of His birth, His life, His death, and Second Coming. The Gospels in the New Testament speak in detail about His earthly ministry and so on. And finally, Revelation shows His judgment on sin and final victory over Satan, culminating in His rule and reign for all eternity."

"That many people over that span of time writing a single book with one main theme – it could only be possible with God!" Drew whispered in awe. Alexander handed over his Bible so the boy could hold it in his hands. "And this clue, if it leads to these copies or original documents, what does it mean for our Bible?"

Alexander scooted closer in his seat when Santiago's soft snoring sounded behind him. "Besides what I have told you, there is an overwhelming amount of evidence that proves the Bible had to be written by God. While the book of Mormon and the Koran are filled with inaccuracies and contradictions, the more a person studies the Bible, the more they discover that it is truth."

"How?" Drew asked.

"The archeological record provides confirmation of thousands of detailed statements and facts documented in the sacred Scriptures. Scholars have not found one single confirmed archeological discovery that absolutely disproves a statement from the Bible."

"And what about all the prophecies in the Bible? I've heard something about them..." Kaci asked curiously.

"An excellent question," Alexander pointed out. "Every predictive prophecy given in the Bible from the past has been fulfilled without a miss or exception. And, did you realize there are over three hundred prophecies in the Old Testament about Jesus Christ that He fulfilled in His life from His virgin birth to His bodily resurrection? To accomplish something like that is humanly impossible, but Jesus was the Son of God." He smiled at their captivated faces. "Furthermore, did you know that there are dozens of scientific facts discussed in God's Word thousands of years before they were discovered by men? Their findings only proved that God *had* to have written the Bible as He claimed He did."

Alexander settled back in his seat as his niece and nephew absorbed his lesson. He knew not every person he met wished to discuss the Bible. It could be a touchy subject for many, but he himself always found it fascinating and wanted to constantly learn all he could about what was held within its pages, what it could tell him, show him about his life and the world around him. He was thankful these two young people had a love for and a genuine interest in God's Word. He prayed that God would give him more opportunities to teach them everything he could, to help them become firmly grounded in the truth of the Bible.

"It's incredible, all of it," Kaci said quietly. "That it's managed to be preserved for so long..."

"Because He has helped preserve it. He promised that He would," Alexander told her. "Since the time the Old and New Testaments were written, the Bible has been expertly translated into multiple languages, including English. Like I said before, if – and that's a huge if – we can ever find these scrolls, it would be crucial evidence that the version here in our hands actually *was* translated from accurate Biblical texts, and it would prove that modern English translations came from corrupt ones...but, all of that is a topic for another time."

"Aw, come on," Drew pleaded as Alexander chuckled.

"No, I suggest you both get some rest. We still have a little while before we land, I'm sure, and you will need your strength."

He closed his eyes, folded his hands over his chest, and listened to Drew and Kaci whispering excitedly back and forth. He couldn't hear everything they said, but the adventurous energy flowing from them reminded him so much of himself back in his younger days. His worry over his decision to bring them along now seemed pointless. They were meant to be here as surely as he was meant to be on this path. God had a plan for all of them, and their faith would be their strength and their guide to see them through whatever came next. He was sure of it.

Alexander hadn't remembered drifting off, but a hand shook his shoulder and he groggily blinked his eyes open. "We're going to land in twenty minutes," Drew said.

"Wonderful. Santiago, you awake, my friend?" He turned around with a yawn to see his friend wide awake and staring intently out the window. His skin was pale and his hands rubbed anxiously up and down the armrests. "Santiago?"

"Hmm? Sorry, I was simply thinking of something else," he said with a weak smile.

"This is gorgeous!" Kaci exclaimed. "Look at the water and the old fortress! Drew, are you seeing all of this?"

"Yeah, I'm seeing it," he laughed as he joined her in looking out the window as the plane began its descent.

Alexander leaned over and began to point out the remains of the ancient lighthouse, one of the seven wonders of the ancient world, within the construction of the fortress below them. But then the plane dipped and he quickly grabbed for his armrests and scrunched his eyes shut, counting the seconds until his feet were firmly planted back on solid ground.

CHAPTER V

Alexander, Kaci, Drew, and Santiago stepped out of the local airport and searched for their Cambridge contact who had been arranged to meet them. Hopefully this time, the professor thought to himself, they would be able to check into their hotel first and then carry on with their search for answers as to what this clue meant.

Alexander noticed more nervousness on Santiago's face, but before he could question his friend, Drew called out, "I think that man's waving at us." He pointed to a middle-aged man with olive skin, light brown eyes, and short-cropped black hair, smiling at them and waving his lanky arm in greeting. In his other hand was a sign saying Cambridge Professor. He hadn't put Alexander's name on it for which the professor was grateful just in case they were being followed. "Should we go?" Drew asked.

"Yes, head toward that man and stay by your sister's side," he said, then he waited for Santiago to catch up. "Is there something going on you're not telling me?"

"No," he hesitated then let out with a sigh, "Just problems at home."

"Is that why you wanted to come? To get away from the family? Santiago, you shouldn't be here if you're needed back there. Your family should always be first."

"No," he snapped, and Alexander frowned. "I'm sorry, it's just…things are complicated."

"I wish I could say I understand. I'm here if you need to talk, you know that."

Santiago gently placed a hand on Alexander's shoulder, "Yes, my friend, I know."

They reached the man a few seconds after Kaci and Drew; he held out his hand to warmly greet Alexander. "I know you," the professor said slowly, squinting his eyes in thought. "Omar, right?"

"Yes!" the man agreed excitedly in his heavy middle-eastern accent. "We met many years ago on a dig in the Sahara. I'm surprised you remember."

"You were quite impressive on that expedition and hard to forget. I see you've met my niece and nephew and this is Santiago, a professor and fellow archeologist from Spain."

Omar shook all their hands and motioned behind him. "We will be taking the metro bus. Would you like to check into your hotel first or—"

"Library!" Drew and Kaci said together, bouncing on their heels.

"Please, Uncle James?" Kaci added, smiling. "We already wasted so much time on the flight here. Plus, we all got naps; we should be recharged and ready to go!"

"Easy for you to say," he laughed. Then as she and Drew tried to give him the pleading, puppy-eyed looks they'd used as kids, he gave in. "Fine, fine. I guess it's off to the library first." At least the only luggage they had was a knapsack each, so it wouldn't be a pain lugging their things around the city with them.

Omar led them to the bus station, wading through the thick crowd of people. Kaci and Drew were a step behind him with Alexander next and Santiago bringing up the rear. Street vendors sought their attention to purchase their wares, holding out jewelry and leather goods. One man with a broad half-toothless grin held up a Boston Red Sox T-shirt in front of Drew and asked, "You like?" The young man politely waved him off, and the merchant immediately snarled and sulked back to his canvas tent.

Amidst the loud talking and bartering, they could hear the soft sound of an ethnic flute, and Kaci tapped on Drew's arm as she eyed a snake charmer working with a cobra. A small crowd had gathered and some were dancing in anticipation of what was to happen. The two young people wanted to stop and watch but their uncle hurried them along. Omar looked over his shoulder and grinned, "There are many sights here in Egypt that are strange to the Western world."

After they bought their passes at the barred station window, they made their way to a bus that Omar gestured to. Black smoke billowed from its exhaust. Some of the paint was faded and chipped on its side with Arabic letters scribbled all over it. Alexander smiled to his niece and nephew and said, "Welcome to third world transportation."

Men in turbans and women in hijabs looked up at them as they boarded the bus. Some held small wooden crates of fluttering, flustered chickens; others had cloth sacks with fruits and vegetables they had purchased from the market. A small boy happily waved at Kaci as she passed by, his large brown eyes intrigued with her, not having seen tourists ride the public transportation before. The seats were old and worn; the bus smelled of farm mixed with body odor. Dust hung in the air as the sun pierced through the windows. Drew and Kaci took seats near the middle while Alexander and Omar found two more empty ones right behind them. Santiago glanced at the empty seat across the aisle but mumbled something about buses making him sick, so he moved a few more rows back and sat down.

"Your friend appears distracted," Omar mentioned as the bus finally moved away from the curb.

"Family matters, I think," Alexander replied.

"Ah, happens to the best of us. But, I am thrilled to have you in Alexandria, Professor, though the reason was quite vague."

Alexander grinned, but stayed on his guard. "I'm afraid it's sort of a need-to-know basis type of trip this time. I hope you can understand. We had some trouble in Spain and with my niece and nephew with me, I'm being extra cautious."

Omar nodded in understanding. "You've given me no offense. I only hope the library here can help you with whatever it is you seek."

"As do I."

Alexander watched the other passengers on the bus. After what happened in Spain, he kept his eyes peeled in case anyone else managed to find them or was following them. Behind, he heard Santiago's familiar ringtone and glanced over his shoulder to see him answer it. He was too far away to hear what was being said, but Santiago's eyes widened in fear and narrowed just as quickly in anger. His hand holding the phone shook but when he happened to catch Alexander's gaze, he suddenly smiled and waved him off, mouthing something about his wife. Alexander nodded and turned back around, but continued to check every few seconds. At one point, he saw

Santiago lower the phone from his ear as his jaw dropped in response to whatever was on the screen. He placed the phone back to his ear, said something else, and hung up. He sulked in his seat, jaw clenched, and hands fisted on his legs. Alexander's concern deepened. He made a mental note to try and talk with Santiago as soon as possible about his family troubles which seemed to be escalating by the minute.

The bus came to a stop near the library and their group disembarked along with several other people. Once they were away from the crowd, Alexander pulled Santiago aside.

"Is everything alright? Be truthful with me."

Santiago rubbed his forehead, laughing nervously. "Everything is fine, my friend. I promise you. Everything will be just fine. We are here. Should we not get going?"

Alexander frowned at the dismissal, but they had much work to do and he was anxious to get inside, as were his niece and nephew. "Very well. Kids? Stay close and let's go figure out what this clue of ours means."

As they neared the library, Kaci and Drew stared wide-eyed at the impressive site. The main structure of the building appeared as a disk, angled up from the ground. Windows lined it and skylights gave natural light to the room within. A statue stood outside while the stone part of the building was carved with hieroglyphics and other symbols. Kaci spun around on her feet, wanting to stay outside to admire the uniqueness of the architecture. Off to the side was a rounded structure with a sign beside it she couldn't read.

"What's that?" she asked Omar.

"That is a planetarium. You could spend all day here exploring the library, but I think your uncle may have other plans."

"Sadly, we do. Come along," Alexander said and held open the door. "Welcome to one of the most famous libraries in the world. This place has been in existence since the Greek Empire founded it in the 3rd century B.C.!"

Kaci and Drew hurried past him inside and skidded to a stop as they tried to take in every detail. The slanted ceiling stretched high over their heads and sunlight poured in from every skylight, dotting the shelves and tables filling the massive space. Balconies extended farther inside the library, following the slant of the ceiling, lined with so many books Kaci couldn't imagine ever having enough time to finish reading them all.

"This is crazy," she said to Drew.

"Yeah, that's a good word for it," he agreed. "Check out the columns for the structure support and all these halls and balconies. You could get lost in this place."

"Easily. Wonder where we'll find the texts Uncle James needs."

"Not here," the professor whispered behind them making them both jump. "This way, monsters," he chuckled. "Our destination lies in a very special part of the library."

They followed Alexander and the others up three sets of stairs, pointing out relics and artwork hanging on the walls and displayed in glass cases the deeper into the library they walked. On the upper floor more artwork, religious paintings, and antiquities filled the walls and floor, being admired by other tourists moving quietly along. Drew stopped to admire a very ornate and old dagger before Kaci rolled her eyes and grabbed his arm.

"What? That's incredible. Almost looks like one from a dig Dad told us about."

"It might be," Alexander said as he stopped to look at it with them. "Items he helped uncover are on display all over the world in museums and libraries like this."

Drew felt a sense of pride fill him knowing that the piece he stared at could've been brought to light because of their dad. The thought stayed with him and kept a smile on his face, until they reached a large desk placed before a room with a locked door and a restricted access sign on it.

Alexander pulled out his Cambridge ID and handed it over. The man at the desk swiped it and nodded, handing visitor passes to Santiago, Kaci, and Drew. Omar said he would wait outside for them. "I have some e-mails to take care of, but I wish you luck," he said and sat down in a comfortable armchair off to the side.

Alexander waited until everyone had their badges displayed and the man behind the desk made a phone call to whoever was working down below. He reached out and swiped another card on the door and it popped open. They moved around the desk to go through the restricted access door. Beyond it stood two elevators and only a down button.

"Where do these go?" Kaci asked curiously.

"The crypts beneath the library where they keep all the dead bodies," Drew teased in a guttural voice until Kaci playfully smacked his arm.

"No more crypts or dead bodies, please!" she laughed.

"Actually, we are headed to the sub-basement," Alexander explained, and Kaci stopped smiling. "I don't think there are *too* many dead bodies down there." He winked down at her as he pressed the lone button on the wall. When the elevator doors opened, they stepped inside. He then hit the down button and waited as they rode down below the main level of the library.

Kaci watched the digital numbers drop and couldn't decide if she was more scared or excited to see what was beyond the doors. The elevator came to a stop and the doors dinged open.

"This is the sub-basement?" She stepped out, her mouth falling open in surprise.

"Yes, welcome to one of the many hidden gems here in Alexandria," he said.

Drew stepped up beside his sister, equally wowed by what surrounded them. The bookshelves upstairs had been modernized, but these–these were created out of bronze and dark metals, carved with ornate etchings and stretched so far in either direction, he imagined them reaching miles beneath the city. "We're going to find what we need here?" he finally asked, tilting his head back to stare at the twisted metal sconces and chandeliers that lit the room. "How? It'll take hours."

"That is why you have me," a woman's voice replied.

Drew and Kaci turned around to see a beautiful woman wearing a flowing black skirt, crimson red blouse, and black framed glasses walking toward them. Strands of gray ran through her dark curly hair, which hung over her shoulder in a loose braid. She pushed her glasses up on top of her head as Alexander roughly cleared his throat and stepped forward.

"James Alexander," the woman said, holding out her hand. "It has been too long."

"That, my dear, is an understatement," Alexander replied and kissed the back of her hand.

Drew grinned and Kaci tried to cover up her giggle with a cough.

"I see you have brought guests?"

Alexander blinked a few times then turned around and felt his face flush to see Drew and Kaci grinning from ear to ear. "Yes, Drew, Kaci, this is Gabriella Moretti. This is my nephew and my niece, and of course you already know Santiago."

Gabriella held out a hand for both Drew and Kaci and waved at Santiago. "It is a pleasure to see you again and to meet the two of you for the first time. Tell, me, what new adventure has brought you to my library?'

"Your library?" Kaci glanced around then back at the Italian woman.

"It might as well be," Alexander clarified. "She has been running the special collections department for a quarter of a century now. Knows where every book, relic, and artifact is without needing a fancy computer system to tell her."

"You flatter as always," Gabriella murmured and Kaci giggled again. "What do you need, James?"

Drew glanced between the adults. They had to have been a thing at some point. No one else called their uncle 'James' except them. Alexander rubbed the back of his neck and his cheeks reddened even more.

"We are in need of the second volume of the Commentaries of Irenaeus," he managed to say.

Gabriella replaced her glasses, but her face remained blank. "That is certainly an interesting piece. May I ask why?"

"You may," he replied, but didn't elaborate.

Gabriella winked. "You and your secrets. Very well, you know the drill."

"Cell phones everyone," Alexander said and turned around to face the guards Kaci and Drew hadn't even noticed flanking the elevator. They'd been too enamored by their surroundings and the mysterious woman.

All four of them removed their phones and handed them over to be placed in a lock box behind the guards. Then they were patted down for weapons. Once the guards cleared them, they stepped back to their posts, looking straight ahead.

"Are they always down here?" Drew asked quietly as they walked away, following Gabriella's flowing skirt between tables and chairs for study. Whispers drifted out from the shelves, but no matter how hard he and Kaci searched, they could find no one else down there.

"Yes, their job is to protect these ancient texts," Gabriella explained. "There are many precious items down here. There are more guards further in, but you will soon see that for yourselves."

Drew nodded absently, tapping Kaci on the shoulder and pointing at the far walls. Egyptian statues of what he recognized as the old Egyptian gods and goddesses lined the intricately carved columns. Some of them were done in marble and other columns had colorful glass and stone tiles showing immaculate detailing of landscapes and scenes from history. It was too bad they'd had to leave their phones at the entrance. Drew would have loved to take pictures, but he bet the flash of any photography could do severe damage to many of the ancient texts down here.

Gabriella turned left at a specific shelf and the others followed behind. "So, James, you don't call, you don't write for years and suddenly you appear in my library. What is a woman to think of that?"

Alexander shoved his hands in his front pockets. No other woman on earth made him as nervous or caused him to trip over his words as Gabriella always did. "Time, I will admit, got away from me. Can you forgive this old fool?"

"I forgave you for being a fool the day we first met," she said with a wink.

"And here you are helping the fool again."

"I would rather help a fool than some of the others who come here," she said angrily, a frown creasing her brow. "Treasure seekers, cultists, men with darkness in their hearts. They claim to be scholars, but they know nothing except greed."

Alexander cringed. "I am here seeking out something that was once lost, a treasure of sorts."

"But you are a scholar. If and when you find this item, what will you do with it?" she asked, leading them down another long line of shelves towards a large set of old, stone doors guarded by four men this time. "Will you sell it for profit?"

"No, never," he argued, but she was smiling. "I have missed you."

"As I have missed you, but we are the same, James. We are both forever seeking knowledge and the truth. Your path has taken you one way and mine another." This time, there was sadness in her eyes when she turned to him, but also an understanding. "The books and texts here keep me company and they will continue to do so when you have to leave again."

Alexander had met Gabriella even before he knew Santiago. They studied at Cambridge together, traveled for months on digs across the ancient world, sharing in their love of the Bible and history. But then life happened, and they drifted apart. He had never actually told her, but he never thought he needed to. She knew without words what she meant to him and vice versa.

"Through these doors," she announced as their group gathered, "are the rarest and oldest manuscripts on the planet. Please do not touch anything. Ask me and when you do handle anything we take off the shelves, you must use extreme care and gloves at all times. Do I make myself clear?"

They answered yes as one and she nodded to the guards. One from each side reached out and unlocked the doors before pushing them inward. The doors gave way into a long stone corridor and Gabriella marched forward. Kaci and Drew admired the artwork on the wall that soon turned to pieces of pottery and other Egyptian and Mesopotamian pieces. The farther they walked, the more impressive the artifacts became until the corridor emptied into a large, square room. Three stories of books lined the perimeter, but in the middle the shelves were filled with parchments and scrolls.

"I feel like I just stepped back in time," Kaci whispered, amazed. Four columns took up the corners of the room, carvings covering them from top to bottom and the ceiling was painted to look like the night sky with constellations and a full moon. Several more display cases marked the end of each aisle and she hurried to one holding pieces of clay cuneiform from the time of King Hammurabi. She recognized it from pictures her dad showed them.

The smell of the room filled her nose and she breathed it in, the strong scent of aged and weathered pages and pages of historical texts, leather-bound books, and something sweeter. Cinnamon and vanilla. She knew many artifacts were packed with certain spices when transported from digs to museums.

"Now then, you said Irenaeus," Gabriella mused, removing a pair of black silk gloves from her pocket. "That is quite far back in history."

"Is that a problem?" Alexander asked, already knowing the answer.

"Ha! Have you forgotten? I love a challenge."

"Kids, take a look around, but remember, don't touch anything. Let us know if you see something," he reminded them, and followed Gabriella. Santiago meandered around the room in the opposite direction.

Kaci and Drew started at the far end of the racks of scrolls, tilting their heads to read tags hanging off the ends of wooden or metal knobs. Many of them were in languages neither recognized so they moved on to the next rack and the next as Gabriella and Alexander kept up the search on the other side. Within five minutes, though, Gabriella let out a triumphant laugh and gingerly removed a scroll from the rack, carrying it to the table.

"There are several. I'll bring them all to you, but remember, use the gloves. These pages are fragile and can easily be damaged."

As they slipped on gloves similar to Gabriella's, she carried over four more scrolls and gently set them on the table. Starting with the first one she pulled, she unrolled it, stretching it across the large desk, followed by the next three until they could all be seen. The crinkling of the aged animal hide scrolls was the only sound in the still room and the musty old smell mixed with cinnamon wafted up. Drew tried not to sneeze and buried his nose in his arm when he failed, turning away from the scrolls.

"Bless you," Kaci whispered and he nodded in thanks.

"This is Latin," Alexander told his niece and nephew, his fingers hovering just above the scrolls. The lettering was faded, but still legible. Gabriella turned on a special low UV lamp on the desk to help brighten the text as much as possible so they could read it. His lips moved as he translated line after line as the others stood by with bated breath. But by the time he reached the last scroll, he hung his head and placed his palms flat on the desk. "I don't see anything pertaining to a clue.

These writings are simply defending Bible doctrine against Gnosticism."

"There *has* to be something," Santiago urged, almost begging.

"I'm sorry, but I don't see anything that would relate to a path, or a hidden tomb."

Drew and Kaci moved around to Alexander's side of the table, neither ready to give up. They squinted at the manuscript, not able to read the words, but maybe...maybe there was something else...

"There!" Drew said excitedly. "The symbol in the corner! It's very faint."

Kaci found it, too and pointed. "The torch symbol, the one we saw on the other parchment from Mikhos. They're a match, aren't they?"

Alexander leaned down and studied the faded symbol. "What would I do without you both?" he murmured with a smile. "Check for more symbols...there must be more."

Kaci, Drew, Alexander, and Gabriella each took a scroll, examining every inch of it from top to bottom. Santiago stood by, anxiously shifting on his feet. Something was wrong. Alexander felt it, but they were on their way to finding the next clue. Once they solved this next mystery, he would pull his friend aside and see what was really going on in his life.

"Drew?" Kaci said, nudging his arm. "Do you see this?"

He squinted. "Is that...that's a marking of some kind under the letter," he mused and together they found five on her scroll. "Hang on, I need a pen." He pulled his knapsack around the front of his body and dug around until he found a pen and a small pad of paper. He jotted the Latin letters down that the symbols were under then moved back to his scroll. He found five on his as well and moved down the line to Alexander's.

There were only three on his and the same on Gabriella's. Drew wrote down the last letter and frowned. "What does it mean?"

"These here," Alexander said as he pointed, "these are numbers, five and five. Could mean fifty-five."

Drew nodded and wrote the number down. "And the rest?"

Alexander frowned as he waved Gabriella over. "Any ideas?"

She pushed her glass on top of her head and they whispered words back and forth, rearranging the letters. They wrote down words, but then would shake their heads and cross them out again. Drew and Kaci wanted to help, but neither knew Latin and translating the letters to English wouldn't do them any good.

"Wait, that's a name," Gabriella whispered. "Look, right here. *Andriace.*"

"*Andriace*...and the rest...the rest form the word *petram,* or cliff in English," Alexander turned to include his niece and nephew. "If we rearrange them like this..." he continued to organize the scrambled letters, writing down the two words followed by the number. He swallowed hard, "We get *Andriace cliff 55.*"

"The ancient port to the city of Myra in Asia minor," Gabriella said.

"Which is now in modern-day Turkey," Alexander finished, grinning madly. "We found it...we found it! This is it! This is our next destination!"

"Turkey?" Kaci asked. "We're going to Turkey?"

"Looks like it," the professor put his arm around her shoulder. "It seems you two are going to get a true and thorough tour of the ancient—" Santiago suddenly reached out and snatched away the paper, shoving Alexander hard in the chest. He staggered backwards and fell, taking Gabriella down with him.

"I'm sorry, my friend," Santiago whispered sadly. "So sorry!" He turned and sprinted out of the room. Doors slammed shut, locking them in the inner room and Santiago didn't stop sprinting until he reached the closed door. He knocked once and gripped Alexander's badge that he had swiped, along with Gabriella's, to show to the guards outside.

"Good day, Professor," one of the guards said as he pulled open the door. "The others remain?"

"Yes, for a little while longer," he explained and thanked them. He whistled as he walked, hiding his shaking hands in his pockets as he backtracked to the elevators. Those doors wouldn't hold them long and he needed to get topside. He nodded at the guards by the elevators and swiped Gabriella's badge on the keypad to call one down to the sub-basement. The security was created so if an intruder did manage to get inside, they would have no way out.

He impatiently waited for the elevator.

Back in the room with the scrolls, Alexander bashed his shoulder against the doors, but they wouldn't budge. The four of them smacked their hands on the door, yelling at the top of their lungs hoping the guards would hear.

Back at the stone doors leading to the corridor, one of the guards turned with a frown.

"What's wrong?" his partner asked.

He held up his hand for silence and then his eyes widened. "Stop that man!" he bellowed and hurried to unlock the stone doors as the other three guards raced to track down the man who left, the one they assumed was the professor. He opened the doors, running for the second set as the yelling grew louder. "Ms. Moretti!"

"We're alright," she yelled back. "Where's that man?"

"They're after him," he informed her and opened the door. He tried to ask what happened, but they sprinted down the corridor and the guard sucked in a deep breath before he took off after them. Voices echoed back to them, but by the time they reached the elevators, Santiago was gone and the guards were waiting for the other elevator doors to open.

As soon as they did, Alexander, the kids, Gabriella, and three of the guards rode up together. Alexander willed it to go faster, but the seconds felt like minutes as they waited to finally reach the upper floor again.

"Alexander," Omar said in confusion as they exited. "Santiago ran out, mumbling something odd."

"Where is he?" Gabriella yelled. "Where did he go?"

Omar pointed. "Down the stairs. What's going on?" But the others didn't respond. Alexander reached the stairs and scanned the library, searching for his friend.

"There!" He spotted him running down the last set of steps and bolting toward the front doors. "Santiago, stop!" he bellowed, and his friend skidded into a few people, knocking them down to the floor. Alexander sprinted down the steps, skipping a number of them as he tried to grab the man before he ducked outside, but he was too late.

Kaci and Drew were right behind him and burst outside onto the bustling sidewalk.

"Where is he?" Drew yelled, jumping up to try and see over the surrounding crowd.

"Wait, I see him!" Kaci yelled and before Alexander could stop them, they bolted out into the street.

Alexander yelled to Gabriella, "Wait here!" and took off after the kids. He had thought he was in shape, but quickly found he was not as agile as his niece and nephew who were already a couple blocks ahead.

Drew kept right beside his sister as they wove through the crowd of people, and quickly found themselves rushing through the center of a busy market. Merchants yelled and customers haggled over prices around them. The strong smell of manure hit their noses, but they pushed forward, trying to be as polite as possible, but frustrated that Santiago would get farther away each time they had to dodge around people. The Spaniard glanced over his shoulder and when he saw them, lowered his head and took a sharp right turn. Drew and Kaci followed, tracking him down an alleyway filled with crates. Kaci dug in deep and pushed herself to run even faster. They had to stop him. They had to get that paper back! She couldn't believe Santiago, one their uncle's closest friends, would turn on them. But here they were chasing him through the streets.

"Kaci!" Drew yelled and she felt his arms close around her middle and yank her back as a car whizzed past.

She hadn't even seen the roadway. "Thanks," she mumbled as they found their feet.

"Pretty sure Mom would ground me for life if I let you get hit by car." He squeezed her shoulder and after checking the street, rushed after Santiago once more. They could barely make out the tails of his shirt as he sped around another corner. They took the same turn, but he'd knocked over crates and stacks of pallets, blocking their path. Drew grabbed them and kicked them out of his way, but when they made it through, Santiago was gone. "I can't believe he got away," he muttered, kicking at a pebble on the ground.

"Well, we can't keep wandering the streets. We'd better get back to Uncle James," Kaci took a deep breath and looked around. "I hope your sense of direction is better than mine."

"Hey, you two," Alexander panted. "Hold on a second and let an old man catch up."

"Sorry for running off like that," Drew apologized. "We were sure we could catch him."

Alexander continued to gasp for breath, hands resting on his hips as he paced back and forth. "You two stick close to me from now on, especially after what happened in Spain, and now here. I don't know what I'd tell your mum if I lost you."

The kids nodded and assured him they wouldn't run off again. Alexander wiped the sweat from his forehead as they walked back down the alley, across the street, and into the market. A few of the vendors who saw them run through before glowered at them, lecturing them loudly in their foreign tongue.

"Sorry," Kaci offered. "Really, we're sorry!"

A few of the vendors nodded in acceptance, but others waved the teenagers on, wanting them away from other customers and potential sales. When they saw the library, they broke into a jog again and met Omar and Gabriella out front.

Gabriella rushed to Alexander, a look of concern in her eyes. "Are you hurt? What happened? Where is Santiago?"

"He got away." Drew hung his head. "Uncle James, he's your friend. Why would he turn on you?"

Gabriella held out a cell phone. "The guards brought me your phones, including Santiago's. James, you need to see this."

Alexander's lips thinned as he stared at the screen. "He did not turn on me. He did what he had to do to protect his family."

Drew and Kaci frowned, but then their uncle turned the phone around and their blood ran cold. "Is that...is that his family?" Kaci whispered, horrified.

"Yes. It appears the brotherhood has his wife and kids."

Drew covered his mouth and regretted thinking anything bad about the man as Kaci shook her head, staring at the image of the woman tied up and the kids beside her. They were a few years younger than she and Drew from the look of it.

"They must have forced him to find out what the next clue was and bring it to them," Alexander said. "Gabriella, I'm so sorry we brought this trouble upon your library."

"No, James, don't apologize. You have plenty to worry about besides the mess in my library. That is easily fixed. This...this will be a bit more complicated. Do you remember what it said at least? The clue?"

"*Andriace, cliff,* and *fifty-five,*" Alexander repeated. "I'm not sure where to go from here."

"The hotel won't be safe," Gabriella agreed. "And the airport may not be safe either."

"Professor? Where is it you're needing to go?" Omar asked.

"Turkey," he said. "But we can't fly out, not from Alexandria."

Omar shook his head. "That will not be a problem. If you'd like, my brother could fly you out. He has a plane, but not in the city. It's a small plane, very small."

Alexander gritted his teeth together and thought to himself, *How small is small?* Oh, how he hated flying. "Can it make it from here to Turkey?" he asked, clearing his thoughts and hoping they might make it out of Alexandria without being seen or running into any more trouble. "We'll pay whatever he asks if he can get us there in one piece."

"All he will require is fuel, but we must take the train out of the city. The ride is only a few hours. He keeps his private jet at an old airfield," Omar told them. "And he can fly you into Antalya. Would that suffice?"

"Hmmm. Yes. But are you *sure* he'd be willing to do this for us?"

"Not to worry! My brother often has business in Turkey. He deals with many sellers there for his shops here. Let me call him and I will see." Omar pulled out his cell and walked away for a few minutes of privacy.

"I guess this is goodbye again," Gabriella said with a sigh.

"I suppose it is. I'm sorry we couldn't stay longer," Alexander said regrettably.

"You have important matters to take care of, I know that." She allowed him to take her hand in both of his. "Look after yourself and come back and see me in one piece, sì?"

He grinned and lightly kissed the back of her hand. "I'll do my best."

She patted his shoulders and with a wave of farewell to Kaci and Drew, she and the guards made their way back inside the library. Alexander watched her until she was out of his sight, wishing he could follow and take that job she had offered him so long ago to work beside her amongst those rare and ancient texts.

"Professor?" Omar said, pulling him from thoughts of a completely different life. "My brother, Menefer, says he can take you, no problem." He checked his phone. "There's a train leaving in twenty minutes that will take us within driving distance of his home. The ride is several hours long."

"I guess it's off to the next leg of our adventure," Alexander said, hoping to boost some of the old enthusiasm they'd had when they first arrived in Spain.

They followed Omar to the train station, bought four tickets, and made it to their seats as the conductor called for everyone to clear the platform. The old train shuddered as it came to life and then pulled out of the station. Kaci and Drew's eyes were glued to the window as they watched the changing scenery, leaving the slightly modernized city mixed with the ancient buildings to buildings spread farther and farther apart until it gave way to views of the Nile River, stretching far out before them. Palm trees lined the banks and boats moved in a constant stream up and down the river.

Alexander wished he could lean back and enjoy the view, but he pulled out Santiago's forgotten cell phone and brought up the image of his family again. He scrolled back through the messages, searching for any hint of where they were kept, or when they would be released, but there was nothing.

"Don't worry," Alexander whispered, tucking the phone away again. "All will be well. Somehow, this will turn out as it should. We'll get them back."

He closed his eyes and as people talked around him, he prayed for the safe return of Santiago's family and for God to watch over them on what was quickly turning into a very treacherous journey.

◊ ◊ ◊

A grin lifted Kadir's lips as he tapped his long black nails on the arm of his throne. "Good. That is very good news. Send men ahead of them, now."

"We don't know exactly where they'll be," the cloaked messenger replied.

"That train will make several stops, will it not? Call our men and tell them to board. They are to apprehend the professor and whoever is with him."

"Yes, my lord," the man said and bowed his head before he stood and exited down one of the four elevated stone pathways that led out of the lair, leaving his master to gloat over finally getting one step ahead of this Professor James Alexander.

"We'll stop him," he whispered to the empty room. "No matter what the cost, we will stop him."

CHAPTER VI

Evening settled in as the train made several more stops before finally leaving the city behind and heading out toward a more desert-like landscape. Alexander moved his group to a dining car when they decided they were hungry enough to eat. He wasn't sure if he'd be able to get anything down, not with all the worries weighing heavily on his heart, but he needed his strength, as did the rest of them.

"What's a *Hawashi?*" Kaci asked, looking over the simple menu at their table near the front of the car.

"Meat pie," Omar said. "You would like it, I trust. As would you, Drew."

"Same for me," Alexander said absently, glancing at Santiago's phone again. He hoped it would go off and give them another idea as to what was going on, but no such luck. When a waiter came by to take their order, he settled on a cup of coffee instead, not wanting the uneaten food to go to waste.

"What do we do once we get to Myra?" Drew asked after their food was delivered and he and his sister happily dug in. "The clue didn't say much. But at least there *was* a clue!"

"Andriace is a place and I'm guessing the number has to do with something in that place," Alexander told him, running over the clue in his mind again. "We might not be able to figure out anything until we're actually there and can look around for ourselves."

Kaci finished off her dinner and downed her bottle of water. "At least we'll get there with full stomachs," she commented. "I think I'm going to freshen up quick." She pushed back from the table, looking toward the car behind them where the restroom was located.

"If we're not here, we went back to our seats," Alexander told her.

"I'll try to hurry." She walked through the car, smiling politely as she moved around waiters and other passengers. When she reached the next car though, she sighed to see a line for the restroom. The only other car with a bathroom was at the very back of the train and she didn't want to stray too far away from her brother and uncle.

She patiently waited, trying not to stare at the other passengers in this car, and busied herself with thinking about the clue they found in the library. She froze when she thought she heard someone say *James Alexander*. She glanced about, only to suddenly make eye contact with a creepy-looking bearded man whose eyes shifted away from hers as he spoke with his friend sitting next to him. Kaci shuddered. She continued to strain her ears, trying to hear anything else, but the restroom opened up ahead of her and she had to duck inside.

When she stepped back out, she swiftly made her way back to the dining car, careful not to make eye contact with anyone. She just wanted to get back to Drew, Uncle James, and Omar. The table they'd eaten at was empty, so she pushed on to the next car where their seats were. The door opened and closed behind her as she reached the end of the dining car. Turning around, she saw the same bearded man with his long-haired friend who had just been in the other car. Both wore leather jackets and gloves. *They don't look like everyone else here; they're different,* she thought to herself. They stopped halfway through the car, glancing down at something in their hands.

When they sharply looked up, Kaci turned back around and hurried through the door separating the cars. She quickly slipped into the passenger car and spied her group toward the very front. The three of them were engrossed in conversation and didn't notice that she had entered. This car was considerably longer than the dining car. A handful of people sat in sporadic places; most of them had their eyes closed in attempts to take a late afternoon nap. Her heart jumped when the door opened behind her before she'd hardly gone ten feet; but it was just a lady, her hands loaded with snacks, rejoining her family. Yet, Kaci could see the two men still standing there, and this time, they weren't trying to hide where they were staring.

It was directly at her.

As the connecting doors slowly closed, she saw them tuck away what appeared to be phones into their pockets and begin working their way through the passengers of the dining car toward her, all the while never breaking eye contact.

The passenger car was too long for her to run down to reach her brother and uncle in time, and instead of causing a scene, like Drew always jokingly accused her of doing, she sank underneath an empty row of seats, watching for the men's boots to pass by. As they entered, their feet shuffled when they realized she was gone. They moved their way along a bit further but then sat down. Kaci frowned. *Okay, now I've really complicated matters.*

She had left her phone in her knapsack, which was currently in Drew's possession, so she couldn't text him. And she couldn't exactly stand up and yell. *That would be the ultimate scene causing,* she scowled. *For all I know,* she tried to convince herself, *I'm just being paranoid.* But in the back of her mind, her conscience was screaming at her to be cautious since these two men had been acting very suspicious.

She decided to count out another full minute before getting to her feet and casually moving farther down the car. When she popped up, Drew noticed her and gave her an amused but puzzled look. Now that he'd seen her, she felt more confident to walk toward her group. As she passed by the two men, she saw the phone they were holding. The intricate tattoos on their hands caught her attention first. Then she gasped.

There on the screen was a snapshot of her uncle, Drew, and herself in Mikhos' crypt in Spain. The men's conversation stopped immediately and their hate-filled eyes locked onto hers. Kaci found herself unable to move from fright. She barely opened her mouth to scream when suddenly she was shoved to the floor of the car. Then the men vaulted over her and she almost shrieked in relief, watching as they charged past her down the car toward Alexander and Drew. Omar sat on the opposite side of the aisle and they ignored him, going straight for the professor. Alexander yelped as they grabbed for him, trying to pin his arms behind his back as he struggled, but he was a big man and his nephew was right there to help fight them off.

Drew grunted as he grabbed the man with the ponytail around the middle and dragged him backwards. Kaci sprinted up to the commotion and joined him. Together they managed to tear the villain away. Omar leapt into action, smashing the one still holding Alexander into the window.

"Run!" he yelled, but earned a punch to the face, throwing him back across the aisle.

By now, some of the passengers in the car had started screaming and frantically scurried back from the fight. Others still kept their eyes forced shut so as not to be involved.

Alexander ducked under the man's fist as it swung at him. He heard Kaci scream, but when he tried to see, she and her brother had the second attacker down. She was sitting on his legs as Drew tried to hold down the rest of him. Omar was still shaken from the hit, but he waved at Alexander to run.

"*Go!* Get him out of here!"

He needed to lead one of these attackers away from his niece and nephew. Without wasting another second, Alexander bolted out the door of the car toward the front of the train. He quickly wove past passengers in the aisles, loudly saying, "Excuse me" in their native tongue, as he went from one car to the next. He could hear his assailant pursuing him as the man gruffly shoved people out of his way. Finally, Alexander came to an end when he found himself up by the locomotive. He slammed the "staff only" door shut that led to the engineering part of the train, but couldn't lock it from his side. *Seriously? You have got to be kidding me,* he sarcastically thought to himself. The man leered through the window, brandishing a wicked-looking knife.

"Oh God, help me," Alexander prayed and spied, through the nearby door, a ladder along the outside of the train leading to the roof. He quickly opened the door, latched onto the ladder and climbed up, struggling to keep his balance as the train took a turn on the track. The door leading into that car burst open and the man growled up at him as he began to follow him up the ladder, holding the knife blade in his teeth.

Alexander stepped backwards, holding his arms out wide to try and keep his balance as the man approached looking ready to kill. He walked along the top of the train, struggling to stay upright with the rough jostling as it hit bumps and uneven railroad ties. He could hear the assassin behind him shouting viciously for him to stop and fight. They leaped from car to car until finally they were on top of the one where the chasing all began. Alexander turned to face his opponent.

Back inside the train, the other assailant kicked out hard and Kaci somersaulted down the aisle to avoid him as Drew shouted to draw the man's attention away from his sister. The man backhanded him hard and then wrapped his hands around the boy's neck and squeezed. Drew beat at his arms, but the attacker was nearly twice his size.

"You shouldn't have gotten in the way," the man growled, crushing Drew's neck.

"You...should learn...to look...behind you," Drew gasped with a smirk.

The man frowned. "Huh?"

Kaci screamed as she brought down a large glass bottle from a nearby passenger over the man's head. His hands released Drew instantly, but he didn't fall to the floor as she hoped. She stepped backwards, dropping the rest of the bottle as the man shook his head, sending glass flying everywhere.

"You...I'm going to kill *you* first!"

The golden rays of the setting sun glistened off the knife he suddenly pulled on her. Kaci gulped and wondered if this was going to be the end of her adventuring days. A thud from above followed by yells made everyone look up and she feared her life might not be the only one ending on this night.

Alexander jumped back another step nearly falling off the train as his opponent swiped at him with the knife again and again, laughing madly each time. "This would be easier if you would simply let me kill you!" the man shouted.

"I'm not one for giving up easily," Alexander yelled back, watching the knife closely.

The man lunged forward again, and this time Alexander grabbed hold of the man's wrist with the knife. He bashed it against his leg, trying to loosen the man's grip and to his surprise, the man yelled in pain and the knife clattered to the roof of the train before sliding off and disappearing over the edge. Excited that he disarmed the man, Alexander forgot to pay attention to the man's other hand and it swung around, clocking him in the side of the head. His vision blurred as his arms spun around, trying to regain his balance. The man came at him again, hitting him once in each side until Alexander was gasping for air. He shifted on his feet the best he could and threw the man down with him, wrapping his arms around his middle. They rolled, hitting and kicking each other furiously when suddenly the train turned again and Alexander slid closer to the edge. His hands grappled for anything to hold onto as his body was flung over the side of the car. At the last second, his hands caught the metal pole that ran along the top of the train and his shoulders were jerked hard as he tried to hold up his weight.

The ground rushed by below his dangling feet and he gulped, praying he wouldn't lose his grip and fall.

The man's shadow loomed over him and Alexander glared up at him.

"You should have left well enough alone, Professor," the assailant yelled over the noise of the train. "You should have never interfered!" He stomped his boot down hard on

Alexander's right hand and he grimaced in pain, forcing his fingers to stay wrapped around the pole. The man stomped down again on his other hand and Alexander nearly lost his grip.

The train rattled on and he thought he heard Kaci yelling from inside. He had to get back in there! But when he tried to pull his weight up, the man was right there to kick him back so hard both hands almost let go.

"Say goodbye to this world," the man sneered, lifting his boot again. He pulled another knife free, the blade glinting in the sun's orange glow. "Your time is over!"

Alexander was debating if he should let go and risk breaking his neck or be stabbed, when suddenly a gunshot rang out. He flinched, but it was his opponent who stared down at his chest confused. A dark spot bloomed against his blue shirt and he slowly turned around, his body wobbling with each step. His lips moved, but whatever he said was lost on the wind rushing past. The man crumpled to his knees and with a thud, hit the roof of the car. Alexander hoisted himself up, swinging his legs high enough to latch onto the pole. He rolled his body over and stared up at the sky.

"Professor?"

Alexander jumped and sat up quickly to see Omar before him, a short snub revolver held loosely in his hand, aimed away. "The kids?" he asked in a panic.

"Oh, your niece and nephew can handle themselves just fine. They are crazy!" Omar muttered, shaking his head. "You'd think they weren't afraid of staring down a man ready to kill them both. Come on, let's get back inside. We should be nearing the station in a few minutes."

"Won't we be arrested?" the professor asked, following Omar off the roof of the car. "What about the body?"

Omar hurried back toward it and with good shove, sent it sliding off the roof to land in the sand. "I doubt anyone has called the police. We'll make it out as long as we hurry."

Alexander's mind raced as he hit the platform and stepped into the car. The place was trashed, but what made him smile was the sight of Kaci and Drew tying up the man who attacked them with curtains torn from the windows. The man had a gash on his forehead, and appeared to be dazed. Kaci finished knotting up his wrists as Drew shoved him between a set of seats, cramming his body out of sight.

"Definitely my little monsters," Alexander announced and the kids rushed to him, embracing him tightly. "Or should I say *grown up* monsters! How did you two do it?"

"Omar helped," Drew told him, coughing harshly when his voice came out so rough. "He pulled a knife out toward the end but Omar and I jumped him. We got him down and a gun slipped out of his waistband. Omar hit him over the head with it and then went up to help you. Sounded like you were having a rough time of it," Drew smiled.

"You could say that. I'm an old man who can't be fighting like this on top of trains." He grimaced, feeling his bruised face and ribs. He was going to be sore for the next few days at least. "You both sure you're alright?" He noticed the marks on Drew's neck, but his nephew nodded and smiled.

"Yeah, we're fine. It's them though, isn't it," Kaci stated. "The people who chased us in Spain."

"You were attacked in Spain?" Omar asked surprised. "By these same men?"

"You know who they are?" Alexander asked when he saw concern forming in the man's eyes.

Omar glanced at the man the kids had gagged with a piece of curtain shoved in his mouth. "I recognize their clothes, but I could be wrong. Once we are off this train and on my brother's plane, we will discuss it more."

They gathered their belongings and stood by the exit waiting for the train to stop at the station. No other passengers returned to their car, probably afraid of being dragged into whatever fight had broken out between these strange people. Omar led the way off the train as soon as it came to a stop, not slowing as he raced through the station and out the main doors. The worn-out group followed as he pulled keys out of his pocket and unlocked a banged-up old truck in the sandy parking lot.

"Get in, quickly," Omar insisted when yelling followed them. He started the engine and floored it out of the lot, sending gravel and sand flying everywhere. "My brother's home is not far. We'll be out of sight there."

"How did you have a vehicle here?" Alexander asked.

"My brother said he would leave his truck. I have the extra keys. This way, he could ready the jet and we would be able to leave as soon as possible."

Kaci and Drew were still shaken from the fight, the latter a mix between pumped-up and realizing how close he'd come to death. His throat ached and when he'd spoken earlier, it hurt even worse. The raspy sound of his voice he assumed would go away. Kaci's eyes were wide and he reached over to hold her hand. Neither sibling said a word as Alexander whispered to Omar in the front seat. Their first real life-and-death encounter and they came out mostly unscathed. Drew was proud of himself and his sister. She was pale and shaking now, but she had stood her ground during that fight. He wondered how proud their dad would be, too, seeing them take down bad guys and help save Uncle James' life.

"We're here," Omar said barely ten minutes later. He pulled up a long stretch of road to a set of wooden gates. Alexander offered to get out and open them so Omar could drive through. As the gates closed behind them, Alexander rejoined them in the truck and they bounced down the road to a modest home surrounded by what looked like a beautiful oasis. Far behind was an airplane hangar. "Welcome to my brother's home. We'll get inside and wash up, then discuss our plans for leaving."

Kaci and Drew simply nodded. Both were suddenly drained and passing out in a bed sounded like a fantastic idea, but they couldn't stay in Egypt, not with men tailing them so closely.

A man who looked like he could be Omar's twin stepped out of the house, warm light spilling out behind him. He greeted his brother warmly and held out his hand for Alexander's. "I am Menefer; and you, my friends, look as if you had a very rough train ride." He flashed a good-humored toothy grin as his eyes flit from each of them. "Please, come in. Welcome to my home!"

"Thank you. I don't think we can ever repay your kindness, or your brother's." Alexander was overwhelmed with emotion as he turned and clasped Omar's arm. "I owe you my life."

Omar patted him on the shoulder. "No, you owe me nothing. Let's get inside. Your niece and nephew look ready to fall over."

The group traipsed inside the house. Menefer secured the door behind them as Omar led them into a living room. Kaci and Drew collapsed on the couch and just sat there, staring blankly ahead of them. Alexander sat across from them as the two brothers said they would make tea to help soothe their nerves. Alexander rubbed his eyes and flashes of the fight filled his mind. He'd been in scuffles before, but this one was different. Those two men, they wanted to kill him and they were willing to kill Kaci and Drew, too.

"I'm sending you two back to England," he whispered. "First thing in the morning."

"What?" Drew asked, shaking his head. "No, you can't do that."

"I can and I am. This is too dangerous for you both. I should never have brought you along after what happened in Spain. If anything happens to either of you, your mum will kill me."

"We're not leaving you behind," Kaci argued firmly. "We can't."

"We all almost died!"

Drew glanced at his sister and shrugged. "Almost, but we didn't. If we hadn't been there, what would've happened, Uncle James?"

The man scrambled for words. If he'd been attacked by two men, alone, they would have overpowered him in the end, he knew that. "I can't overlook what happened," he pushed on, trying to hold strong.

"You said it yourself earlier, you felt we were meant to be here with you," Drew reminded him, holding a hand to his sore throat. "What would happen if you sent us home now? When we've only just begun?"

Omar and Menefer brought over a clear glass teapot and small glasses for them all.

"Your niece and nephew are right," Omar said as he poured Alexander a glass of the steaming liquid. "Without them today, where would you be?"

"They're kids."

"They are not kids, not anymore," Menefer said and handed a glass to Kaci and Drew. "I know I have just met them, but they seem, how do you say...*mature* to me. Sometimes it's hard for adults to accept, but it happens. They are meant to be with you. I can feel it."

"And if those evil men come after us again?"

"Then we fight them off, together," Drew insisted. "We started this journey together and we're going to end it together." He hesitated, sucking in a harsh breath as he added, "I refuse to get another phone call from some strange man saying someone we know is dead."

Alexander's chest crushed like a vice as he saw the pain in Drew's eyes. He stood and made the three steps to close the distance between them and embrace Drew and Kaci. He hadn't been thinking of what they'd already gone through, losing their dad on a dig, far away and overseas. He kissed the top of their heads, murmuring he was sorry. He wasn't going to leave them and he wasn't going to die on them either.

"You're right, our chances are better together."

Kaci and Drew were smiling, the first wiping tears from her eyes, as Alexander resumed his seat and drank his tea. It did indeed calm his nerves and made him feel better. It was green tea with a hint of ginger and clove.

"Now then," Menefer said as he sat down in another chair beside Omar, "tell me what happened on the train."

Omar retold the story with the others filling in when he wasn't sure how something happened. Menefer's face darkened with each new bit of the tale as Alexander explained what happened before they were even on the train, and then back to what was found in Spain.

Menefer was silent for a long while, stroking the black beard he had which his brother lacked.

"You know, I just remembered," Kaci said suddenly, "they had tattoos on their hands! I saw them right before I saw the picture of us on their phone."

"Do you remember what the image was?"

"I...I think so."

Omar stood and hurried away. When he came back, he had a pen and paper for her to use. She sketched out a simple circle and placed a crescent shaped moon on either side of it so they opened outwards.

"There. I think there were words in the center, but I'm not sure what they said. I think they were in a foreign language."

Alexander leaned in along with the brothers and frowned. "At least we know for certain who's been chasing us. This," he said, holding up the paper, "is the symbol for the Demeons. It is them."

"Who are the Demeons?" Drew asked confused. "Are they the men who chased us in Spain?"

"Most likely. And probably the ones who are holding Santiago's family hostage." Alexander held his hands together and rested his chin on them. "We have managed to find ourselves in a very sticky situation."

"But *who* are the Demeons?" Kaci asked the question again, eyes filled with some curiosity but mainly with concern.

Alexander looked to his niece and wished there was an easier explanation, or that he knew more, but it wasn't he who answered.

"They are rumored to be a cult," Omar said quietly. "They have been around for centuries, formed by a man named Demetrius. They worshipped the goddess Diana back in the early days and according to what people say, they still do. That tattoo? That is a symbol of the goddess herself."

Kaci and Drew exchanged a nervous look as Alexander's heart pounded in his chest. "And now they're after us? Why?"

"You said you came to the library to find something important," Omar clarified. "What exactly did you find in Spain? Does it have anything to do with Christianity in any regard?"

The three nodded as one.

"That is why. Whatever you are searching for, they probably want to find it first."

"What for, if they're a cult?"

Omar turned to Drew, his lips thin and eyes filled with anger and sadness. "To destroy it. Their goal for many, many generations has been to corrupt Christianity at every possible turn. Some hoped they would simply fade away with time. It's true no one has heard of them in decades, but apparently they are still around, hidden somewhere in the world."

"Where is it you are headed once we reach Turkey?" Menefer asked.

Alexander pondered his trust of the brothers, but then recalled Omar saving his life. He easily could have let him fall off the roof of that train car and let the kids be taken, or worse. He could feel God telling him he could trust these men. "Myra. We need to get to Myra."

"And you said this friend of yours, Santiago...he knows this, too?"

"Yes, which means the Demeons will by now. Probably why they were on the train," Alexander muttered, annoyed. "They might beat us to Myra, too."

"They might, but whatever happens, you cannot let them reach the end of this path first. Whatever lies there waiting to be found, they will never let the world see it. They will do whatever they must to destroy it." Menefer finished his tea and stood. "Drink your tea and then we must depart. The flight is close to eight hours long."

Alexander inwardly groaned. The train ride had taken them farther south than he thought, but he couldn't find reason to complain. For the moment, they were among friends and safe. As requested, they finished their tea, took turns washing up in the restroom, and then made their way through the house toward the back where the airplane hangar stood.

"Who exactly is your brother?" Drew asked at the sight of the fancy jet waiting in the hangar.

Omar winked. "My family used to be merchants and traders. They have held onto their wealth for many, many generations. We live a comfortable life."

"I see that," Drew grinned. He couldn't believe he was getting to ride on a fancy, private jet. Despite how rough the evening started out, his night was ending on an awesome note.

"You're already thinking of how to tell this story to some girl back home, aren't you," Kaci teased as she followed him into the jet and sat down on a plush leather seat. She closed her eyes and relaxed. She could easily sleep in this seat, but sleep had to wait a bit longer.

Alexander and Omar joined them, talking quietly about where exactly they would be landing and if the professor had contacts he could trust somewhere nearby. "Istanbul. I have a friend there. Haven't seen him in a few months, but he should be in the city. We can connect with him after you take us to Antalya, and we find out what we can discover there."

"And you're sure you can trust this man?" Omar asked as Menefer was outside opening the large hangar doors leading to his private runway.

"I hope so," Alexander said as he found his seat.

Everyone buckled themselves in and Menefer climbed inside, closing the door behind him and latching it. "Next stop, Turkey. I suggest you get some rest while you can. The flight should be smooth enough."

But once they took off and were in the air, Alexander watched Drew remove his iPad from his knapsack, pull it out of its cushioned case, and turn it on. "If you're hoping for Wi-Fi, you're out of luck," Omar laughed.

"Nope, no Wi-Fi needed. Dad bought us an entire copy of the Encyclopedia Britannica a while back." He turned it on and grinned when he pressed on the app, opening it up. Drew mouthed the word 'Myra' as he tapped it into the search bar and waited. "I want to know where we're headed."

"Well then, Professor Howard, you have the floor," Alexander told him, waving his arm wide.

Drew scrolled down the page, taking in the ancient carvings and paintings of the city versus what it looked like today. "It says Myra was the perfect city to be a point of trade by ship. It sat on a hill formed by two valleys," he explained, tilting the iPad so Kaci could see the pictures, too. "The ships would come from Egypt and Cyprus and it later became the capital of the province." He moved his finger down the page further, skimming for useful information. "Something about grain from nearby plains and from Egyptian cargo ships...carried to Greece and Rome...nothing else there."

His brow furrowed as he continued down the page. Why were they going to Myra? Definitely not for farming. He hated to think his uncle was wrong, but then he found something quite interesting and straightened in his seat.

"What have you found, Professor Howard?" Alexander asked, his lips lifted in a crooked smile.

"Myra was a crossroads for the Roman Empire." His eyes brightened even more when he read the next portion. "And they have a necropolis!"

"Necro-*what?*" Kaci's leaned over to see the screen better.

"Tombs. There are tombs in Myra." Drew scrolled down. "It looks like the main necropolis is at the bottom of a hill, or rather a cliff. I'm seeing openings to these tombs - quite a number of them actually. Check out this picture."

As Alexander peered over, Kaci sat back in her seat and thought over the rest of their clue. "How many tombs are there?"

"There appear to be hundreds if not more," Alexander told her. "I have heard of these. They are still finding new entrances and corridors within the necropolis, but it's dangerous. The walls and interior structure are quite unstable. Tourists are only able to view it from the top of the cliff."

"Are they numbered? The tombs? We still don't know what the number five and five means."

Alexander tried to remember if they were numbered, but shook his head. "Not that I recall. Drew? Any information on a numbering system there?"

"Well, this is the image of the most famous necropolis where a majority of the tombs are, but I just counted and there's not fifty-five." He handed the iPad to Kaci and wrote down the number on a piece of paper. "Maybe it's a year? Or maybe...maybe it's something else..."

"Drew?" Kaci watched as her brother drew a straight line between the two fives. "What are you doing?"

"Five and five. It didn't say fifty-five. Those two weren't on the same scroll." He tapped the paper and looked at the picture. "Could it be...a grid, maybe?"

He took the stylus from the iPad and counted out the images of the tomb openings in the side of the cliff. Alexander and Omar moved closer so they could see what he was doing. He counted five down and then five over, circling one of the tombs.

"There, it could be this one, unless you're to count from the bottom then it would be…this one," he added and circled a second option. "What do you think?"

Alexander took the iPad and beamed. "I think you are a very smart young man."

"Don't tell him that," Kaci joked. "His ego's already big enough."

Drew ruffled her hair and she shoved his hand away annoyed. "Hey, at least we have a better idea of where we need to go."

"Good. When we get closer, I will arrange a car for you," Omar said. "Someone who can discreetly take you from the rural airport we're landing at to this cliff. From there, though, you are on your own, Professor."

"That is more than enough. Thank you," he said and held out his hand. Omar shook it warmly and they sank back into their seats. "Now, get some sleep. We'll need all our energy tomorrow if we're going to explore those tombs."

"How are we going to get down there? There aren't any stairs," Kaci pointed out.

Alexander closed his eyes, leaning his head back and crossing his legs at his ankles. "I'm sure we'll figure something out. We always do!"

◊ ◊ ◊

"I want to see my family," Santiago pleaded, kneeling on the hard marble floor.

Kadir stalked around the platform, his steps growing heavier with every passing second of listening to this blubbering fool. "I told you, you will see them when this is over."

"But I've done what you asked! I recovered the clue. They have *nothing* to do with this!"

Kadir paused, but only for a second then resumed his pacing. "They have everything to do with this. The whole world is blinded! And we...we are the cure to that blindness."

Santiago clasped his hands and held them out as Kadir neared. "Let me speak to them, just to tell them it's going to be alright. I'm begging you, please." Tears burned in his eyes, but Kadir had no sympathy for this pathetic man. He stood in the way of progress, in the way of their end game. He was useful, but when the time came he no longer was, Kadir would either find a new use for him or get rid of him. He made another circuit around the platform, but the man's persistent begging ate at him.

"*Enough!!* Take him to his holding cell!"

"No wait! Please, I only want to talk to them! *Please!*" He kicked and yelled as two men dragged him away, his cries echoing off the stone walls of the massive chamber.

Kadir rubbed his forehead and felt a headache blooming. "Leave me," he said to the remaining men in cloaks. They bowed their heads and filed away, leaving their lord alone with his thoughts.

He rested his hands on the altar and focused on a single candle flame flickering before his eyes. Turning his back to the altar, he sank to the floor, folded his legs, and rested his hands on his knees with his head tilted back. The hard stone pressed into his back and the energy flowed from the ancient stone into his body.

He breathed in deeply, letting the souls of men who stood here before him fill him with strength and focus his mind.

"Goddess Diana," he whispered and his words slipped away in the shadows of the room. "Come to me, Diana. Fill me with your power, with your righteous indignation. Fill me so that I may do your bidding."

A faint flicker of wind brushed over his face and then was gone just as quickly.

Rustling of robes sounded nearby and when Kadir's eyes opened, the faces of his two albino counselors stared down at him. "What are you doing here?" he demanded. "I said to leave me."

"We have word," the one on the right said, his eyes more pink than the other's, the only way Kadir could even tell them apart. "Word of a train and a fight."

Kadir stood gracefully. "Explain."

"It appears our men found the professor," the one on the left said. "And it also appears the professor and his companions have been underestimated, again. This will not please the Goddess. Too many failures. Far too many."

Furious at losing this man yet again, Kadir roared in rage. "Where are they?"

"They are headed to where the clue pointed them."

"No, not them, where are the men from the train? Where are they?"

"Still in Egypt. Would you like them brought here?"

Kadir snarled as he turned on the two men, but neither flinched at the sight of his anger. Some days, he truly did wonder if they were human at all or something more. "Yes, I want them brought here, immediately. I want to know how they managed to lose a professor and two teenagers!"

"I'm afraid only one will be able to tell you what happened."

"And why is that?"

The albinos shrugged as one answered, "Because one of them has died. Shot, I believe."

"Shot? By the professor?"

"We are unclear of the details. The man who lived said his companion went up after the professor, but only the professor came back down."

"And where was he during this fight?"

"Detained. By the two teenagers."

He swore the albino's cracked lips widened in a slight smile for a moment before his face resumed his serious expression. "You call him and you tell him he is needed here. I want everyone gathered in the next five hours and he had better be here by then. Do I make myself clear?"

The two men bowed their heads. "Yes, my lord," they said in eerie unison and walked toward the throne, disappearing through the hidden doors behind it.

Kadir trembled furiously. He sank back into his meditative pose trying to collect his thoughts and soothe his anger, shape it, and hone it to be used later. *Mistakes must be paid for*, he whispered to himself. *And soon, they will be.*

CHAPTER VII

Menefer landed the jet smoothly on the rural airstrip outside of Demre, modern-day Myra in the Antalya province. Alexander was jostled awake on impact to see Drew and Kaci already wide awake and staring out the windows excitedly. Omar greeted him with a sleepy smile as well. Alexander rubbed a hand down his face and flinched when the jet came to a stop a little more roughly than he expected.

"Did you two get any sleep?" he asked as he unbuckled himself from the seat.

"A few hours," Kaci replied. "Too excited to sleep."

"Excited or nervous?" Alexander asked when he saw the way her eyes darted around uneasily.

His niece took a deep breath and smiled. "I'm good. I have you and Drew. We already proved we're a pretty good team." She nodded confidently and slung her knapsack onto her back. "I'm ready. Let's go find this tomb."

Drew grinned along with his sister and Alexander felt a sense of pride swell in his chest. If only their father could see them now. "Then I guess we should get going."

Menefer stepped from the cockpit a few minutes later and opened the door. The group climbed down the small aircraft's steps one by one and headed toward the exit.

"I have a car waiting for you already with instructions to take you wherever you need to go," Omar informed Alexander as they walked through the small, private hangar. "And you are sure you have someone you can trust? Someone you can truly trust?"

Alexander shook his hand. "I do. I'll contact him once we check out this clue and see if it's what we need or not."

"For your sake, I hope it is," he added. "Come with me quickly, if you please."

Curious, Alexander followed Omar through the hangar to a table set against the wall.

"We were unsure of what you might need on this next part of your journey, but I had a friend deliver several items that may be of use to you." Omar waved his hand over the ropes and rappelling gear along with a map of Turkey, a guidebook, a train schedule, food and bottles of water. "In case you are there longer than you anticipated."

"How did you know we needed climbing gear?" Alexander said, happy they wouldn't have to waste time finding somewhere to purchase what he needed.

"I saw the pictures of where you're headed and have been to similar locations myself," Omar said with a knowing smile. "There are no stairs and no easy way down the cliff. Be careful, my friend, and for all your sakes, I hope you beat the others to this place."

"It'd be nice if we could find the clue and leave before they even saw us," Alexander added. A nervous flutter hit his stomach. *Although something tells me that is wishful thinking.*

He packed up the climbing gear in his bag and called Drew and Kaci over to pack the water and food in their bags. The day could either go as planned and take only an hour or so, or they could be out there for a very long time searching through those tombs. They thanked Menefer and Omar again before climbing into the all-terrain vehicle, an older middle-eastern man with a white scruffy beard and a battered baseball cap at the wheel.

"Where to, my friends?" he asked.

Alexander sat up front and told the driver where to go. Drew and Kaci waved out the back window until Menefer and Omar disappeared from their sight.

"You ready for another adventure?" Drew asked as they turned back around in their seats.

"What do you think?" Kaci wished she didn't sound so unsure. She wanted to have the same type of life their dad had, but she doubted he was ever chased around by these brotherhood people. "Drew, you don't think Dad got caught up with people like the ones chasing us now, do you?" she whispered.

"No, no, I don't think so. Dad wasn't anywhere near where we've been, and he wasn't like Uncle James."

"I know, but remember his last postcard? He said something about a group of men in cloaks, didn't he?" she asked, wishing she had the postcard in front of her so she could just read what he wrote instead of wracking her brain. "Maybe it was nothing."

"I'm sure it was nothing," Drew agreed firmly. "We need to focus on what we're doing today. Getting down to those tombs won't be easy. You saw the climbing gear Uncle James shoved in his bag."

Kaci had seen it and was thankful their dad had taken them rock-climbing so often. "Do you think you can rappel without falling on your face this time?" she asked, wiggling her eyebrows until he playfully shoved her.

"Of course."

"Hmmm...you sure?"

"I only fell the *one* time," he replied defensively.

"Yeah but it was a great one time. I'll never forget it."

As they laughed, Alexander glanced back to check on them and smiled to see them still in such high spirits. The ride to the cliff didn't take as long as he thought and soon the driver was parking. The kids jumped out the back doors to stare down over the edge, no railing to stop them from tumbling over if they weren't careful.

"That's awesome," Kaci exclaimed, staring down to see the outcroppings and columns built into the side of the stone cliff. Nature had taken over and trees and shrubs covered much of the doorways, but far below, very far below, was the room she assumed they were headed for. "How far down is that?"

"Far enough, so please both of you, be extra careful," Alexander begged.

"Where would you like me to wait?" the driver asked, scratching at his beard as if this was the most normal thing in the world for him to do.

"There's a road that runs near the bottom of the necropolis, yes?" Alexander asked.

"There is. I shall park down there and wait for you."

He helped them remove their knapsacks, wished them luck, and then drove off leaving Alexander with his niece and nephew staring down the side of the cliff. They walked toward the edge and he peered over, whistling as a stone tumbled from under his foot, bouncing off stones and trees as it went.

"There's a clear path," he said, pointing, "but we'll have to take it one at a time."

"I'll go first," Drew volunteered. "That way if anything goes wrong, you can pull me back up."

Alexander wanted to argue, but his nephew had a good point. Drew and Kaci were strong, but Alexander was a large man. If he faltered and they had to drag him back up, he wasn't sure they'd be able to do it, especially if he was unconscious. He set down the knapsack and pulled out the gear. Drew and Kaci fastened a good, solid anchor around a large boulder that wasn't going anywhere anytime soon. Alexander rigged up the harness for Drew as they laid out the coiled rope he would toss over the cliff and use to rappel down. Drew stepped into the harness, one leg for each loop, and hooked his personal anchor to the main one until they set up the other rope with the belay device. Alexander tossed the two strands of rope over the cliff, doing his best to shake it out so it hung straight.

"It's steep," Alexander told Drew. "Make sure you watch where you plant your feet." He double-checked his nephew's harnesses and they tested to ensure the rope would hold his weight and the brake would stop him if he slipped or accidentally let go. "Take your time. We're in no hurry."

"Right, no hurry," Drew said laughing. "I'll just take my time and soak in the sights, because we definitely don't have a brotherhood of crazy men chasing us, trying to kill us."

Kaci stifled a laugh and Alexander managed to hold back his own smile for about ten seconds before he watched Drew carefully remove his personal anchor. He stepped back, making sure his feet were planted a bit farther apart than his shoulders and his backside was down, like he was sitting in a chair with his feet up on a coffee table. One hand holding the ropes at his hip, he fed the line through and walked his way down the cliff. He focused on where he placed each foot as he lowered himself down. The necropolis grew closer and soon he could swing himself over a few feet and peer into a doorway, crumbling and overgrown with bushes and vines.

"How does it look so far?" Alexander called down to him.

"Good!" He glanced over his shoulder and saw he was nearing the place where more of the openings to the tombs were located. He had already figured out which opening was the fifth one down and the fifth over. "About fifty more feet to go!"

When he had made it near the fifth row, he carefully began to step over to the correct opening. He noticed that the ledge in front of the opening had eroded. He wouldn't be able to land there. His hands grew slick, but he kept his grip firm and touched down gingerly on the small outcropping of rocks above the opening of the tomb instead. He waved his arm over his head and unhooked himself from the harness so Alexander could pull it back up for Kaci to come down next. Drew knelt as he pulled his knapsack from his back and took out a flashlight, shining the beam around the opening below him. He hoped this was indeed the correct opening and they weren't wasting precious time.

"Rope!" Kaci called and he stepped aside as she tossed it over the cliff again.

He watched her intently, holding his breath nearly the whole time as his sister maneuvered skillfully down to join him. When she was about thirty feet away, the stones beneath her foot crumbled and she yelped in alarm as her body slammed into the cliff.

"Kaci!" Drew yelled and rushed to stand beneath her. "You all right?"

"Careful!" Alexander called from above, but she called back that she was fine.

She steadied her footing, focused on her grip, and dropped the rest of the way down to her brother. She climbed over to the rocky ledge and breathed a sigh of relief.

"Can you not scare me like that again?" he muttered as he helped her step out of the harness.

"Just seeing if you were paying attention," she teased, but something was off in her voice.

"Kaci?"

"Uncle James and I saw two cars drive by while we were watching you go down," she told him and waved her arm over her head for Alexander to tug the rope back up and let himself down next. "We have enough rope to get all the way down, right?"

"Looks like it. If we had to, we could climb," Drew said, peering over the far edge of where they stood. "There used to be a very steep set of stairs there, it looks like."

"Good, we might need a fast escape route."

"Uncle James thinks it's them?" he asked, alarmed. "Already? How did they get here so fast?"

"I'm guessing the same way we did."

Alexander tossed the rope down again and joined them after a few tense moments of practically falling all the way down the cliff. He unhooked himself from the harness with a wink at their disapproving frowns. "I'm an adult, I'm allowed to rappel like that. You two are not."

"Whatever you say, Uncle James," Kaci muttered.

"Now then, shall we find our next clue before we have to make another run for it?"

Drew handed Kaci his flashlight. "You go first. I'll be right behind you."

Kaci climbed to the edge and let her uncle gently lower her down. As she entered the tomb, she shone the light around the shadows and cringed at the cobwebs floating everywhere she looked. Her shoes crunched across the rocky floor as she quickly made her way around, searching for something, anything that could possibly be their clue.

"Kaci, don't mean to rush you," Alexander said, leaning into the doorway. "But we might have company."

"They're here?"

"I heard car doors. Stay out of sight. I'm sending Drew down now," he told her.

A couple seconds later, her brother landed in a crouch in the beam of sunlight. "Find anything yet?"

She shook her head. He started searching with her as she shone her flashlight on all the walls, floors and ceiling making her way deeper into the earth. They came to the grave and Drew began to search it when something else caught Kaci's eye. Off in the shadows, a two-foot boulder sat up against one of the walls. It seemed so inconspicuous, and Kaci almost didn't give it a second glance. But just as she was about to move her flashlight beam back to the tomb in front of them, she thought she saw the light catch on something etched into the front of the rock face. Running over to it, she quickly rubbed away the dust and dirt and gave a little shriek when she saw the familiar torch symbol staring back at her.

'But where's the clue?'

Perhaps the boulder was a seal, set in front of an opening where the clue was hidden. Kaci had to move it and see for herself. She tried to budge it, but even though she used all her strength, she only managed to move it about an inch.

"Drew! I need your help!" she hissed, not wanting to yell. He quickly ran over and knelt down next to her in front of the boulder.

"The symbol!" he whispered excitedly.

"Hurry. Help me move this," she grunted as she shoved her body against it again.

He tried with her and it moved further, but still not enough to see what was behind it. "Find something we can use as a lever," he instructed and they hurried around the room, searching for anything, when Kaci spied part of a tree protruding through the stones. She called for Drew and he rushed to her side. Together, they kicked and tugged until the branch was free. "This might work."

"Hurry up, you two," Alexander whispered as his shadow fell over the opening. "We're about to have company."

The siblings ran back to the rock and managed to wedge the branch into the crack they opened so far. "It won't hold," Kaci said anxiously.

"It'll hold," Drew insisted.

"How do you know?"

"I have faith," he said and together they moved the boulder. It slid over another six inches and they hastily shone the flashlight beam inside the small cubby carved into the stone wall. "Wait, what is that?"

"Drew, Kaci!"

"Grab it!" Kaci urged as another voice that was certainly not their uncle's yelled down from high above. "Hurry!"

Drew snagged the strange marble statuette, shaped like an ancient ship, no bigger than his hand, and pulled free. They would have to examine it later. He gripped it tightly as Alexander reached down a hand to haul him up and Kaci next.

"Ah, there's the happy family," a man yelled down sarcastically.

Kaci couldn't see his face, he was too far away, but his robe billowed out behind his body as the wind rushed past and the malice in his voice sent a chill down her spine. Two more men, hooded in dark blue cloaks, flanked him. The sunshine that had shown so brightly only minutes ago seemed to fade.

"Go," Alexander whispered to Drew and Kaci. "Take the rope and go."

"We're not leaving you here," Drew argued, but their uncle gave them a sharp look and, grabbing Kaci's hand, Drew rushed to the rope and the single harness. He strapped himself in and handing the statue to Kaci to shove in her knapsack, told her to grab hold of his back. She held on tightly and he moved around the ledge to head further down, praying the rope would get them safely to solid ground. For one moment Drew's eyes met his uncle's before he released the brake and slowly lowered them out of sight.

"Where are they going? Oh no, I'm afraid I can't let any of you leave!" the man yelled. "Stop them!"

Alexander watched as more men appeared above and ropes were tossed over. He looked for another way off the ledge and spied the crumbling steps, if he could even call them that. The rope Drew and Kaci were on was still anchored at the top of the cliff and just as Alexander was readying to climb down the cliff without any rope support, he saw the man who spoke reach for the anchored rope.

"No! Don't you hurt them!" Alexander bellowed.

The man drew something from his hip and the sun glinted off steel before he knelt and began to saw the rope. It frayed and Alexander heard Drew and Kaci cry out in alarm as their rope jerked. The man sawed faster and Alexander rushed to try and grab hold of the rope before it could fall with the kids on it. Gunfire erupted around him and he was forced to back away, watching it sway, helpless to do anything without getting shot. He scooped up his bag and leapt over the side, praying he'd hit a solid steppingstone somewhere along the way.

He grunted in pain when his feet slipped and he skidded down across hard stone and plants before coming to a stop under another ledge, giving him some protection from the gunshots still ricocheting around him.

"Drew? Kaci?" he yelled, trying desperately to see. "Answer me!"

But he couldn't hear anything over the gunfire. He spied the rope through the leaves blocking his face and watched horrified as one piece fell completely. They now dangled by only one rope. It wouldn't hold their weight for long. As Alexander watched the second rope start to twitch and sag, Kaci and Drew clung to the cliff face below their Uncle.

"Kaci, see that vine?" Drew said. She was still on his back for the moment, but they both knew they had to do something or plummet to the ground.

"I see it!"

"I'm going to move you toward it. Grab it!"

He moved his feet across the cliff, clinging to the one rope to keep them both from falling. Kaci stretched out her hand, but she missed by a few inches and he had to walk them back to try again. He felt the rope fraying and knew they were running out of time. He refused to look up and see what the men were doing, but then Kaci tapped his shoulder frantically.

"Drew! Drew, they're coming down here!"

"Grab the vine!" he urged and swung her over again. He held his breath as she stretched and with more bravery than he expected, she jumped off his back and clung to the vine. It held her weight and she gave it a hard tug to be sure it was safe.

"The harness! Unhook yourself!" she told him, eyes glued to the men above them rappelling down the cliff.

Drew struggled with the carabiners, his fingers fumbling over themselves. He was still trying to detach himself when the rope gave way. Kaci screamed as he fell, arms scrabbling to catch onto something, anything! This was it. He wasn't going to make it. He wondered how far the fall really was when he was jerked to a sudden stop by a strong hand gripping his arm.

"I've got you." Alexander hoisted him up to the ledge he had managed to find beneath them. He quickly embraced his nephew, thankful he'd gotten down there in time, and then looked up the wall. "Kaci! Where is she?"

They heard rocks falling in the silence left by the absence of gunfire and a moment later her sneaker came into view and she continued her downward descent with the vine. "Are you two going to hide there all day, or what? Let's go! They're almost to the tomb!" She let her hands go slightly and glided faster down the vine, ignoring the stems and leaves that got in her way, pricking her hands. She could deal with the scratches later when they weren't about to be killed.

Drew climbed onto the vine next followed by Alexander. He worried about it holding their weight, but the ground was closer. A fall from this height wouldn't hurt them, or so he hoped. They moved quickly, but when Alexander heard a furious yell from above, he saw one of the men on the rock ledge above the tomb, preparing to slice the vine with a large ceremonial dagger.

"Hold on!" he called down to his niece and nephew and a second later the loud *clink* of the blade against stone echoed around them.

Kaci screamed as she fell, Drew and Alexander right behind her, but the ground sloped and they landed with grunts and gasps, rolling away from the necropolis. The men continued to yell down to them, but that wasn't what made the three of them jump.

A car horn honked behind them and the driver was there, waving for them to hurry.

"This isn't even the road!" Alexander exclaimed as he painfully climbed to his feet.

"I heard gunshots," the old man explained. "Menefer and Omar told me there could be trouble. I was not about to wait and come back later to find your bodies…or find nothing at all."

Gratefully, they piled into the car. A few more shots pinged off the car and Kaci and Drew ducked down as the driver floored it through the trees and bushes, and swerved back onto the road. He was grinning like a madman, glancing in his rearview mirror every few seconds.

"Who are you?" Drew asked with a grin.

The man barked a laugh. "If I told you, I would have to kill you." He winked as he said it, but Drew sensed the man wasn't completely joking.

"Are you two alright?" Alexander asked, turning around to check on them.

"Fine, just some scratches," Kaci said, holding up her hand with a wince. "And bruises. Lots and lots of bruises." Her sides ached and her calves were scratched up badly. Drew's arms had bruises and scratches, too, but it could have been a lot worse. "They shot at us. Why were they shooting at us?"

"They really don't want us to find whatever's at the end of our path, I guess," Drew replied ruefully.

"Or they want it for themselves," Alexander corrected lightly.

"But why? They're a brotherhood for Diana."

"Maybe to destroy it? I don't know, but we can't let them get it." Alexander cringed as he tried to shift in his seat, his back throbbing in pain. He was getting too old for running around and falling off cliffs. "Did you find anything? Inside the tomb?"

Kaci dragged her knapsack onto her lap and dug around in it, searching for the small, marble ship. "This was all that was in there, at least from what we could see. We just grabbed it and ran."

She pulled out the marble carving and handed it to her uncle. "Remarkable," he whispered, running his fingers over the smooth surfaces and the intricate detailing. "Simply incredible."

"It was stashed behind a boulder that had a torch symbol on it," Drew told him. "Crazy!" Then, looking at the artifact, he commented, "It looks like an ancient type of vessel from Greece."

"Perhaps it would be best to discuss the item once you are safe, Professor," the driver said gently. "Those men may be following us."

"I can't ask you to drive us all the way to Istanbul," Alexander argued, handing the piece back to Kaci for safekeeping. "It's too far!"

The man was grinning. "I know the drive, and so do they. We will take a more scenic route along the coast before we turn inland. Trust me, I have spent many years evading people. They will expect you to go to a large city and they will expect you to take the fastest route, or fly."

"And we're going to do neither," Alexander shook his head. "They'll surely get there before we do."

"That is the point. I have contacts in the city. Tell me your friend's address and I will ensure his place is safe before we even arrive," the elderly driver insisted.

Alexander shared a glance with Drew. "Seriously, who are you?"

"It's who I used to be, Professor. I am a man of many names and many faces. Retired now but I won't lie, this sort of adventure does get the blood pumping all over again."

"And this trip continues to surprise me," Alexander whispered to himself. The driver laughed and only then did the professor realize he didn't even know the man's name.

CHAPTER VIII

Kadir glared down the cliff, waiting impatiently for his men to report what they found. They were close, so close to catching these three religious fanatics and yet again they managed to slip between his grasp and escape. He dared not think they had divine intervention on their side, but he was quickly losing faith in the men under his command to get the job done.

"My lord," one of his men said, bowing his head as he returned to his side. "They're in the tomb." He handed over a handheld radio to Kadir.

He held down the button. "What did you find?"

"There is nothing inside," the man replied.

Kadir fought the urge to fling the radio off the cliff and paced along the edge. "Search the entire tomb. Now! You find me something, understand?"

"Yes, my lord," the man nervously responded and Kadir handed the radio back to the other robed man standing close by. The two albinos watched him intently, their hoods pulled so their faces were in shadow in case the sun broke through the overcast sky. "We also heard back from the tail we tried to put on them," the messenger said reluctantly. "I'm afraid they lost the vehicle and the team at the airport hasn't seen any sign of them yet."

This wasn't happening. *I refuse to be outwitted by a professor and two children!* Kadir's fury rose along with the breeze and he halted his pacing. "Where is Emel?"

The albinos lifted their heads at his words. "He is here, awaiting your judgment."

"Bring him...bring him *now!*" Kadir commanded.

One of the albinos snapped his fingers and Kadir waited impatiently for Emel to be brought to him from the back of one of their parked black SUVs. His men needed motivation and there was no better motivation than fear. Fear of failure and fear of what would happen if they could not follow orders. If they could not find a clue to lead them to the professor, if they lost the trail completely, they would lose their chance to stop this great discovery from happening. Back at their base, his men were busy researching James Alexander and his connections to anyone in Turkey. The moment they found an acquaintance, his men would be there ready to follow and capture them.

"Here he is, my lord," one of the albinos announced.

Kadir turned to see the long-haired man already fallen to his knees in the grass, bowing his head low enough to touch the ground. "My lord, I beg for mercy. Please."

"Mercy. You failed me in Egypt, Emel," Kadir muttered. "You failed to capture a man with no training, no fighting expertise, and two worthless teenagers. You have nothing to offer me or the Demeons, not any longer. An example must be made."

"No, wait! Please!"

Kadir heard his cries for mercy, heard the quiver in his voice as the man pleaded for his life, but his failure had been the start of the plan unraveling. One weak link could bring down an entire empire if one wasn't careful and Kadir was always careful. He turned back around and both albinos nodded in unison. Not that he needed their permission, but those two had been around longer than Kadir and he did very little without their approval, most of the time at least.

"Stand," he ordered and Emel clambered to his feet. Sweat mixed with tears ran down his deeply tanned face.

Kadir reached out, smiling, and held the man's arms, turning him so his back was to the cliff. "You are right, mercy would be preferable."

Emel sighed in relief, but then Kadir drew a blade from his hip and stabbed the man in the chest so fast, he didn't comprehend what happened until his leader yanked the weapon back out and held the bloodstained tip before his face. "But I never promised to be merciful." Emel blinked in disbelief as his life drained away and blood soaked his robes. A gentle shove sent the man tumbling backwards off the cliff. Kadir wiped the dagger on the sleeve of his robe and sheathed it at his hip.

"I have said it before, and now allow me to say it again. Failure will not be tolerated!" he yelled to his men on the cliff and far below him. "That is what happens when you fail the brotherhood! Goddess Diana does not show mercy to those too weak to serve her!"

A few of the men stared at him in wide-eyed fear, but others nodded in agreement with his actions. They continued their search of the necropolis, but uncovered nothing to tell them what the professor had discovered and where he was headed now. If the men back in Ephesus could find no acquaintances of Alexander's, he might never find them again. Kadir stormed back to their convoy of vehicles, the albinos with him, and ordered the men to drive him to the airport. They would stay in Istanbul and wait to hear any news.

Perhaps luck would be with him and he would simply bump into the cursed professor and the elusive teenagers who were so greatly testing his patience.

◊ ◊ ◊

Alexander stared up at the stone building, stretching his arms over his head as the kids climbed out of the vehicle behind him. The aroma of ethnic food and the bustling sounds of a nearby outdoor market filled the air. The ten-hour drive had been long, but they'd managed to get some sleep and see a bit of the countryside before entering the city of Istanbul. His friend and old classmate, Oliver Winthrop, was currently out of the country, but had told Alexander to make himself at home. His cook and personal assistant were there to help them with anything they needed.

"Thank you for driving us here," Alexander said, shaking the driver's hand as he walked around the car with him. "No sign of the bad guys yet at least."

"That's good. Stay out of trouble, Professor."

"I'd like to say I usually do, but these past few days have been a bit more exciting than normal. It'd be nice to hole up for a few days and get some actual rest instead of running off to our next destination, but I doubt that's going to happen." The marble piece in Kaci's knapsack had him curious and he was eager to discover what it meant. Another large yawn reminded him that a full night's rest in a bed was needed before he'd be able to think clearly.

The driver held out his callused hand. "I wish you the best of luck." He saluted with two fingers to the kids and climbed behind the wheel to drive away.

"What do you think he used to be?" Drew asked as the three hurried up to the front door of the building and Alexander rang the bell. "A spy maybe, or a wheelman?"

"Or an angel unawares," Kaci cleverly grinned and nodded toward the car as it drove off down the street.

"In a baseball cap instead of wings," Drew mused. "I could run with that. He certainly was God-sent!"

Alexander heard someone unlock the door from inside and smiled as a kind-looking older gentleman wearing a butler's tuxedo appeared before him. "Hello, I'm James Alexander. Oliver said you were expecting us?"

The man grinned and waved them inside. "Yes, yes, come inside please," he said, his accent matching Alexander's. "Oliver won't return for another two weeks."

"Where is he?" Drew asked as the man closed and locked the door behind them.

"On a dig in southeast Asia," the man informed them. "I'm Carter, his personal assistant – posh title for butler." He winked at them and extended his hand toward the stairs. "I'll show you all to your rooms and if you need to shower before you eat, just let me know. Zehra, our resident cook, is ready to make you whatever your heart fancies."

"I could eat a cow," Drew said and his stomach rumbled loudly in agreement.

"Ah, well I will let Zehra know to start cooking then." Carter took them up a narrow set of winding stairs to a large, open hallway. He pointed out the two guest rooms and told Alexander he was more than welcome to use the master bathroom as well, since Oliver was away and it would give them more space to spread out. "I'll be downstairs if you need anything."

The siblings filed into their guest room. Drew let his sister shower first as Alexander hurried to freshen up in the master bathroom. The décor reminded him of back home. Though the outside of the building was traditional Turkish architecture, the inside had been renovated to reflect Oliver's English heritage. The hot water felt rejuvenating and when Alexander was in fresh clothes, he wandered downstairs to the kitchen, letting the smell of freshly baked bread and fish lead him.

"That smells fantastic," he mused and Carter motioned for him to take a seat at the table.

"Please, help yourself," he announced as Zehra brought a basket filled to the brim with fresh rolls. She smiled warmly at Alexander and laid out the rest of the dinner. Carter joined him and once everything was out, so did Zehra, leaving open seats for the kids.

After Alexander thanked God for their meal, Zehra commented, "You must be on quite the adventure."

"That we are," Alexander agreed, loading up his plate as she poured him a glass of water. "I'm afraid what started as a simple discovery has turned into a rather dangerous situation."

While he ate, he filled them in briefly on what had happened so far and before long Drew and Kaci joined them. They loaded up their plates and ate quickly. Alexander wanted to ask Kaci about the statue, but he decided to let her eat a bit before he finally brought it up. Drew grinned and set the small marble ship on the table.

"That mark is on it!" he told his uncle. "The symbol with the torch is on the sail."

Kaci tried to contain her excitement, "Then we must be on the right track!"

The professor picked up the artifact and noticed the faint etching, letting his thumb run over its ridges. He smiled.

"There are words on the bottom of it, too," Drew mentioned. "I was looking at it upstairs. Not sure what language, though."

Alexander shoved his glasses up on top of his head to study the words carved into the marble. "Greek...this is written in Koine Greek." He squinted, turning the small statue over in his hands to catch the light differently. "It's another riddle! Write this down, if you can," he motioned to Drew to grab a notepad and pencil. "It says something like this..."

> *'The weight of four*
> *Upon the ocean floor;*
> *Only one bears the mark*
> *Like a light in the dark.'*

"Interesting, very interesting," he mused.

"What does it mean, the poem?" Kaci asked.

Alexander sat back in his chair and lowered his glasses on his nose again. "It means we are in for a very interesting day in our near future," he said as he handed the statue to Kaci. "However, I'm making all of us take a few days of rest. We've been on a nonstop groove and a few days to recoup from our excursions would be a good idea."

"What if the Demeons find us?" Drew asked.

"I'm sure we weren't followed this time. Besides, I need some sleep. I'm an old man, remember?" he joked.

Drew and Kaci glanced at each other, and then sighed. "Yeah, you're right."

"Are you going to make us wait to talk about the ship?" Kaci asked through a huge yawn.

"Yes, because we all need rest," Alexander said. "Off to bed, both of you. I'll see you in the morning."

Drew and Kaci thanked Carter and Zehra and then trudged back upstairs. Alexander remained at the table a while longer, speaking with Carter about making arrangements for a flight out of Istanbul.

"As discreetly as possible," Alexander added.

"And where is it you are going now?"

Alexander played through the poem in his mind again and grinned. "Malta. We're going to Malta. I think there's a sunken ship somewhere in the Mediterranean with our name on it."

"I can get you tickets for two days out. That should be sufficient rest time, do you not agree?"

"Yes, thank you." The professor grunted as he stood, his tired muscles from the day's activities throbbing in protest. A ten-hour car ride hadn't helped, but they made it here safely and without being followed. He'd take the pain if it meant a few days of being safe. "Thank you both again, and thank Oliver for me when you speak with him."

"Of course. Have a good night's sleep, Professor. I'm just down here on the ground floor if you have need of anything."

Alexander tiredly nodded, turned, and slowly climbed the stairs, each step taking more effort than he expected.

"And Professor?" Carter softly called up after him. "There is no reason to worry, sir. You know the nature of Oliver's work and some of the things he might store here in transition..." The butler beamed reassuringly. "We have the most sophisticated security system available, like a museum. We're locked down tight, and even if something happened, the police would be at our doorstep in less than two minutes. You *are* safe here!"

Alexander kindly thanked him, his mind becoming more at ease. He peeked in on the kids and smiled to see them both passed out in their beds, Drew snoring quietly. He closed their door and walked down the hall to his own room. After kicking off his boots, he collapsed on the bed and poured out his heart to the Lord with overwhelmed gratitude that they had made it through the day in one piece.

◊ ◊ ◊

Kadir opened his eyes at the sound of rushing steps. A robed man fell to one knee before him and held out a slip of paper. Kadir took it and as he read the words, a grin spread across his face. He settled back in his chair and closed his eyes. Today was not such a waste after all.

CHAPTER IX

Alexander stretched in the plush bed and smiled at the warm sunlight falling through the open window. A cool, Turkish breeze ruffled the curtains and church bells chimed somewhere in the city announcing the hour. It was earlier than he thought, but he'd slept soundly. Though his body was rested, his achy joints from yesterday were now stiff and he spent a few minutes stretching before he finally felt ready to face the day. He was thankful they all had decided to stick around for another day at least.

On his way down to the kitchen, he knocked on Drew and Kaci's door, but neither answered. He opened the door a crack and grinned to see them sleeping, faces down in their pillows, arms resting in mirror of each other. He considered letting them sleep longer, but figured they were anxious to know what their next clue was.

"Morning, sleepyheads," he wryly announced, rapping his knuckles on the doorframe.

Drew grunted and Kaci dragged the blankets over her head.

"Fine, keep sleeping. I guess I'll make plans without the two of you. Figure out where we have to go next...in the middle of the Mediterranean."

"What?" Kaci bolted upright, shoving the covers from her face.

"I'm awake," Drew chimed in, trying to stagger to his feet. "No planning without us!"

Chuckling, he promised he would wait and said he would meet them downstairs for breakfast. The smell of freshly baked bread met his nose along with some strongly brewed coffee. "Good morning, Carter, Zehra," he said in greeting.

"Ah, we did not expect you up so early," Carter said, smiling back. "Coffee?"

"Yes, black, if you please."

Carter brought him a steaming cup. "How did you sleep?"

"Better than I have since this trip started," he confessed and took a long sip of the hot brew. "This is fantastic. And breakfast smells amazing."

"Traditional Turkish breakfast for you today," Zehra said as she bustled to the table with a tray bearing an assortment of food. "Boiled eggs, sesame halvah, tomatoes, sweet peppers, sucuk, and feta cheese. Oh, and olives, almost forgot the olives." She hurried back to the counter and laid out the final dish as Carter set plates around the table for Kaci and Drew as well. "If you think the kids might want something different, let me know."

"Oh no, they're quite adventurous, the two of them. Fairly certain they'd eat anything."

Alexander placed a piece of the sesame-based halvah on his plate along with a boiled egg and some olives. He had just finished expressing to God his gratitude for the food, and was about to dig in when his niece and nephew joined him. They thanked Zehra and Carter before sitting down and looking at what was offered for breakfast. Drew shrugged and started putting one of each item on his plate to try. Kaci stuck with the tomatoes and olives and a piece of the halvah. Zehra poured them some juice as they prayed silently for their meal, and then turned to stare expectantly at their uncle.

"What?" He looked at them innocently.

"You made us wait until morning to hear what the clue meant," Kaci pointed out. "Come on, Uncle James, you can't expect us to keep waiting!"

Alexander grinned and winked, but when they both groaned, he gave in. "Very well, but first let's pray and thank our Heavenly Father for the protection He has graciously given to us these last couple of days." He bowed his head and held out his hands. Drew and Kaci each took one. He didn't expect Carter to join them, but the older man stepped forward and gripped Drew's other hand, and Zehra closed their small prayer circle. Alexander smiled at them and closed his eyes. "God, we wish to thank you for granting us this day, for keeping us safe beneath your wings, and for the hospitality of our kind hosts. Please look over us and them as we continue on our quest. Amen."

The word was echoed around the table and everyone returned to breakfast, quietly eating their food as they waited for Alexander to pick up the statue Kaci brought down with her. It set on the table by his plate.

"You know what I find fascinating," he started and both kids leaned forward eagerly. "How there are such grand similarities between God's protection of us and preservation of His Word through the centuries of time."

"What do you mean?" It wasn't his niece or nephew who asked, but Zehra who was also leaning closer, genuinely intrigued.

Alexander reached around to his hip where he kept his Bible. He held up the worn leather volume for them all to see. "People don't realize it, but there's a battle, a spiritual warfare that's constantly raging, seeking to undermine and destroy the Word of God." He set the Bible on the table, resting his hand on it reverently. "Empires have tried to burn it, stamp it out forever. Kings have sought to banish it, and men have eagerly scoffed at it. Translators have spent their days hunched over the pages, finding new ways to pollute His Word and yet…yet it still stands."

No one made a sound. All their eyes were glued to the Bible beneath his hand.

"No other book in the history of mankind has been attacked more than this Book here," he continued quietly. "But it has survived, despite all the intense efforts to annihilate it."

"Really?" Kaci asked, her eyes bright with curiosity.

"Yes," the professor smiled. "For instance, in 175 B.C., the King of Syria ordered the Jews to destroy their Scriptures and worship the Greek gods. But a man named Judas Maccabaeus led a revolt and saved the books, winning independence for the Jewish nation."

Kaci and Drew leaned in closer, drawn in by the history lesson.

"The Roman emperor Diocletian outlawed Christianity during his rule, its leaders killed and their Bibles burned. And yet, as a sign of God's providence, the following emperor, Constantine, legalized Christianity and even went so far as to pay for fifty new hand-copied Bibles to be taken around the known world." Alexander leaned back in his chair as the rest at the table stared in awe at the Bible before them.

"Do you believe the Devil is behind these attacks?" Drew asked.

"Absolutely. I believe God's Word has been Satan's number one target for generation after generation. Even now, he seeks to rip its truth apart – either destroying it or somehow diluting it. Why do you think there are so many translations existing today? Because he wants to throw people off the right track. He knows the Bible is the key to all life's questions." Alexander paused and smiled, feeling his faith fill him and warm him from the inside out. "The Bible holds the answer to everything, if people only knew how to trust God's every word."

He slid the Bible across the table for Drew to pick up and examine. "It's truly amazing once you start thinking about it," the boy mused.

"Quite incredible," Carter agreed.

"*'The grass withereth, the flower fadeth: but the word of our God shall stand for ever,'*" Alexander recalled from his memory. "Isaiah 40:8. And it's true. The Bible *has* stood through all these long centuries, never changing, never wavering. Psalm 100:5 promised that *'His truth endureth to all generations.'* And the Son of God vowed *'my words shall not pass away.'* Furthermore, He claimed in Luke 16:17, *'And it is easier for heaven and earth to pass, than one tittle of the law to fail.'* Isn't that astounding?" Alexander took a pen from his pocket, began to draw a couple of letters on his paper napkin, and continued. "He was saying that it would be easier for the universe to be no more, than for this dot over the 'i' or the tail mark of this 'Q' to fail in being preserved in the Bible for us!"

Everyone at the table was speechless, enthralled with the preciousness of God's Word.

Alexander suddenly chuckled, remembering a story he knew from his studies of the Bible and of those who scoffed it over the years. "What's so funny, Uncle James?" Kaci asked, smiling at him.

"Just thinking of some people in history who didn't love the Bible like we do."

"Like who?"

"The French philosopher Voltaire. He was a skeptic who destroyed the faith of many people. He boasted that within one hundred and fifty years of his death, the Bible would disappear and the only copies of it would be in museums." He chuckled again as he added, "Twenty-five years after his death, the Geneva Bible Society moved into his former home and used his printing presses to print countless Bibles that were distributed across the world."

The others laughed with him, seeing the irony in the situation.

"But...how did God preserve the Bible over thousands of years?" Kaci wondered aloud. "Obviously, *someone* in each generation had to be a part of helping with this."

"You are precisely correct, my little monster," Alexander commented with a lop-sided grin. "The amount of work and sacrifice God's people have made for His Word is staggering. Nevertheless, they considered it a privilege and an honor."

He leaned forward with his arms crossed on the table. He was thinking to himself how he could give a condensed yet concise answer. He began, "It all started with the Levites. Of course, God used Moses to write the first five books of the Old Testament; they were called the Pentateuch. He charged these men with the responsibility of protecting these scrolls. And they did it, very seriously. As the Old Testament was being assimilated over the generations and copied for people to use, Jewish scribes were given specific and meticulous guidelines in how to copy it to maintain its complete accuracy."

He flipped to a random page and turned it around so all at the table could see. "For example, copyists would count and compare each sentence, each word, and each letter to make sure everything was an exact match. They'd say the words aloud, never copying from memory, as they wrote it down. If an error was found on a page, they would immediately tear it up and rewrite the whole thing again. Before they wrote the name of God, they would wipe their pens and say His name in prayer. Every time they came to God's most precious and holy name – Jehovah – they would wash their whole bodies as if they were unclean vessels, unworthy to write it."

"Wow! That would take a very long time," Drew reflected, imagining sitting in a room for that long copying from one page to another. "And patience, lots of patience."

"Hence, patience being a virtue. And, they had enough to do it the right way," Alexander told his nephew. "Nothing else mattered to them. These people devoted their lives to ensure its accuracy down to the letter. After they were done copying a book of the Bible, it was then compared with the ancient manuscript from which it was copied. If there was one wrong letter, the entire copy was rejected." Alexander smiled. "Yes, through the faithfulness of His children, God has preserved His inspired Holy Word so we could have a copy of it today."

"I feel so convicted," said Kaci. "I have not been as grateful for my Bible as I should be."

Drew nodded that he felt the same way. "But, I'm so thankful that since we were kids Mom has encouraged us to read our Bibles every morning before we get on with our day. And..." he paused. "And Dad, too...when he was alive." His voice trailed off.

Seeking to bring the kids' attention to the matter at hand, the professor quickly remarked, "Yes, all of this – how God has preserved His Word – is just as incredible as this path we're on. We have been divinely guided and protected so far on our journey. Luck had nothing to do with it. God has been good to us!" Alexander rejoiced, Drew and Kaci warmly agreeing with him. He picked up the marble statue that was resting off to the side on the table. Zehra began dishing out seconds on breakfast for everyone. "Let me read the poem again."

'The weight of four
Upon the ocean floor
Only one bears the mark
Like a light in the dark.'

"Any ideas?" he asked.

Kaci and Drew mouthed the words repeatedly, staring at each other in confusion. "Weights upon the ocean floor…anchors?" Drew said and his eyes widened. "Anchors! Of a ship!"

"That is exactly right," Alexander smiled. He took his Bible and opened it up to a specific passage. "I have been giving this some thought. It is quite a stretch, but after what we have seen and experienced already, it is not impossible…"

"What do you mean, Uncle James?" Kaci asked, leaning over to see what book and chapter he had turned to.

"In Acts 27, Luke has a very interesting story to relay here," he said, nodding to the pages. "About a voyage with Paul once when they were taken prisoner and an unpredictable, horrible storm came that was nearly the end of them all." He skimmed through the passage to summarize for the others listening in. "Paul was arrested in Jerusalem, but after not being cleared by the authorities in Caesarea where he was tried, he decided to appeal to Caesar in Rome. He and Luke set out on a ship under the guard of the centurion Julius and eventually reached Myra, where they transferred to an Alexandrian grain vessel that was headed for Rome. Of course, you know the story. They were shipwrecked before they were able to get there."

He paused, looking over to Drew, who had suddenly and quickly pulled out his iPad and typed something onto it. After a brief moment of silence, his eyes widened, and the professor – intuitively knowing what he found – asked, "Drew, would you mind showing the others what you have just discovered?"

Drew flipped over the tablet. "It's the same kind of ship!" he exclaimed. On the screen of his Encyclopedia Britannica app was a painting of a grain vessel that matched the marble statue resting on the table before them.

Kaci's eyes narrowed with astonishment. "So wait, we're looking for Paul's sunken ship? Really?"

"No one's found it before?" Drew asked excitedly.

"Not to my knowledge. For the past five hundred years, tradition has held that the shipwreck of Paul occurred in a bay on the northeast side of the island of Malta, which is south of Sicilia, Italy. Yet nothing has been found to-date, in spite of extensive exploration. I believe that is simply because no one has ever taken the evidence that exists on the pages of the Bible and connected it all together!"

Drew held up his hand. "This is incredible! We're going to need a map."

"Ah, I have just the thing! Give me a moment." Carter set down his teacup and hurried from the kitchen, and they heard him rummaging around in the den - a vintage room with wall-to-wall bookshelves stacked high with old volumes. Kaci and Drew helped Zehra clear the last few dishes and cups that lingered on the table. When Carter returned, he carried a large map of the Mediterranean with a backer board, along with a box of pushpins. Mumbling under his breath, he pushed a pin at Myra. "There...and also another one at Malta, here. Continue if you please. Drew?" Carter handed him the pins and together they stood over the map as Alexander picked up the story.

"Luke recorded that it was not until they sailed along the southern coast of Crete that their voyage took a radical turn for the worse. Gale-force leading winds of a disastrous Mediterranean weather phenomenon known as *'Euroclydon'* swept down from the northeast and slammed into their ship, threatening to capsize their vessel."

Drew found Crete and pushed in another pin. Carter produced a string and wrapped it from the first pin to the second. "The sailors desperately tried to bring her about in order to return to safety, but their efforts were useless as their ship was driven hard into the open sea. However, it appears they found the winds calm enough around Clauda Island, which today is known as Gaudho, to use the ship's cables to undergird it and reinforce the hull."

Drew pushed in another pin at the tiny island south of Crete. Alexander's finger skimmed down the page of the Bible. "Verse 17 says, *'...and, fearing lest they should fall into the quicksands, strake sail, and so were driven.'*"

"*Quicksands*...what does that mean, Uncle James?" Kaci asked, reading over his shoulder.

"Yes, very interesting that you should bring that up. In the New Testament Greek, it is the word *'Syrtis'*. The Bible is actually referring to a specific location here."

"I think I've got something," Drew piped up as he studied a historical article on his tablet. "Apollonius of Rhodes talked about it in his book *Argonautica* written in the 3rd century B.C. He says here that it is a place in *'the Libyan Sea between Carthage and Cyrenaicia off the coast of Africa, full of shallows and sandbanks.'"*

He paused as he silently read on. Meanwhile, Carter drifted his finger over the map, "So it would be located somewhere in here."

"Wow," Drew continued, summarizing what he was reading. "It was the greatest fear of any sailor in the Mediterranean. The water was dark, filled with seaweed and foamy waves. Once a ship got stuck in that region, there was no hope of ever getting out again. They were stranded, with miles of ocean surrounding them!"

Alexander nodded, "This is why the men on Paul's ship were so frightened of the storm blowing them in such a violent southwestern direction. So for the next two weeks, they dumped overboard as many supplies as they could to keep themselves somewhat heading west."

Carter took a pin and put it in the heart of Syrtis. Then he grabbed a black sharpie, circled the region, and crossed it off. Kaci looked at elderly man and smiled, "May I do that next time?"

"Of course, my dear," he answered with a fatherly grin. "So, we know they did not go there."

"What else does the Bible tell us, Uncle James?" Drew asked.

The professor was deep in thought. "There are a lot of key facts here. Verse 27-29 tells us that on the fourteenth night, the sailors sensed they were nearing land. They took a couple of soundings and found that the water was 120 feet deep. A few moments later, they did it again and discovered that it was only 90 feet deep. *'Then fearing lest we should have fallen upon rocks, they cast four anchors out of the stern,'* and waited for daylight. When the morning came, verse 39 tells us, *'they knew not the land:'"*

Alexander took off his glasses to wipe the lenses. He stood, peering down at the map. "Malta is the only island they could have reached in the fourteen days of being pushed across the Mediterranean. Of course, we know where they ended up because we have the whole Biblical account. But, when they were experiencing this, *they* didn't know that it was Malta. If the sailors had been on the north side of the island, they would have recognized where they were. Malta was not an out-of-the-way place. It was a frequent stopping point for many vessels. But all of the main ports they would have been familiar with, like Valletta, were on the northern side of the island."

"Interesting, sir!" Carter interjected. "So we can readily eliminate the traditional shipwreck location of St. Paul's Bay on the north side." And with that, he handed Kaci the sharpie and pointed to a spot on the map. She grinned as she put a big "X" through the body of water.

The professor continued, sitting back down and taking in the youthful excitement of his niece and nephew, "Verse 39 also says, *'but they discovered a certain creek with a shore, into the which they were minded, if it were possible, to thrust in the ship.'* Hmm. The wording here sounds a little cryptic, but..."

"Are we looking for some sort of stream?" Drew frowned, cutting him off, scrolling through his tablet, "Because the geographic description given here is telling me that Malta doesn't have any rivers at all."

Alexander chuckled, "No. Not necessarily. That is what you Americans think of when you hear the word *'stream.'"* He gave Drew a lopsided grin. "Of course, with all that rain from the severe storm for two weeks, they could have spotted some sort of 'flashflood' river that was washing out into the ocean.

But, what I was going to say was that this is an old-fashioned English term that can also be translated as *'a bay of the sea.'* Specifically, according to Scripture, we are looking for a bay with a shoreline – a bay with a beach."

"Do you see that, Drew?" Kaci asked from her position hovering over his shoulder, reading through the description of the island on his iPad. She highlighted the words with her finger.

"Huh!" he mused. "It says here that most of Malta is surrounded by cliffs!"

"Excellent!" Alexander stood back up and leaned over the map. "So I guess we can quickly narrow the possibilities down to a couple of the southern bays with beaches."

"Actually," Drew said slowly, "I'm one step ahead of you. There are two bays that have sandy beaches." The professor looked up quickly, as Drew continued, "St. Thomas Bay and Marsaxlokk." Carter pushed pins into both places on the map. They were on the southeastern part of the island.

Meanwhile, Kaci had pulled out her cell phone; her fingers blurred across the screen. "Here are pictures of them both," she showed the rest of them who gathered around to look. "I also read that both bays are 15 to 20 fathoms deep."

Alexander skimmed back over the pages of his Bible. "Just as described by Luke," he whispered.

"So which one is it?" Drew wondered aloud.

"We must finish going over the facts. The Biblical account concludes that with the storm still raging, they decided to cut loose the four anchors and aim for the shore. Verse 41 states, *'And falling into a place where two seas met, they ran the ship aground; and the forepart stuck fast, and remained unmoveable, but the hinder part was broken with the violence of the waves.'* Luke records that they ran into a sandbar or a reef of some kind and the ship began to break apart. Then, nearly three hundred men on the vessel jumped overboard and swam for their lives. Miraculously, everyone survived. God had promised that to Paul the night before when an angel visited him."

"What a powerful testimony...and such a marvelous opportunity Paul must have had to share the Gospel with these men!" Carter remarked.

"Yes. I believe that many came to know the Lord! So, we must figure out which bay is known for a sandbar or a reef." Alexander observed. "Drew, can you find out if either of these bays allude to one of those two things not far from its shore?"

After a few moments of searching, Drew exclaimed, "Yes!" with Kaci enthusiastically tapping him on the arm. "There it is. Just outside St. Thomas Bay, there is – and I quote – *'a dangerous sandbar called the Muxnar Reef!'* There is a link here to a nautical guide, saying that it is treacherous for boats and must be avoided. It has...two currents running into each other beneath the surface of the water causing violent swirls."

Kaci bounced with excitement, "Could this be the same place the Bible is talking about?"

"Yes, I believe so!" Alexander remarked as he began pacing around the room. His heart was pounding. "But, before we jump to any final conclusions, let's work our way back from the shore. Ultimately, we are looking for four clues: a bay with a beach, a reef or sandbar where 'two seas' meet, a seabed with about 90 feet of depth, and a place the sailors did not recognize."

"Uncle James, St. Thomas Bay fits *all* of those descriptions!" Drew exclaimed.

Kaci took the sharpie from Carter's hand and crossed off Marsaxlokk and made an emphatic circle around St. Thomas

Bay. Carter tied string from the Clauda Island pin to the final destination at Malta. *Could this be it?* Alexander wondered to himself. He closed his Bible, studying the path and staring in awe as he realized they could be following the same path Paul took so many centuries before. "I'm not sure what's there, but if that's where the clue leads us, then that's where we go. We're going to be diving for anchors. Are you both in?"

Kaci and Drew stared at him like he was crazy. "No, no, I think we're ready to give up. What do you say, Kaci? Had enough?"

She rolled her eyes. "Yeah, I think we're so close to the end that I'm just going to throw in the towel right now and call it a day." They laughed when Alexander sighed and took his seat again. "We're leaving in the morning, right?"

"You'll have to ask Carter; he booked our tickets."

Carter smiled as he studied the map. "Everything is set for eight o'clock in the morning. You'll be in Malta by lunch."

"And in the water soon after!" Drew announced. "Wonder what's down there?"

"What do you mean, what's down there?" Kaci asked and the smile slipped from her face.

"You know, we're going diving in a very mysterious location. Probably a sea monster or two," Drew teased.

"You just think you're so funny, don't you?" Kaci grumbled. "There're no such thing as sea monsters. So don't start trying to scare me now."

Alexander listened to their banter as he finished his coffee and looked forward to at least one day to actually relax and enjoy this semi-vacation. Just one day to recoup and then they would be off again for Malta and St. Thomas Bay.

CHAPTER X

C arter saw the professor and the teenagers off early the next morning. He was just cleaning out Oliver's study, something he rarely had a chance to do when his boss was home, when the bell rang out. *The plane for Malta should be on its way by now,* he reasoned to himself, but his gut still nagged that something was terribly wrong as he rushed downstairs.

When he pulled the front door open, however, it wasn't Alexander he saw on the stoop.

"Good day, sir," a man with a strange accent said, bowing his head. He wore a wool cap, but the dark lines of a tattoo peeked out from beneath it. "I'm looking for Oliver Winthrop. Is he at home by chance?"

"I'm afraid he's out of the country," Carter said politely while his eyes searched the sidewalk behind the man. The hair on the back of his neck stood up. "If you would kindly leave me your name, I'll be sure to tell him you stopped by."

The man bobbed his head when a thud came from inside the house. Carter turned, wondering if Zehra dropped something in the kitchen when the man shoved him backwards into the house, with four other men rushing in after, slamming and locking the front door behind them. Zehra screamed and Carter tried to fight his attacker off, but the man pressed a blade to his throat and he stilled immediately.

"What do you want?" he seethed, watching as they dragged Zehra into the foyer with him.

"You had visitors the past two days, did you not?" the man asked gruffly, and Carter glanced at the scar on his face, turning up his lips on one side.

"I don't know what you're referring to..." The blade pressed in harder and he winced as he felt a small trickle of warm liquid roll down his neck.

"Don't make me hurt you, old man."

Carter's eyes darted to Zehra, but she subtly shook her head at him until one of the men close by told her to look away. "I don't know anything."

The man lowered the blade from his throat with an angry sigh. He reached up and removed the wool cap covering his head and Carter saw the tattoo. His eyes widened as he realized who these men were, based on what Alexander had told him.

"I wanted this to go smoothly, but you, you just don't want to play along, do you?"

"Let her go at least, please," Carter pleaded.

The man narrowed his gaze at him. "Are you lying to me?"

"No, no, I'm not. She knows nothing about what's going on, so please let her go."

The man nodded and two others dragged Zehra toward the front door. "No, Carter! Carter, I'm not going to leave you! No!"

"Get out of here," the butler yelled at her and they shoved her outside, locking the door behind her. He knew exactly what she would do and where she would go, but he worried the authorities wouldn't make it in time. Carter gritted his teeth, irritated with the foolish mistake he'd made in not resetting the security system after Alexander and the young people left. He wasn't sure how long he could hold out. Though he had been a military man, those days were long behind him and the look in this man's eyes promised him pain.

"Now then, tell me where the professor and the two brats are and we'll be on our way."

Carter squared his shoulders and braced himself for whatever would happen next. "I will not tell you anything that could harm them," he replied firmly. "They're just kids."

"I gave you a chance, old man," the tattooed man replied. "Guess it'll be the hard way for you then. Hold him."

Carter struggled as two men came toward him and held his arms. The knife glinted in the light and Carter stared the man down, praying for strength.

◊ ◊ ◊

As soon as the plane landed at the Malta International Airport, Alexander and the kids took a taxi to a scuba rental shop in Marsaskala, in the southeastern edge of Malta. They couldn't go straight to St. Thomas Bay, but had to head to the area just north of it to find a fisherman willing to rent his boat to them and take them out to where they were pretty sure they needed to go. With their gear in tow, they headed to the docks and found a few locals near their boats, talking and laughing loudly.

"Excuse me," Alexander hailed them as he neared and spoke quickly with one of the men. Kaci and Drew watched from a little ways off, each searching the surrounding buildings and people's faces for any sign they were followed. "Kaci,

Drew!" Alexander called and waved them over. "This is Aiden and he's going to be our guide for the day."

The man, looking older than Alexander with his frizzy greying hair, held out a hand to each of them, offering up a warm smile that revealed a couple missing teeth. "Good day to you both. Out for a bit of diving then?" His accent was interesting and Kaci found she liked hearing the old man talk.

"Yes, a bit of a treasure hunt, I guess," Drew replied as they followed the man down the docks to another fishing boat.

"Treasure hunt, eh? Best be looking out for the beast that's down there. Horrible stories."

"Beast?" Kaci asked, her voice slightly high-pitched. "What beast?"

"See, I told you," commented Drew slyly, elbowing his sister.

"Just a local legend is all. Say a great beast lives beneath the waters. It's why not many fishermen go to that bay. Say it's cursed and the beast eats all the fish near there anyway." His clear blue eyes peered off into the distance, and his gnarled hand rubbed his stubbly chin.

"Has anyone...died?" Kaci dared to wonder.

The man snapped out of his reverie and winked. "It's only a legend, my dear."

But his words stuck with Kaci and Drew and they whispered about it as they walked, one excited while the other wished the sailor hadn't said anything at all about a beast.

The boat wasn't large by any means, just a typical fishing vessel with a winch, which was what Alexander needed. The boat only needed to hold the four of them and get them down to St. Thomas Bay. Once their gear was on board, Aiden shoved off and moved them out of the narrow bay before turning south, following the coastline. The crystal blue waters stretched out before them and the smell of salt made Kaci wish this was a vacation and she could find a beach to bum on for a few days. The running around was exciting, but part of her wished for more days of rest. Staying in Istanbul an extra day returned a lot of her energy but it also made her long for more peaceful times. She wasn't going to say anything to Drew or Uncle James, though. They needed her.

Alexander showed the picture of the map to Aiden and the old man nodded, steering the boat out a bit further from the shore until a sandy beach came into view. "Just beyond the Muxnar Reef, you said?"

"Yes," the professor replied, "and the seabed needs to be about 15 fathoms."

The vessel steered wide of the reef, but Drew and Kaci could see through the blue water that the coral was teaming with schools of fish and bright colors. Drew shouted to her over the loud engine, "This is so unbelievable!" She nodded excitedly as she pulled her windblown hair into a ponytail.

After keeping a close eye on the depth finder, Aiden killed the engine. He remarked, "This is as close as we can get you. Going any further could put us in danger of where the water collides together. No one knows where that is exactly, but I think we are at a safe distance. And, this is around 15 fathoms," His weathered face cracked open in a smile.

"Perfect!" Alexander gave him a lopsided grin in return, slapping him on the back.

"This will be close, but without an actual location, you'll be guessing down there," the craggy local told them. "What is it you're looking for?"

"Anchors," Alexander replied. "Forgotten anchors from many, many years ago."

"Anchors, eh? Interesting treasure," he said with a wink.

The boat creaked and rocked as the waves moved it about and the three suited up in their wetsuits, tanks, and masks. Their flippers went on next and Alexander made sure Drew had the small metal detector in his hand. He and Kaci fell backwards off the edge of the boat, splashing into the water. Aiden took the edge of the chain and handed it to Drew, minding the hook at the end. Alexander was getting ready to join them when Aiden held up his hand.

"Just in case," he said and lifted open the top of an old, wooden chest. "Take this with you."

"For what?" Alexander asked, concerned, as he took the old harpoon gun. He already had a bowie knife attached at his belt in case they had to cut away seaweed. "I thought you said the sea creature was just a legend."

"Oh, that?" The fisherman cackled with laughter. "That *is* a legend, but sharks sometimes wander into the sea. Best to be safe, eh? Take it and keep an eye out...for sharks *and* for that beast." He patted Alexander on the shoulder.

Alexander frowned beneath his mask, but made sure his gear was good to go before joining the kids in the water. He slung the harpoon over his back, careful of his tank, and hoped they had everything they needed. They gave each other thumbs up as they dove down into the water. The water was a clear bright blue, but the farther they descended, the more the bay was filled with kelp and seaweed, obstructing their view ahead. Alexander led the way, going deeper until he saw the sandy floor beneath them. Brightly colored fish swam about, catching the rays of sun that filtered through the water above. The further out into the bay they swam, however, the darker the water seemed to become until they reached a ledge and had to swim down through the standing seaweed. They had to be getting close and he paused so Drew could swim up beside him, moving the detector around in a wide arc beneath his swimming body as they reached the sandy bottom again.

Drew squinted through his mask when the detector lit up briefly. He couldn't see much, for it was darker down here than he expected. He tapped Alexander on the arm and flipped on the tiny lamp on his head, motioning for his uncle and Kaci to do the same. Drew swam on, trying to aim his light in the right direction.

When a hand clamped down on his leg he flinched and whirled around in the water to see Kaci, staring intently to the right of them. She opened her arms wide then motioned something swimming. Alexander and Drew looked, but after a few moments of nothing, they placed her between them and swam further along. The detector lit up again and then Drew's light caught something shiny through the seaweed. He swam faster, pushing himself ahead and through the kelp and seaweed to see the top of an old anchor sticking out of the sand. Alexander smiled behind his mask and swam closer, brushing sand from around it. It didn't take much to find another beside it to the right and another, and another.

Four anchors. All four anchors were right here. Alexander couldn't believe it! They'd found the anchors of Paul's ship. He couldn't even begin to describe the elation he felt as he nodded excitedly to Drew.

But it was Kaci who he should have been watching. She had tried to tell them that since swimming over that ledge, she hadn't spotted a single fish. Not one. She watched Drew take the chain as he and Alexander examined each anchor. They seemed concentrated on the last one, pointing to something on it, but Kaci stopped watching them when something created a cold current behind her. She turned, aiming her light at the darkness surrounding them. Had it been this dark before?

The harder she stared, the more the shadows seemed to consume everything around them. There! She saw it again, a lurking shape shooting through the water. It was too skinny to be a shark, and she hadn't seen any fins. As far as she knew, nothing that big should live out here.

The legend – could it be? But the old man teased her, surely.

Her legs moved in a steady rhythm, keeping her where she was in the water, watching.

She should have looked down.

Something suddenly dragged her downward and she screamed, but it was muffled by her mask. She kicked, trying to break free as her light fell on a long, purplish tentacle jerking her through the water and down to the bottom of the sea floor. She reached down, frantically trying to yank it off, but it stuck to her leg, wrapping even tighter. Drew and Alexander were too far away to hear her, but her light! Reaching up she flashed her light on and off a few times, aiming it in their direction.

Alexander was closely studying the marking of a torch on the last anchor when he noticed the light from behind him. What was Kaci doing? He turned to see and instant panic erupted in him. She was being dragged away by a large, hulking shadowy form in the seaweed. He grabbed Drew's arm and they swam after her. A tentacle was wrapped around her leg and as Drew grabbed his sister's hands to pull her back, Alexander swam toward the creature and with his bowie knife, cut the tentacle in one clean swipe. He watched the rest of the tentacle recede, but the beast wasn't gone.

Drew pulled Kaci to him, keeping her hand in his as they swam in a tight circle, searching for the beast. Drew couldn't believe what he had seen. Nothing that big should be down here. He glanced back at the anchors and quickly grabbed

Alexander's arm when he saw the beast hovering over the one they needed, wrapping its tentacles around it, and lifting it up out of the sand.

They couldn't let it take the anchor! They all started swimming toward it, Alexander pushing himself harder and arriving before the kids. He noticed the anchor must have been too heavy for the beast, because it slipped through his tentacles, thudding to the floor and shooting a plume of sand up into the water making it impossible to see. Drew lost sight of Kaci and Alexander, holding his arms out trying to feel for them. A hand grabbed his and held it tightly. Kaci. But where was their uncle? Kaci tugged on his hand and when the sand cleared enough, Drew saw her pointing to where Alexander, with a tentacle wrapped around his middle, was being dragged away into the black abyss. He'd dropped his knife and the harpoon was no longer on his back. Drew and Kaci searched for it, knowing that if they didn't find the weapon, they had no chance of saving their uncle from this creature. They dove down deeper as the beast continued to mercilessly pull Alexander away.

Kaci grabbed Drew's arm and pointed again. There, in the sand was the harpoon gun. Drew grabbed for it and Kaci directed her light on the creature, searching for the best place to hit it. The light moved up its purple skin and finally to a large, black eye with a narrowed slit for a pupil staring back at them. Drew didn't waste any time lifting the harpoon gun, his finger finding the trigger to discharge it. He said a quick prayer that he wouldn't hit his uncle and then fired the weapon.

The harpoon shot through the water and the creature immediately released Alexander when it was struck square in the eye. It quickly swam off, squirting black ink in its wake. The three watched the seaweed, waiting for the beast to return, but it never came back. The ink took a while to clear and when it did, the three stared at each other and smiled, shaking their heads. Nothing could be easy about this adventure. Nothing at all.

Thankfully, the winch Drew had attached to the anchor was still in place and they gave it a tug to let Aiden know to pull it up. The chain grew tense and they helped lift the anchor out of the sandy bed so it could be brought to the surface.

They followed the anchor through the water and up to the surface where Aiden waited. "Well now, that's some piece of metal you found," the fisherman said, using the controls of his fishing trolley winch to lift the heavy anchor and bring it onto the deck of his boat.

Alexander and the kids swam around to the ladder and the standing platform at the rear of the boat. He made them climb up first before he joined them and they all sank onto the deck.

"What happened down there?" Aiden asked in alarm. "The harpoon...you had to use it?"

"Yeah," Drew said after he removed his gear, struggling to catch his breath. "That beast of yours was there, guarding the anchors."

Aiden cracked a smile, thinking he was joking, but the serious looks on Alexander and Kaci's faces said otherwise. "You actually saw it?" he asked.

"Saw it, got in a fight with it, and won," Drew said and held his arm up in the air. "Yay team."

Kaci gave him a weak high-five, offering up a grin. "You shot it in the eye. Did you mean to shoot it in the eye?"

"Nope, just pulled the trigger."

Alexander grunted. "Don't tell me that."

"What? It worked, didn't it?"

Aiden eyed the three of them like they were crazy. "Well, get yourself out of your gear and we'll take a closer look at this treasure of yours and later, later I want more details about this beast. No one will believe me."

After they caught their breaths, they took off their diving gear and then moved in to examine the anchor. Aiden had already removed the chain and was gently brushing off sand and what coral and barnacles he could without damaging the surface.

"That's brass," he told them. "Not rusted except in a few small places."

Alexander ran his fingers over the torch signet on the upper part of the anchor. There was nothing else carved into it, nothing at all. "I don't understand."

"What were you hoping to find?" Aiden asked.

"I'm not sure, but there has to be something besides this mark. A clue to lead us onward."

Aiden had no idea what they were talking about, but he ran his hands over his frizzy hair and shrugged. "Depending on what you're looking for, sailors back in the day used to smuggle things in all sorts of ways. One of those ways was by hollowing out extra anchors on the ship."

Alexander frowned. "Hollowing them out?"

"This here thing, it's what, Roman from the design?"

"You know your ship anchors," Alexander mused, impressed.

"Ha! I was raised on the water. Come from a long line of sailors." He held up his hand as he added, "Besides, everyone knows this was a stop for the Romans. If any anchors are going to be found down there, chances are they're Roman."

He started knocking his knuckles against the anchor, listening closely. Alexander watched the old man move over every inch of the anchor. When he neared the top part of the shaft, the only place where the brass had completely worn away, the sound changed. All four of them stared at the place as he knocked a second time. To be sure, he knocked all the way down the shaft until the sound changed. He moved back to the top and tried again, grinning at the hollow sound.

"I think we may have found your treasure."

Alexander examined the top of the shaft, running his fingers around the rim searching for a way to open it. There was a ring where the chain would have passed through. He gave it a tug, but it didn't budge. "Do you have a pole of some kind?"

Aiden snapped his fingers and hurried to the side of the boat where he had a long, metal pole with a hook at the end. He removed the hook and slid the pole through the ring. He and Alexander started to push the rod, and after a few long moments of pushing, grunting under their breath with muscles bulging, the top gave. A grinding sound made them pause, but only for a second. Kaci and Drew hurried over to join them and together, the four pushed, walking around the anchor as the top twisted free until finally, it was off altogether.

"You think water got in there?" Kaci asked. "It could've damaged whatever they hid."

"For our sake, let's pray it didn't." Alexander reached his hand down into the anchor and felt around carefully. At first, he though there was nothing, but then his fingers brushed over the edges of something smooth, almost like leather. He gripped it gently and dragged it out of the anchor for all of them to see.

"What is that?" Aiden asked curiously as Alexander looked for a place to set it down. "Inside, there's a table and a light."

They followed Aiden into the bowels of his boat where a circular table was bolted to the inner deck and a lamp hung overhead. Alexander set the container down and popped open the end. No water spilled out and the cylindrical container was dry. He pulled out a rolled-up parchment, setting the container aside.

The parchment crinkled as he unfurled the first one and set the others aside. "It's in Greek," he said and began to slowly translate the rough writing. As the words became clear, his eyes lit up and his hands trembled with excitement.

"What does it say?" Kaci asked. "Is it another clue?"

"It's a letter," he told them. "From the church in Myra to the church in Rome. This is incredible!"

"Church?" Aiden repeated then his eyes widened. "Anchors...wait! You found Paul's shipwreck?"

"No, not the wreck, but the anchors," Alexander said. "I take it you know the story well?"

"Ha, what person on Malta doesn't? This find, this is amazing. I don't believe it."

"Believe it." Alexander translated the rest of the page and when he reached the end, he started back at the top to let them know what it said. "There is no mention of the lost scrolls or clue to where to go next, but this makes it quite clear the church in Myra used these ships to send messages back and forth across the Roman Empire. This one here details safe houses and mentions a map. Is one of these a map?"

"Safe houses for Christians?" Kaci asked as she slowly unfurled another page.

"Yes. They were being persecuted so many tried to set up safe houses and hidden churches for their followers. That night when they took Paul, someone must have replaced one of the anchors with their own. These were meant to get to Rome, but they never made it."

The fact that Alexander was holding an actual piece of history, one much like what was found in the tomb in Spain, untouched by man for thousands of years, astounded him. So much lost history in the world, but here he was, able to discover and hold onto a tiny piece of it.

"Here," Drew said, pointing to a scroll that he'd unfolded. "This looks like a map of a city."

"That's Rome," Aiden said before Alexander could. "No doubt about it."

"But it doesn't say anything about the scrolls, does it?" Drew asked, disappointed. "Why would they lead us here if there's not another clue to take us further? I don't even see the torch image on any of these pages."

"Patience, Drew, we must have faith and patience." Alexander set the letter down and studied the map before him. On the right-hand side was more writing. He translated the first part and his brow wrinkled in thought. "This ship was headed for Rome and it can't be a coincidence that Paul was on board at the same time."

"You think he knew what they were doing when he was taken?" Drew asked.

"It's possible. It may be part of the reason why he was so willing to go to Rome. These safe houses listed, they could have been new locations needing to reach the underground church there." Alexander tried to work out the situation, but all he could come up with was that they needed to go to Rome. His eyes gazed down the listings again and he paused when he recognized two names: Aquila and Priscilla. He found the corresponding number on the map and grinned, pointing out where their house would have been in ancient times. "We're going to Rome and we're starting our search right here."

"What's there?" Kaci asked, peering at the place he pointed to.

"The next stop on our tour of ancient history," he informed them brightly. "Aiden, I think we're ready to return to shore if you'd be so kind. We have a plane to catch."

"My pleasure, sir," the fisherman said with a toothy smile and a few minutes later, they were on their way back to the mainland.

◊ ◊ ◊

The scuba shop stood before him and Kadir forced a friendly smile to his face before he entered. The bell on the door rung annoyingly in his ear, but he ignored the urge to shoot it and approached the desk. A scruffy man who smelled of fish and salty sea air grinned through a thick beard.

"Can I help you, sir?"

This was the fourth attempt to find the professor, and Kadir's patience was wearing thin. "Yes, I believe you can. I'm actually looking for a group of people. We became separated when we arrived here and I've been trying to find them."

The man tugged at his beard. "Hmm, and who exactly would you be looking for?"

"James Alexander? He's an old friend, you see. He's traveling with his niece and nephew. Teenagers."

"I see. How is it you became separated for that long of a time?"

"I'm sorry?"

"They came in here a few hours ago for gear and never mentioned they were supposed to be with anyone else." The man wasn't believing Kadir's story, not even a little. He crossed his arms and nodded toward the door. "If you're looking for trouble, I think it best you just leave, sir. Now."

Kadir nodded. "Of course, I was just hoping to find them again."

"Yes, well, best head off to the local authority. They'll help you find your missing friends."

Kadir glanced toward the front of the shop and saw that two of his men blocked the door. He reached to his lower back and removed the pistol there. The shop owner's eyes widened, but before he could yell for help, Kadir leapt over the counter and shoved him hard against the wall, pressing the muzzle of the gun against the man's knee.

"You are going to tell me what you know of the professor and the teenagers, or you're going to start losing body parts. Do I make myself clear?" he seethed.

The man's eyes darted wildly around the shop and he even tried to move, but Kadir pressed the gun harder into his knee.

"One move and I pull this trigger. No one can help you, so tell me what I want to know and this will go easier for you. Much easier. You might not even have to clean up any blood from the floor."

"All right! They were here, like I said, but they only rented gear and then returned it an hour ago!"

"Where did they go? Who were they with?"

"I do not know, I swear! They got on a boat with a single fisherman, that's all I could see from the window. They didn't say anything except how incredible the water was. That's it! Please, that is all I know!"

Kadir stared intently into the man's eyes, but he saw no lying in them. With an angry grunt, he stepped back from the man, who sighed in relief. Kadir's fury got the better of him and he whacked the man hard across the face with his pistol, knocking him to the floor with a pained groan. He had missed them yet again. Each time, his need to find this James Alexander and stop him only grew, turning into a rage he feared he wouldn't be able to control when he finally did catch up with the man. He opened the door to exit the shop and when the bell rang above his head, he snatched it and with a snarl he threw it across the room, ignoring the jingling as it clattered across the floor.

"We missed them by one hour," he bellowed to his men. "I want these sorry excuses for humanity found, do you hear me? We will tear this island apart until we find someone who knows where they went!"

But as his men made ready to move out and begin scouring the city, another ran up to him, panting and holding up his hand to stop Kadir from leaving. "Sir…sir!"

"What is it?"

"We…we found something…one of the fishermen said they got onto a boat, *The Spartan*. It's tied up at dock and the sailor, he's still on it."

Kadir patted the man on the shoulder. "This is how you rise within the brotherhood, my friend. Come, we have someone we must speak to." He marched toward the docks, his men slowly falling into line behind him. A man was singing, off key, at the top of his lungs, as he untangled nets on the deck of the fishing vessel with the name *The Spartan* hand-painted on its side. He was alone when Kadir knocked on the railing of the boat and the man turned.

"Ah, good day to you, sirs. Something I can help you with?" he asked politely, a few missing teeth causing a lisp when he spoke.

Kadir did not wait for permission but stepped onboard, causing the man to frown.

"I'm afraid you can't be on my boat, sir."

"I'm afraid I must insist," Kadir replied and drew his pistol for the man to see. To his credit, the old sailor didn't even flinch or make a sound. He simply glanced from the gun to Kadir as if he'd seen worse in his time.

"Well then, I guess welcome aboard. Did you need me to take you somewhere?"

Kadir paced around the deck as the rest of his men closed in. He searched for any sign of what the professor had done while on board this ship. They went out to scuba dive but what were they looking for? What could possibly be...

"What is that?" he asked, pointing the gun at a brass anchor situated at the far end of the deck.

"Nothing. Scrap metal from some ship is all."

"Then why do you have it?" Kadir hurried over to it, running his hand along the outside, and when he neared the top, he frowned. "It appears a piece is missing." The inside of the shaft was hollowed out and from the way the anchor was shaped and aged, he could assume this came from a ship hundreds of years old. Thousands maybe. "What was so interesting about this piece that made you haul it onboard?"

"Got tangled in my nets," the man said simply. "Figured I'd sell it for scrap, like I said."

"I'm afraid I'm in no mood for lies today," Kadir said and straightened. "A professor and two teenagers were on board your ship and you are going to tell me why." He leered as he closed in on the man, the rest of his men following suit.

CHAPTER XI

"Welcome to Rome's Antiquities Department," Alexander announced as they stepped inside off the busy streets of the ancient city. "My friend should be here to greet us any minute now."

"Who are we meeting with this time?" Kaci asked, her head on a swivel as she took in the artifacts and paintings surrounding them. She could spend all day in here exploring and seeing what secrets this place hid, but they weren't here as tourists. They were on a mission. She just hoped this one didn't involve them going back underwater.

"Lorenzo, an old friend from my University days," Alexander explained. "He's a great historian and cartographer dealing solely with Ancient Rome. If there was ever an expert who could help us find our way to Priscilla and Aquila's home, it's him."

"Alexander! In the flesh and whole," Lorenzo said cheerfully from the doorway and the small group turned. "And I see you've brought friends. *Benvenuto in Roma!*" The man with immaculately combed salt-and-pepper hair and deep brown eyes held out his hand to all three and bobbed his head. "Now, what can I do for you? Your message was very short."

"We were in a bit of a hurry and I'm afraid we still are."

"So this is not a fun social call?" Lorenzo teased, dramatically placing a hand to his chest and pretending to swoon. "You are always on the run. What trouble have you gotten yourself into this time, *mio amico*?"

"Oh you know, hunting for manuscripts and being hunted by a brotherhood bent on stopping us," Kaci quickly replied.

"Or killing us," Drew added.

Lorenzo was still smiling, but when he saw the serious look on Alexander's face, it disappeared. "You are not kidding."

"I'm afraid they're not. We're on a modern-day quest, Lorenzo, and we need a guide."

"Then you have come to the right place. I'm assuming this involves maps of ancient Rome or you would not have called upon me?" he asked, leading them behind the desk and through a door after flashing his badge. "What are you looking for?"

"We have an old map and we need to find where a house would be now," Alexander told him.

Lorenzo nodded and steered them into a large open room with a table in the center. Wooden cabinets lined the far wall, dated and given codes for locations. He murmured under his breath in Italian, running his fingers along the labels. "Ah, this one will do." He slid open a drawer and pulled out a large map of Rome, modern day, framed. He laid it on the table and waited for Alexander to reveal the map they found tucked away in the anchor.

Alexander delicately unrolled it and laid it beside the other map.

"Where did you find this?" Lorenzo asked in awe.

"In an anchor at the bottom of St. Thomas Bay."

"This won't work. Give me a moment," the Italian told them and hurried to the other side of the room. "If you want a more accurate idea of where to find something from that map in today's Rome, we'll have to line them up."

He returned wearing gloves with tracing paper in hand. He asked Alexander to situate the map beneath the tracing paper and Lorenzo slowly but accurately traced the old map so he could lay it over the modern-day city of Rome. When he was finished, Alexander removed the parchment, carefully, and watched as Lorenzo laid the transparent page over the map.

"Now, the rivers and certain roads should align," he whispered under his breath as he moved the transparent map around. "Buildings have come and gone throughout the years of course, but if we do this just right…" He trailed off and grinned when the old roads lined up almost perfectly with the map. "There you have it."

"Neat," Kaci said, and Drew nodded in agreement.

"We're looking for this home," Alexander said, pointing it out on the old map before him.

Lorenzo stared at it then turned back to the transparent one and found it. Using his finger, he marked the place and read the address on the map beneath the old one. "I know this place well. It's an old antique shop. I believe they renovated the house many times so there's not much left of the original structure. I'll find you a copy of the city and mark the location for you."

He left them alone to study the maps. "If the house is gone, any clues might've been destroyed, too," Drew mumbled. "What if we don't find anything?"

"There'll be something there, I'm sure of it. Have a little faith," his uncle squeezed his shoulder.

"Yeah, guess you're right. We've made it this far on nothing but faith, I feel like."

Lorenzo returned a moment later, holding out a folded-up map to Alexander. He frowned as he handed it over. "You know, I've had a thought. Whatever you seek is from ancient times. It may not be found above ground."

"What are you suggesting?"

"That you look below the surface. This city is riddled with catacombs and underground tunnels and passageways," he laughed, "It's a wonder the streets don't collapse in on themselves with what lies beneath, or rather, what doesn't."

"Yay, more dead bodies," Kaci murmured, but Alexander knew his friend was right.

"There are so many beneath our feet, and even more have yet to be discovered. When you reach the shop, I suggest you try heading down."

"Thanks, we'll keep that in mind." Alexander tucked the map away in his back pocket. "I promise when this is all over we'll come back and have a proper social visit."

"I look forward to it. *In bocca al lupo!* Or as you say it, good luck!"

The three left the building behind and set out into the old streets of Rome. Alexander pulled the map from his pocket and unfolded it, pointing out where they currently were. They could take a taxi, but they weren't too far away from the antique shop and the kids were eager to see the sights of the famous city. Alexander kept their pace brisk, but gave them a modified tour as they passed by shops, markets, and old stone buildings that had been around for thousands of years. The architecture was incredible and nothing like what they could see back in the States. When lunchtime rolled around, they stopped at a café with an outdoor patio and ordered platters of cheeses and meats, enjoying the warm breezy weather.

"You know, I'd almost believe for a minute we were actually on vacation," Kaci mused around a mouthful of garlicky buttered bread.

"One of these days, I'll bring you guys back here and we'll do a proper tour of Europe," he promised them. "One where we're not being shot at."

After lunch, they decided they were too full to walk, so Alexander hailed a cab to take them the rest of the way to the antique shop. When they arrived, the professor stared up at the eighteenth century structure and frowned. This was definitely not the original home of Aquila and Priscilla. This part of town was much older and seemed forgotten compared to the rest of Rome that was lively and filled with tourists and locals alike. They walked up to the shop to find a closed sign on the front door and after peering through the windows, saw no sign of life anywhere.

"What do we do now?" Drew asked.

"Now we look for any sign that might lead us to the old catacombs," Alexander suggested, tucking the map away. "The building may have changed, but the underground might still be intact."

"You really think there are tunnels here?"

He nodded at Kaci's confusion. "Many old churches had places to hide or ways to sneak out and away from the Romans should they ever come knocking. With a little guidance from above, we'll find the one that hopefully resided beneath this house."

They walked the length of the front of the building, but finding nothing, moved to the left side, following it around the block until they were met with a high stone wall and no easy way to get over. They considered climbing it, but Alexander didn't want to be caught climbing over a wall with a sign that stated 'no trespassing' in Italian. They headed around to the front of the store again and jogged around to the right side. It led to an alley, narrow, but Drew waved them over when he came to a stop at the end.

"What about these?" he asked, pointing to old, wooden cellar doors. Wood rot covered the edges and a few holes let light from outside filter down into the depths. "Should we try it?"

Alexander couldn't think of a reason not to. As he pulled on the left door, Drew grabbed the right, and together they heaved them open. "Not even locked," he muttered. "Odd." He told the kids to let him go down first, using his cell phone as a flashlight to shine around the gloomy interior.

The air was cool and musty as he moved around the cellar that was much larger than he first anticipated. Something delicately brushed across his face and he swiped at the cobwebs hanging from the ceiling as he shuffled slowly around. The floor beneath his feet was dirt and stone and the walls were lined with broken wooden shelves, mostly empty.

"Anything down there?" Drew asked, peering over the edge.

"Nothing yet, but it's safe for you to come down," he called up and Drew and Kaci joined him in the cellar, both pulling out LED flashlights from their knapsacks. The beams of light joined the one from his cell phone. "Some books over here and a statue." He frowned, leaning closer, brushing dust away from the face.

"Who is that?" Kaci stood beside him, pulling a handkerchief from her bag to clean it off better.

"Looks like renditions I've seen of Paul," Alexander whispered. "We're on the right track, we have to be. Look for the torch symbol, on the floor or the walls maybe."

Kaci moved to the right and Drew to the left, running their lights around the walls along with their hands. Alexander trained his flashlight back over the statue, but there was nothing else on it. He crossed the floor, his boots stomping against the dirt and stone...but then he stopped and backed up a few steps, shining the light at the floor.

"Uncle James?"

He nodded toward the floor and Drew hurried over. "Hear that?" He stomped his boot on the floor and grinned when he heard a hollow sound beneath the dirt. "Trap door perhaps?" Crouching down, he brushed his hand over the dirt and revealed the wooden planks of a door. Drew dropped down beside him, finding the outline of the door along with the hinges and what looked like a place for a key to go. Alexander frowned, jerking at the door, but despite how decrepit the rest of the cellar appeared, the trap door held firm.

"There's no way that key is still down here," Drew grumbled, annoyed.

"Are you sure?" Kaci rushed back to the statue and held it out to Alexander. He glanced at it, not sure of her meaning, when she shook it and something rattled inside the base. "Have some faith, right?"

Alexander took the statue and shattered it on the stone floor. Careful not to cut his fingers, he pushed the broken clay aside and found a bronze key hidden beneath. It glinted in the light as he moved it to the keyhole in the door and turned it. With an excited glance at both of them, he grabbed the handle embedded in the door and tugged. The door pulled open and a narrow set of stone steps was there to greet them, the depths below far darker than the cellar. Alexander put his boot on the first step and yanked it back quickly as the stones crumbled and gave way beneath his weight.

"We can't walk down that," he said and laid down on his stomach, peering into the shadows. "It's not too bad of a drop. Drew? Want to go first?"

Kaci kept her light aimed down as Alexander lowered Drew carefully down around the rubble that had been the stairs. He staggered, but managed to climb down the pile of rock and look around.

"It's a tunnel leading that way," he said pointing as Alexander glanced around the cellar.

"Runs north," he told them both. "Does it look open?"

"As far as I can tell. And no dead bodies yet, so you're safe, sis."

Kaci rolled her eyes as she stepped forward and Alexander helped lower her down next, Drew remaining close by to help steady her on her feet as she skidded down the stones and nearly toppled over. Alexander glanced up at the cellar door, wondering if he should close it, but fear of being locked in made him leave it and the trap door open. If the tunnel was closed ahead, they would have to turn back and he wanted to ensure they had one safe way out. With the key tucked in his pocket so no one could lock them down there, he tucked his phone away and gingerly hunkered down into the hole. Stone crunched beneath his feet and he sort of half ran down the mound of rubble.

"On to the next leg of our journey," he mused, wiping the dirt from his hands to his pants.

"Where do you think this leads?" Drew asked as he led the way, shining his light along the wooden beams in the ceiling and the walls. "One of those underground churches?"

"Maybe. Just take it slow. I don't know how stable this tunnel is."

The further they walked, the muggier the air became and the noise changed. Before, it was utter silence except for the shuffling of their feet. They couldn't even hear the traffic on the streets overhead. But when they reached the end of the long stretch of tunnel, Alexander shone his light along the walls, reaching out to feel the wetness there.

"Water running? Is that what I hear?" Drew peered right and then left, straining his ears.

"We could be close to an old aqueduct," Alexander said, pulling out the map from his pocket and opening it up. "Everything appears damp and it sure feels more wet here."

"Well, which way?" Kaci motioned her light right and left. "Any idea?"

Alexander shook his head. "We can't just wander around aimlessly. There has to be a clue around here somewhere, so everyone start searching." He shown his light along the floor and the walls, but it was his nephew who let out a yelp of excitement a minute later. "What did you find, Drew?"

"The torch symbol! It's on the wall to the right."

He used his flashlight to illuminate it and the three turned and headed in that direction. Fifteen feet later, they saw another symbol, and then another. Their excitement grew with each torch engraving they found as they followed the winding tunnel, which began to grow wider the farther they went, sloping downward, taking them deeper into the earth. They'd been walking for nearly twenty minutes and Alexander wondered if they hadn't missed a turn somewhere when he nearly ran into Kaci and Drew who had stopped suddenly in front of him.

"What's wrong?"

But they didn't answer. He frowned, following the beam of their flashlights and gasped in awe at the sight before them. The wall, stretching as far as he could see, was filled with mosaics covered in dust and grime from years beneath the ground, but still mostly intact. Alexander reached out and gently ran his fingers over the smooth glass tiles.

"Incredible," he whispered. "It keeps going."

"What is it of?" Kaci tilted her head and stepped back a few steps, letting her light illuminate more of the wall. "Is that Rome?"

They stepped back even further until their backs were flush against the wall on the opposite side of the corridor. Drew and Kaci adjusted the beams of their flashlights and the colors of the tiles came into better view. A vision of Rome's ancient skyline reached from the floor halfway up the wall before the tiles changed to bright oranges and reds, shooting up into the inky sky above, dotted with stars.

"The Great Fire of Rome," Alexander told them reverently. "It's depicting the fire."

They admired the segment before moving along where the image shifted and changed as if it was coming to life before their eyes. The ancient tiles still showed Rome burning, but two figures, shrouded in cloaks, had been added to a street, glancing over their shoulders as if being chased by someone. In one of their hands was a satchel filled with what could possibly be parchments or texts of some sort. Alexander leaned in closer, studying the two figures, when his eyes widened and he stepped backward in disbelief. He reached out again and rested his palm near the figures, bowing his head to thank God for letting him know he was on the right trail.

"Uncle James?" Kaci asked. "What's wrong? Do you know who they're supposed to be?"

"Yes," he whispered. "Yes, I believe these two brave men are the ones who smuggled the scrolls out of Rome the night of the fire. They're the reason why we're on this path to begin with. It's almost as if...they've been placed here to guide us."

Kaci and Drew smiled in excitement. "How has no one else found these tunnels or the mosaics?" Kaci asked.

"Lorenzo said there are many of these underground passageways that have yet to be found," Alexander said. "It's possible no one's been down here for centuries, or if they were, they didn't understand the significance of what they saw." He encompassed the mosaic-covered wall with his arms. "If this was placed here for a reason – and I think those two men are proof that it was – then there must be a clue somewhere."

"There's more," Kaci said, jogging a little farther down. "Here, it changes again."

The image shifted, but Alexander frowned, confused at what he saw. It was another skyline of Rome, but this one wasn't on fire. It had to be the destroyed aftermath, but there was something strange about it. He squinted, mumbling under his breath as he tried to figure out what threw him off. Tracing his fingers over the buildings he knew well, he paused when the skyline changed to incorporate a grassy hill and atop that...

"A temple?"

"What?" Drew asked.

"This, it's the Temple of Diana," he told them, narrowing his eyes at it. "Why would the artist include this? It's not in Rome. It's not even close to Rome."

"The Temple of Diana?" Drew asked.

"As in one of the Seven Wonders Temple of Diana?" Kaci's eyes were wide.

Alexander nodded. "Yes, that's the one, but it shouldn't be here."

"Where is it actually located, if not here?"

"Ephesus," he answered and his eyes widened as he stared at the image of the temple. "No...it couldn't be."

"What? What is it?" Drew asked, practically bouncing on his heels.

"Paul started the church in Ephesus, and later Timothy pastored there," he told them. "Many believe his tomb is in Ephesus, but the mystery has always been *where*?"

Kaci and Drew shot their hands up with a shout of joy at realizing how close they were to possibly finding the end of this trail. Alexander wasn't sure if what he was seeing before him was exactly what he thought it was, but why else would the artist have included a rendering of the temple here? Lost in thought, he let the light from his phone wander over the wall and it glinted off of something shiny on the other side of the mosaic. He quickly stepped toward it and brushed away the dust and cobwebs with his fingers. This area was not covered in mosaic stone, but instead held a brass plaque with Greek lettering engraved on it. Some of the letters were ruined over the years, but Alexander thought he could read most of it.

"What's that?" Drew asked as he and Kaci appeared at his side. "Greek?"

"Yes, it's in Greek," he said as he translated quietly under his breath. "I believe it says,

> *'The guardians of truth the flames fled,*
> *With holy treasures laid the dead,*
> *Upon a hill six sentinels stand by,*
> *North of the lady doth he reside,*
> *Five and twenty stretch far and wide,*
> *While forty and ten the lines entwine,*

Two hands together to seek and find,
The man who bears the secrets twined.'
L XXV X XXV L

"And beneath it are Roman numerals," he said pointing. "Five in all."

"Those would be fifty, twenty-five, ten, twenty-five, and fifty again," Kaci said slowly. "Right?"

"Impressive! I remember your mum could never get past twenty when she was your age," Alexander's eyes twinkled. "Mathematics was never her strong point." His brow furrowed suddenly as he withdrew back into concentration, and mumbled to himself, "The image of the temple and this message weren't coincidences. They couldn't be."

"Then what does it all mean?" Drew ran his light along the wall and ceiling in case they missed another clue tucked away somewhere they hadn't checked yet.

"If it's referring to Ephesus where Timothy was buried and the scrolls are with him, then it has to be talking about where he is actually buried. The exact location has never been discovered to this day, not even a general area in Ephesus. There was never any evidence to point in a good direction."

"And now?" Kaci asked, pulling her phone from her bag.

"Now, we have a map, or at least I'm guessing that's what this is meant to be."

As Kaci held up her phone to take pictures, the automatic flash lit up the wall even more and she tilted her head curiously. As Drew and Alexander debated their next move behind her, she stepped closer and noticed a piece of the mosaic tile near the brass plaque was crooked and stuck out from the wall. Inching closer, she sucked in a quick breath when she discovered it had the torch symbol on its surface.

She ran her hand over the other tiles near it, but none stuck out like this one. Wondering what would happen if she pressed it, she did so and jumped with a surprised yelp when a stone beneath the plaque popped out of the wall.

"What did you do?" Drew asked, checking to see if she was okay.

"One of the tiles was weird and it had the torch symbol on it." She aimed her light down and, hoping no spiders were hanging around the small drawer-like opening, reached in to pull out another glass tile, the size of her palm. "What is this?" She rubbed her thumb over the tile to clean it off more. "It's another flame, but it looks different, like it's on the end of a torch."

As the three huddled around the tile, none of them heard the men lowering themselves into the tunnel, creeping down along the corridors, spreading out to cover the entire network if need be until they tracked down the professor and the troublesome teenagers. Their orders from Kadir were clear and no one wanted to return to him empty-handed. Not again. Dressed completely in black, they let the natural darkness hide them as they moved in unison. The men were able to see with the night vision glasses they wore, moving swiftly and silently through the passageways.

The man in front heard voices ahead and held up his hand to halt those behind him. Placing a finger to his lips and then drawing a ceremonial dagger from his belt, he gestured for the rest of them to do the same. He sadistically grinned. This was not going to be pretty, but it shouldn't be, he justified to himself. Anyone who would defy the empress of the heavens, his beloved Diana, so blasphemously as these Westerners did, should be brought down by any means necessary. He motioned for the men to carefully move along with him.

But they weren't quiet enough. Alexander's ears perked and he turned around slowly, listening intently as he motioned for his niece and nephew to be quiet for a moment. He thought his acute awareness of sound was simply from being in the muffled silence of the tunnels for so long, but he knew he wasn't imagining it. He could hear them now, footsteps moving closer...and whispers. Kaci paled as Drew took the tile and tucked it in her knapsack, all three turning their lights in the opposite direction. The footsteps could belong to anyone, but the professor couldn't take any chances, especially after all they'd been through.

"Right then," Alexander said loudly, hoping to throw the men he assumed were waiting to ambush them off their game. "We should head back to the surface. They're waiting for us." He could hear nothing but silence in the damp, dark coolness. They must have stopped.

Kaci and Drew frowned at first then played right along. "Yeah, I'd hate for them to miss us," Drew said loudly. "Really looking forward to talking to them."

Alexander nodded for them to quickly continue the direction they'd been headed, praying it would lead them somewhere out of these tunnels. If those men behind them had weapons, there was no way to be able to backtrack and make it past them without someone getting hurt and he wasn't willing to risk his niece's or nephew's life. They picked up the pace, the bouncing beams of their flashlights mirroring their desperation to get out of the tunnels and back above ground, but as soon as they started moving faster, Alexander clearly heard the men's quickened steps behind them.

"Stop them!" a man screeched, his voice echoing around them painfully. "They must not find the scrolls!"

"Run!" Alexander urged the kids on, glancing over his shoulder to see the dark shapes of the Demeons quickly gaining ground. They sprinted as fast as they could, taking a sharp right and another left, following wherever Kaci led them, guided by her beam of light. The solid walls gave way to catacombs and Alexander tried not to think about the three of them disappearing down here, lost and forgotten for centuries. With each pounding step, the mantra in Alexander's mind grew louder, praying that God would keep them safe and make a way of escape. Kaci took another sharp turn and the ground sloped upward as if they were heading back to the surface.

But when they rounded another corner, they crashed into a dead end. The men were far behind them, slowed down by the need to search through every passageway of the maze-like catacombs, but they were not giving up the chase.

"No!" Drew banged his fist on the bricks, but there was no door, no way out. They were trapped with the Demeons only growing closer. Kaci and Alexander felt along the wall, hoping for another secret panel or a way to escape the tunnel when the ground beneath their feet suddenly shook violently. Dust and dirt fell from the walls as they braced themselves, trying to hold steady.

"An earthquake?" Kaci asked in alarm.

Alexander couldn't be certain, but then he heard the thundering sound of...a train? "The underground metro! There was a stop just blocks from the antique shop! We must be right near the tracks." He beat his shoulder against the wall and the bricks slowly started to give way. "We have to break through!"

They could hear the fiendish calls of the brotherhood somewhere behind them in the preceding corridors. They had to be close, but there was no time to look back now. Drew and Alexander bashed their shoulders into the wall as bricks loosened and shifted with the added vibrations caused by the train rushing by. Kaci kicked and dug her fingers into the crumbling surface, dragging pieces of brick out of the way, and finally a section of the old wall collapsed. It wasn't a big opening, but Alexander kicked out a few more bricks just as the men called out behind them, one of them erupting with sinister laughter.

"Hurry! Kaci, climb through!"

Hoping it wouldn't drop them out directly onto the tracks, Kaci shimmied her way through the opening, taking more bricks down with her, and landed on her backside on a hard, concrete slab. Lights flickered brightly overhead and she glanced around trying to get her bearings. They were on what appeared to be a maintenance platform that followed the tracks.

"It's clear!" she yelled and reached through to help her brother out next. He struggled a bit more with his shoulders, but Kaci, not about to leave either of them behind, gave him a hard yank. He tumbled out onto the platform and they reached back in for Alexander.

He thrust his arms through and they both grabbed his hands when one of the Demeons, knife in hand, was suddenly behind him, tugging hard on his waist to pull him back into the tunnels.

"No!" Drew tried to get back in to help, but he couldn't reach.

Alexander backed into the man, grunting as he shoved him off and slammed him into the far wall, the knife clattering onto the stone floor. The professor swiftly lunged toward his assassin before he could recover his knife. The man's night vision goggles made him look even more menacing and he let out a savage growl as he dodged Alexander's blow and cut around him, picking up his ceremonial blade. As he raised his weapon shouting a war cry, all of the sudden more lights filled the corridor, aimed directly at the villain's night vision goggles. He let out a pained yell and fell back, squinting at the brightness.

"Uncle James!" Drew yelled.

Alexander turned to see them shining their LED flashlights and the ones from their phones at the man's face through the hole in the wall.

Knowing he didn't have much time, the professor lunged through the opening, landed hard on his hip, and clambered to his feet as the man yelled for the others in the tunnels. The moment their uncle could stand, Kaci and Drew bolted along the narrow platform, following the tracks. A station had to appear soon and then they could lose the men in the crowd. They just had to reach an exit platform. The ground rumbled as another train shot down the tracks and Alexander flinched at the brightness of the lights, but they pushed on. One look over his shoulder told him several of the men had busted through the wall and were giving chase. Once the train passed, the sound of voices echoing off tiles reached their ears and spurred them on even faster until they reached the end of the platform and darted into the crowd of people waiting to board.

"Excuse me!" Kaci yelled as she pushed her way through, Drew and Alexander right behind her. All she cared about was reaching the surface and losing those men. "I'm sorry! Please let us through!"

She ignored the dirty looks thrown her way and the angry replies in Italian. The stairs were in sight and she bolted for them, forgetting about being nice anymore. There were too many other voices for her to hear if the men followed or not and she wasn't about to slow down and check. She took the stairs two at a time and didn't stop running until a heavy hand landed on her shoulder and pulled her around.

"Kaci, we lost them." Drew was bent double, gasping for breath as was Alexander behind him. "We're safe. They didn't follow us through the crowd."

She collapsed to the ground, not caring who saw. "You couldn't...have stopped me...sooner?"

Alexander and Drew stared at her surprised. "We couldn't catch up with you," the first stated with a grin. "You were like a bullet taking off through that crowd."

"Yeah well, I wasn't about to let them catch us."

"We can't stay here, though. We might have lost them back there, but we don't know how many are in the city."

"Guess we don't get to stay in Rome, huh?" Drew asked, disappointed.

"Afraid not. We'll head straight to the airport and catch a flight to Izmir. From there, we'll head south to Ephesus and figure out what this next clue means," Alexander explained, glancing around the crowd. "Come on. I don't like being out on the street like this."

Drew pulled his sister back to her feet as Alexander whistled for a taxi to take them to the airport. He stopped at the ATM first and withdrew enough cash to pay for the plane tickets outright, anything to throw off the Demeons. He wasn't sure how they kept finding him and the kids, but this close to the end, he was afraid of leading them right to the scrolls. They must protect them from the brotherhood at all costs. Once the tickets were bought, they cleaned up in the restrooms and grabbed a quick bite before it was time to board their plane and leave Rome far behind.

◊ ◊ ◊

The bald man with unnaturally pale skin lowered his newspaper when he spied the kids and their uncle headed toward their terminal. He grinned, his sinister smile scaring the little boy passing by in front of him. Pulling out his cell phone, he texted the information to another who would pass it along to Kadir. The men might have failed to snag these religious fanatics in the tunnels, but they were headed to the one place they should have avoided.

The three adventurers were walking right into the lion's den.

And this time, they wouldn't be walking out again.

CHAPTER XII

The flight to Turkey was stressful. Drew caught himself frequently and instinctively looking around from where he sat on the airplane, observing the fellow passengers on their trip. He had tried to take a nap, but it only brought a warped nightmare of the Demeons killing them brutally in the catacombs of Rome. Kaci looked over at him and, seeing his brow furrowed with worry, she tenderly placed her hand on his. Without saying a word, she smiled, bringing momentary relief. Drew loved his sister. They were best friends; he was thankful that their parents had raised them to be respectful of one another and to always remember that family mattered most. Still, from the tension of the day, Drew found that he couldn't relax until they had landed and Uncle James warmly assured them with his iconic lop-sided grin that they were clear of any harm.

After they had secured a suite in a beautiful downtown historical hotel, they took turns freshening up for the evening. Alexander went last, which gave Drew and Kaci time to look over the room service menu. They did their best to suppress laughter while ordering dinner over the phone to a hotel receptionist who spoke extremely broken English. After placing the antique rotary phone onto its cradle, the siblings threw themselves down into the over-sized chairs in the living room to relax, watching out the window as the sun sank below the horizon.

A while later, as Alexander emerged from his room, there was a knock on the hotel room door. Peering through, he could see a friendly bellboy standing there with a cart of food.

"Wow! You both ordered quite the spread," Alexander happily remarked, as he turned back toward them and rubbed his hands together. He opened the door to let the young man in who, in turn, placed their meals on the dining room table and departed. After a moment of prayer, all three hungrily dove into their Turkish feast.

They ate on in silence, thoroughly enjoying their delicious entrees and desserts. Kaci and Drew finished much faster than their uncle and, after cleaning up their dishes, slowly moved to the sofa where they curled up surrounded by plush pillows.

"I am so full," Kaci said with a moan, eyes closed, but a smile on her face.

"Hey, Uncle James?" Drew spoke up after few moments. "Do you mind if we talk some more about the parchments?"

"Not at all!" Alexander responded, wiping his mouth with his cloth napkin and resting it on his empty plate, "You sound just like your father. He loved talking about the historical aspect of God's Word."

"I'm not sure he'd be happy with us running around like we've been," Kaci commented cringing. "If Mom finds out, she's going to ground us for life."

"Maybe she won't, once she finds out what you two are helping me do," he said, pouring himself a hot cup of strong coffee from the carafe and shifting in his chair to face his niece and nephew. "Now, what would you like to know?"

"Well," Drew started slowly, "I know a couple of times we've talked about why these parchments are so important for us to find."

He sat up a little straighter and went on, "And it is so fascinating to learn how God inspired His Word and preserved it over so many centuries. But what will these scrolls help us understand exactly? We already have the Bible. I mean, I understand the archeological side of it...discovering something as amazing as parchments used by the Apostle Paul would be pretty neat." He sighed and stared off into the distance for a moment before continuing, "But, I guess what I'm trying to ask is, what exactly is the significance of these scrolls and why are the Demeons so desperate to stop us?"

Alexander settled into his chair and mulled over where to start. He understood the concern the young man had over what he'd just asked, and grinned. "Well, Drew, I'm glad you asked. I want to take this one thought at a time, but first let me start out by stating that I believe that the King James Version of the Bible is the Word of God for English-speaking people."

"We do, too," Drew agreed. "Why do you bring that up?"

"Well, for the next few minutes, through everything that I am going to share with you as I answer your questions, I am going to ultimately reveal *why* we should believe this. It is more than just a preference or an opinion. It is grounded upon textual evidence and doctrinal logic."

His eyes squinted in thought, his mind sorting quickly through facts. "Do you remember what we had discussed about the preservation of Scripture back in Istanbul?"

Both of the teenagers nodded, and Kaci replied, "That was fascinating!"

The professor chuckled, "Then get ready for a crash course on something that – I do believe – will blow your minds away." Kaci and Drew shifted themselves, Drew now leaning forward on the edge of the couch and Kaci intently clutching one of the throw pillows between her arms. They enjoyed their uncle's dramatic teaching with his expressive hand motions and rich British accent.

"The Old Testament was primarily written in the Hebrew language with the exception of Ezra and Daniel being in Aramaic," he began. "For thousands of years, Israelites and Christians unwaveringly held to a large group of manuscripts generally called the *'Masoretic Text'* as the inspired, preserved Old Testament of Scripture. The word *'masoretic'* comes from the Hebrew word *'mesor'* meaning *'traditional'*. It was comprised of countless handed-down scrolls that were painstakingly copied, as I described to you before." He loved how attentive his niece and nephew were. Their desire to learn spurred him on to give extra details that he normally kept just for his university lectures.

"Well, in 1524, a Hebrew scholar and rabbi by the name of Abraham Ben Chayyim conducted an extensive amount of research into these old parchments. At the time, many manuscripts were just a couple of the Old Testament books compiled together, and scholars would have to track down other scrolls to get another portion of the Old Testament. So he decided to make everything easier by creating one complete, accurate volume of the entire Old Testament for people to be able to use. Today, this work is called the Ben Chayyim Masoretic Text. It was the uncontested text of the Old Testament for over four hundred years.

"But in the early 1900's," Alexander raised up his hands to make air quotes, "a German 'theologian' named Rudolph

Kittel came on the scene who would change everything. This man was a free-thinking rationalist and a religious liberal, who despised the Jews and personally denied many key doctrines of the Bible. He did not believe in the inspiration and preservation of God's Word; nor did he believe in the virgin birth, deity, miracles, or bodily resurrection of Jesus Christ."

"Wow!" Kaci exclaimed. "He was a heretic!"

"Most definitely. Actually, during the 1930's, he called Hitler's rise to power *'a blessing from God.'*"

Kaci and Drew had their mouths open in pure shock. "You're joking, right?" Drew asked rhetorically, already knowing that his uncle was dead serious. Alexander shook his head.

"No. He actually became highly influential in the intellectual circles of Germany. In fact, his son became Hitler's high priest of religious propaganda, providing the theological basis for resolving the 'Jewish question.' After the Second World War, he was one of the few German war criminals selected to stand trial and be imprisoned for his crimes against humanity."

"So what did this Rudolph Kittel and his son have to do with the Old Testament Hebrew?" Kaci asked, trying to connect the dots.

"Ah, yes," the professor nodded while refilling his coffee cup. "Well, unfortunately, many theologians in Europe at that time were drifting from the fundamentals of the faith. They were embracing 'higher criticism', a secular philosophy that justified a person to question God's authority in His Word."

"That's crazy." Drew interjected. "I guess, *'Professing themselves to be wise, they became fools.'*"

"Absolutely. And foolishly they applauded and accepted what Kittel had produced, since he was so popular and well-received," Alexander continued. "He had decided to compile a *new* Hebrew for scholars to work with and translate from. He named his work the *Biblia Hebraica*. His first two editions published in 1906 and 1912 were loosely based on the Ben Chayyim Masoretic text. However, in 1937, he changed it completely for something called the 'Ben Asher' text. This volume of Old Testament Hebrew had been based on a handful of manuscripts that dated around A.D. 1000; and, using the peculiar logic of that day which believed that older scrolls must always be better, Kittel published his 1937 edition based on this 'older' text. But these manuscripts had been rejected long ago for their significant error and discrepancies. His 1937 edition of the *Biblia Hebraica* and every subsequent edition since then has around 20,000 differences in it from the traditional Masoretic text."

"Wow!" Drew let out a gasp, "And people fell for that?"

"Sadly, yes. But God always has a way of preserving His Word and verifying which text is the correct one," Alexander mused as he shook his head and chuckled. "In 1947, the accidental discovery of leather bound scrolls in a cave in the desert hills on the northwestern shore of the Dead Sea in Israel proved once and for all that the Masoretic Text was accurate."

"Those were called the Dead Sea Scrolls, right?" Kaci asked.

"Yes, that's exactly right. A young shepherd was playing with his friends and tossed a rock into an opening on the side of a cliff, surprising them all when they heard a shattering sound. They went up to find out what it was and came across a collection of large clay jars, seven of which contained leather and papyrus Hebrew scrolls of the Old Testament."

"Yeah! I remember hearing about this in our youth group's Sunday School class as an illustration in one of our lessons," Drew commented.

Alexander smiled as he proudly looked at his niece and nephew. "It amazes me how God has used young people throughout history from Bible times to this modern day for some of the greatest things on Earth. Keep your heart tender toward the Lord. He is using you now in your lives and has amazing things, I believe, for both of you in the future."

Drew and Kaci shyly nodded, taking the loving words of their uncle to heart. After a moment of silence, Alexander continued, "Well, the discovered manuscripts were amazingly consistent with the Ben Chayyim Masoretic Text – assuring us that God was indeed divinely and sovereignly protecting His Word through thousands of years of copying and translating. For you see, though no one knows exactly when, these 'Dead Sea Scrolls' were written between 150 B.C. and 70 A.D. They were the oldest documents of the Old Testament ever to be found. Sadly, however, liberal scholars and modern theologians paid little attention to this. And," he paused, peering at his niece and nephew over the brim of his glasses, "all of the modern English translations of Scripture received their Old Testament translation mainly from the *Biblia Hebraica,* not the Masoretic Text."

"What?" Drew jumped out of his seat. "Do you mean to tell us that all the modern English Bibles have an Old Testament originating from that Rudolph Kittel guy?"

"Yes," the professor replied softly.

"I can't believe it!" Drew gestured with his hands as he looked back and forth from his uncle to his sister, "He was a theological and political liberal, and the manuscripts he purposely used were filled with errors!"

"I know. It is incredulous." Alexander agreed. "The King James Version is the *only one* that contains an accurate Old Testament...translated solely from the Ben Chayyim Masoretic Text."

"Wow," Kaci was stunned. "How can people so willingly reject what is so obvious? And why are so many Christians foolish enough to use these different versions?"

"Well, the sad part is that most believers have no clue what Old Testament Hebrew or New Testament Greek texts were used to translate the versions of the Bible they read and study from," Alexander stated.

"Wait," Kaci paused, her brow furrowed, "You're saying that there's *more*? Something about the New Testament and Greek?"

Their uncle smiled with amusement but sighed, "What I've told you is just the beginning, my dear. Get ready for the *really* crazy part!" Drew sat back down and Kaci tucked her feet beneath her and rested back against the couch more comfortably. Now, it was Alexander's turn to stand and for his niece and nephew to truly become two of his pupils. While he looked out the window to gather his thoughts again, Kaci and Drew exchanged excited glances of anticipation. They couldn't wait to take in everything that he was going to share with them next.

The professor began, launching into full lecture mode, "In the first century, the original epistles were penned by the writers through the Holy Spirit. From these original manuscripts came identical copies for other people or churches."

"Are there any originals left today?" Drew quickly asked.

"No, actually. It is believed that they became worn out from over-use rather quickly. We simply have thousands of copies of the New Testament originals that accumulated over the centuries. So keep in mind, if we discover these 'parchments of Paul' that we are on the hunt for, and if they are New Testament books, then they would be the closest thing to an original in existence, preserved by God."

"Wow! This is so incredible!" Kaci whispered excitedly.

"Yes, it is. Now you can see why our find is so spectacular," Alexander smiled. "So, as Christianity spread, the manuscripts spread, but over time some were altered and miscopied. As a result, there developed three different groups or 'families' of copies from these original epistles — the Traditional Text family, the Western Text family, and the Alexandrian Text family. Much, much controversy has arisen among Bible scholars as a result of these three. I will explain in a moment."

He took a sip of his coffee, "Any questions so far?" The two teenagers shook their heads.

He gently placed his cup back down on the table. "As I'm sure you can guess by the name, the Traditional Text family is made up of accurate copies of the original epistles that God preserved of His inspired Word. Toward the end of the Middle Ages in 1516, a theologian by the name of Desiderius Erasmus – who has been claimed to be the most brilliant Bible scholar of the Renaissance period – was burdened to produce a reliable and complete Greek New Testament for study and translation. For centuries this need was great. As with the Old Testament, many manuscripts had only a couple of Gospels or epistles in them, and scholars had to track down other scrolls to read other portions of the New Testament. So he decided to make everything easier by creating one accurate volume of the entire New Testament for people to be able to use. The time was right. Only half a century earlier, Johannes Gutenberg had invented the first movable type printing press, so this finalized Greek New Testament could be a printed volume and not hand-written..."

"Which would allow them to be mass-produced and sent throughout Europe and even the world." Drew interjected, as he caught on to what his uncle was sharing with them.

Alexander smiled brightly, "You're exactly right!" gesturing toward his engaged nephew. "The timing was perfect. I don't believe that it was a coincidence, but rather the providence of God orchestrating things together for the world's good and for His glory."

"How difficult was it for him to do this?" Kaci asked. "To make this Greek New Testament?"

"Well," the professor began to pace around the room. "We are talking about the year 1516. There were no cell phones, computers, or internet." He smiled, "No Google. No *Encyclopedia Britannica*. Furthermore, no modern conveniences like vehicles, airplanes, or indoor plumbing." Kaci and Drew rolled their eyes in agony trying to think back to what it must have been like to live in a time they considered to be so primitive. They could not imagine life without the comforts of modern technology.

Alexander continued, "Though he was limited with what New Testament manuscripts he could locate, he didn't let that stop him from completing what he believed was the will of God for his life. Over the years, he did his best to accumulate and study from as many of them as he could. Of course, it's obvious that he couldn't refer to every scroll in the world...that would have been *impossible*. For instance, it would have taken a couple of months to go just from Germany to Italy over land. Traveling conditions were not good; thieves constantly lurked in the countryside, disease was rampant, and information was unreliable by word of mouth only. Again, no cell phones, email, vehicles, or interstates. So he used what he could, relying upon the Lord, and God was in it all. The manuscripts he used to compile his New Testament were only that of the Traditional Text family and not of the other two families, which we will discuss in a moment."

"Whew!" Drew remarked. "So is this the only Greek text that scholars use today?"

"Yes, it was, for generations. But recently, many modern theologians have become controversial about his work because they don't believe he did a thorough enough job with his compilation. They say he should have consulted *every* manuscript. But one thing I've found to be true is that those who despise the Word of God and the work of God will always seek for ways to accuse it or argue about it."

Alexander sat back down in his chair, leaning forward with his arms resting on his legs. "Nevertheless, history speaks for itself. Of the 5,600 New Testament manuscripts that have been discovered and catalogued, 95% of them comprise the Traditional Text family. They agree with one another and match the *Textus Receptus* compiled by Erasmus."

He pulled his small worn leather Bible out of the leather pouch on his hip. "From this text family and from Erasmus' *Textus Receptus* came the New Testament translation of the King James Version."

A lexander reverently held his Bible with both hands, looking down at it. He could hear the amazement softly ebbing from his niece and nephew's lips as they sat in the stillness. He then slowly passed the Book over to Drew, who, with a renewed awe and appreciation, wanted another chance to look through it.

"As you can see in my custom-made Bible, I have the New Testament Greek on the left column and the King James Version translation on the right. The King James Version is completely accurate, mirroring the original language the Word of God was written in."

Both Drew and Kaci were spellbound by the dynamic truths that their uncle had just expounded upon. Much of this they had never heard before in their lives. As teenagers, they loved God, read their Bibles daily, went to church with their mother, and even participated in the youth group activities. However, though they heard Bible sermons three times a week and learned valuable life lessons from Scripture, they had never actually been taught the history of the Bible. Over the past week, what they had been slowly gleaning from their uncle concerning the inspiration, perseverance, and now translation of Scripture was fascinating to them and invaluable to their

Christian growth. They soaked up as much as they could as their admiration and love for the Word of God continued to grow.

When the professor handed Drew his Bible, Kaci eagerly scooted over on the couch to look over her brother's shoulder. As he thumbed through the worn pages, Drew observed, "So what you are saying is that the King James Version has been perfectly translated?"

The professed nodded, "Yes, the Old Testament from the Ben Chayyim Masoretic Text and the New Testament from the *Textus Receptus* of the Traditional Text family." He paused for emphasis sake. "I fully believe this version *is* the Word of God for English-speaking people."

Kaci peered up and asked, "Uncle James, how *was* the King James translated exactly?"

A lop-sided grin slowly spread across Alexander's face. "Do you remember the maiden name of your grandmother? My and your mother's mum?"

Kaci and Drew looked at one another, each with their brows creased in thought. "Savile, wasn't it?" Drew answered.

"Yes! Exactly right. As I told you earlier in our journey, we are direct descendants from one of the scholars who helped translate the King James Version. His name was Sir Henry Savile," Alexander sat back in his chair, hooking his thumbs around his suspenders. "He was one of the most profound and critical men of education in his time, being heavily involved with furthering fields of science and study. He assisted in translating the four Gospels, along with the books of Acts and Revelation." The two young people glanced at each other again, their eyes alive with excitement.

"There were six other English Bibles before the King James Version was produced in 1611. But *none* of them had been completely and painstakingly translated word-for-word from the original Hebrew or Greek. So in 1604, a man named John Rainolds came to the King with the idea to create an entirely new and final English Bible through a unique system of accountability," he explained.

"King James approved the undertaking and fifty-four men in all were brought together. They were the best scholars and theologians of the day. Of the fifty-four originally selected, only forty-seven remained by the time work actually began in 1607. Some had died; others had to resign due to ill health or other unforeseen circumstances. They were divided into six teams, each with their own portion of the Bible to translate. Nothing would be permanent until *every* man on their committee came to a one-hundred percent consensus on what was translated."

Alexander reached for his coffee cup and held it under his nose, breathing in its aroma deeply before taking a sip. "When the translation was complete, *each* group of men then reviewed all the others' work to ensure that everything was correct. Afterwards, in 1610, a seventh and final committee was formed to guarantee that the King James version mirrored the original languages in its entirety."

He set his coffee down and pointed toward the Bible Drew still held in his hands. "It did. And I believe they took Psalm 12:6 quite literally where God says, *'The words of the Lord are pure words: as silver tried in a furnace of earth, purified seven times.'* After the seventh committee approved the work, the King James Version – the seventh English translation – was mass produced in 1611 after seven tedious years that had started with an idea and finished with a completed Book. Since that time, it's been the most popular

Bible translation ever printed with over one billion copies spread across the world."

"Very intriguing!" Drew exclaimed, now handing his uncle's Bible to his sister. "These men certainly had a love and a respect for Scripture."

"Yes," Alexander remarked, "And they treated it the right way. It is holy, and they handled it with holiness and reverence."

"Wow. So for four hundred years," Kaci wondered aloud, "No changes have been made? At all?"

"Minor changes only, standardized spelling and the like, but the translation has not been changed," he said. "*Not once.*"

The professor shook his head. "But bitter modern scholars would have you to believe otherwise. They claim that the King James Version underwent three revisions incorporating more than 100,000 changes. But it's not true. They have no idea what they're talking about! The fact is that the King James contains a little more than 780,000 words. Since the first one rolled off the press in 1611 to the one you can buy today, there have only been around 420 word modifications. That's it – amounting to only five one-hundredths of a percent of the entire translation! Words like *'towards'* was changed to *'toward'*, *'burnt'* to *'burned'*, *'amongst'* to *'among'* and a few others like that."

"Remarkable," Kaci whispered, as she slowly sat back down and nestled up on the couch, her mind already on a different question as she leafed through the pages and let her eyes flutter from the Greek words to the English. "A while ago, you said something about there being a controversy with the different New Testament Greek families?" She looked up and instinctively tucked her golden brown hair behind her left ear. "What exactly did you mean by that?"

"And why are there like over one hundred different Bibles in the English language today?" Drew sat forward now on the edge of the sofa with his hands folded in front of him and continued, "When we go to the Christian bookstore, it's unbelievable how many different versions there are! I thought the King James was the final one."

Alexander smiled, raising his hands in defense, pretending he was overwhelmed, "Slow down, you two. One question at a time," his playful scolding made his niece and nephew laugh.

"We just want to know everything we can!" Drew said. "This stuff is so fascinating."

"And I'm realizing how important it is for everyone to know about this!" Kaci added. "I don't think very many people are familiar with all of these things, especially teenagers like us."

The professor poured himself another cup of coffee and stared a moment at the steam rising out of the mug before he continued, "The King James Version was the only English translation used for generations. God used it to bring about the First and Second Great Awakenings. America's Founding Fathers used it to establish their country, which in turn changed the world. It was the same Bible that D. L. Moody, Charles Spurgeon, and so many other men of yesteryear preached from, seeing the saving of souls and the spread of the kingdom of God. All was well," Alexander clenched his jaw and spoke with disgust, "until two vile men came on the scene – Brooke Westcott and John Hort."

"Who were they?" Drew interjected.

Alexander's eyes twinkled, "Ah, well, in order for me to explain, we must first address Kaci's question."

Kaci smiled, "Yeah, the Greek controversy."

"Yes." He stopped for a moment, rubbing his stubbled jaw, looking at his niece and nephew. "Are you sure both of you are following all of this?" They nodded vigorously and Alexander chuckled, "You're getting a year's worth of college education crammed down into one conversation. I'm thankful that I have not bored you."

"No, not at all! We're the ones grateful that you are willing to take the time to teach us this stuff," Drew replied.

"Well, 'this stuff' will help you to become firmly grounded in your Christian life upon the Word of God...to *'earnestly contend for the faith.'* As you grow older, many will try to sway you. But, it is my prayer that *you*, rather, will strengthen and help others to *'hold fast the profession of our faith without wavering.'*"

The professor stood and resumed pacing around the living room as he conducted a brief review. "Do you remember the names of the three New Testament Greek 'families' I had mentioned?" He looked to see which of them would say something first. He was pleasantly surprised when they both blurted out an answer at the same time.

The three of them laughed together, and Kaci jokingly threw a decorative pillow hard at her brother. Drew recoiled as it hit his face and fell into his hands. "Okay, okay," he grinned, "Ladies first."

Turning to her uncle with a wide smile, she answered matter-of-factly, "The *'Traditional Text family'*, the *'Western Text family'*, and the *'Alexandrian Text family.'*"

Alexander gave her a thumbs up, "Good memory!" Kaci looked back at Drew and smiled smugly.

He shook his head and sarcastically apologized, "Please forgive my sister's immaturity, I think it's getting past her bed time." All three of them chuckled again, and the two teenagers settled back into their seats, ready to absorb the last bit of history Alexander needed to share with them.

"So the Traditional Text family is made of accurate copies of the original epistles of God's Word. Of all the thousands of manuscripts that have been discovered, 95% of them comprise the Traditional Text family and agree with one another. The remaining 5% make up the other two groups. The Western Text family was the collection of manuscripts gathered and used by the Roman Catholic Church. They altered the manuscripts to fit their belief system by adding doctrine and taking away others, such as the blood atonement and Christ's ascension."

Drew shook his head in disbelief. "That is despicable. I'm not being judgmental, just honest and obvious. How can they justify changing the Word of God like that?"

Alexander sighed, "Unfortunately, they have been deceived into believing that the Pope is the vicar of Heaven, being infallible like God. According to them, whatever he says goes. But, no one is perfect. He's a lost sinner in need of Jesus Christ, just like everyone else. However, as the various popes steered Catholicism in the Middle Ages, they and their councils created or dismissed doctrine, ultimately adding or removing it from Scripture."

"I never knew that," Kaci remarked in deep concentration.

"They believe in a number of odd things: that the Virgin Mary is the mother of God and queen of eternity, and that there are three places where one can go when they die: Heaven, Hell, or Purgatory, though there is no reference whatsoever of that third place in the Bible. Furthermore, they believe that one can earn salvation if he remains good enough in his life and that baptism by sprinkling can wash away sin. It is so terribly sad." The professor shook his head, "Getting back to the subject at hand, from these changed Western Text family manuscripts came the Latin Vulgate Bible and the Roman Catholic Bible. They are corrupt and doctrinally wrong."

"Very interesting." Drew observed. He brought his hand up to count with his fingers, "So we have the Traditional Text family and the Western Text family. What's with this last one, the Alexandrian? Did it come out of where we were recently in Egypt?"

"Yes! You are very astute," the professor responded. "Alexandria was once a powerful center of learning, education, and culture. Of course, its library was quite the draw to anyone seeking to acquire knowledge and research. It also was a hub for copying Bible texts in that part of the world, but the institution entrusted with this task was liberal in its theology. The copied manuscripts they produced actually removed certain passages of Scripture and were worded in such a way that they attacked the deity of Jesus Christ. Over the centuries, most of them were lost or discarded because of their many mistakes and contradictions to the other 95% – the majority Traditional Text family."

Alexander paused for a moment, taking off his glasses and cleaning the lenses with a handkerchief from his back pocket. "But two manuscripts survived, and I believe that was with the help of Satan, the ultimate enemy of truth. I also believe they lasted that long because they were forgotten about and never used." He put his glasses back on, his brow creased with frustration. "Their names are the 'Vaticanus' and the 'Sinaiticus'. Together, they're supposedly one of the earliest manuscripts of the New Testament in existence. I, however, have my doubts about that. Nevertheless, many people foolishly think that since they are 'older,' that somehow it makes them superior and more trustworthy than the rest of the manuscripts available. Clearly that is *not* the case...especially when they have obvious flaws within them and between them. Nevertheless, these two are responsible for bringing all the controversy that there is today."

Drew and Kaci exchanged concerned glances with each other, as their uncle sat again. Neither of them had heard of these before. "So what were they and how were they discovered?" Drew probed.

"Well, in 1481," the professor began, withdrawn in thought, "the *'Vaticanus'* was found on a dusty shelf in the Vatican library, thus giving it its name. Though discovered there, it had its origins in Alexandria."

"It was just lying there?" Kaci wondered aloud. "How had no one found it before?"

"An excellent question, but one with no answer. A man by the name of John Burgon, one of the greatest textual scholars of the 19th century, took the time to study this manuscript. He discovered and documented that the *'Vaticanus'* left out words, whole clauses, and even entire sentences almost 1,500 times in just the Gospels alone."

"That's insane," Kaci murmured.

"It is," Alexander agreed after taking a long sip of coffee. "But it gets worse. The second manuscript – the *'Sinaiticus'* – was discovered in 1844 by a certain Constantin von Tischendorf. He was a German evolutionist and theologian..."

"Like that Rudolph Kittel guy in Nazi Germany?" Drew interrupted.

"Yes," Alexander replied. "He was at Mount Sinai, at the St. Catherine's Monastery, when he came across it. According to him, the manuscript was in a basket along with other parchments waiting to be burned. He snatched it out and after reading through it, he boastfully assumed that it was written in the 4th century. But, no one has ever found any actual proof that it dated earlier than the 12th century. These pages," Alexander continued, reaching back for his coffee, "were actually written by three different scribes and corrected by countless others. Nearly fifteen thousand corrections can be counted within this manuscript, and the total number of words omitted within the Gospels alone is over 3,400 when compared to the *Textus Receptus.*"

"Then there should be absolutely *no question*," Drew emphasized, his hands a flurry of motion, "that *both* of these manuscripts are garbage. Who cares how old they are?"

"I agree, most definitely. The best part is how much these two texts contradicted each other...over *three thousand times* in just the Gospels!" Alexander watched their faces turn from astonishment to annoyance. "Though they don't match the 95% majority of accurate Greek manuscripts or even agree with *each other*," he went on, "Bible theologians *still* actively use them to this day."

Kaci was visibly flustered, "Why would they do that?"

"I don't know," Alexander threw his hands up in the air. "It blows my mind. I just don't know. It's common sense to any person who studies it out that the *Textus Receptus* is correct." He gently took his Bible from Kaci and opened it to Romans 1:21. "But most of these men are filled with pride and humanism. The Bible says, *'When they knew God, they glorified him not as God, neither were thankful; but became vain in their imaginations, and their foolish heart was darkened.'*"

"Yeah!" Drew declared. "And the next verse is what I quoted earlier, *'Professing themselves to be wise, they became fools.'*"

"Precisely. They irrationally believe that since the Alexandrian text family appears to be older than it must be better. It's like they are living with blinders on. But their blindness is also largely due to the devious efforts of those two men in 1881."

Kaci perched up with a sick feeling in her stomach, "Let me guess. It was those guys Westcott and Hort," her voice trailed off.

"Yes. This is now where they fit into our historical narrative."

"What did they do exactly?" Drew asked hesitantly, knowing that it couldn't be anything good. The two teenagers braced themselves for what they were about to discover.

"They essentially have been polluting the purity of God's Word for the last 130-plus years. Their influence has strangled modern-day Christianity." Drew and Kaci remained still, growing slightly pale.

"By the latter part of the 19th century, modernism was running rampant across Europe, England, and America. Many were criticizing the King James Version and core doctrines of the Bible. During this time, there arose a contingent called 'the fundamentalists' who uncompromisingly stood for truth and Scriptural purity. Well, Westcott and Hort were revered as leading scholars of their day among the modernists. Both of these men greatly despised Erasmus' work of the *Textus Receptus*, even going as far as to call it – and I quote – '*vile and villainous.*'"

Alexander crossed his arms again and leaned back in his chair, "So they decided to take the '*Vaticanus*' and '*Sinaiticus*' and, together, compile a *new* Greek text for study. From it, they produced the first modern translation of the Bible since the King James Version; they called it the English Revised

Version. And many in their ranks quickly heralded their work as the greatest Biblical achievement of the century."

"I feel like I'm going to puke," Kaci mumbled.

"Here's the crazy part," the professor quickly continued. "These two guys were far from decent. They were heretics. They didn't fully believe in the deity of Christ, the infallibility of Scripture, the creation account recorded in Genesis, or in the reality of Hell. After their deaths, it was discovered how truly deplorable they were. They advocated socialism and supported communism. They even delved into the supernatural, dabbled with communicating with spirits in séance, and formed their own secret society called the Eranus Club that turned to occultism. They were *not* men of God as they claimed; but by their own deeds and doctrine it is evident they came from the spirit of antichrist."

Kaci shuddered. Drew clenched his jaw and quietly, yet firmly, said, "These men *were* evil dudes. They *definitely* could not have been trusted with handling the Bible properly."

The professor shook his head in agreement. "Ultimately, I believe it was their secret desire to destroy God's Word. Nevertheless, their work took off like wildfire. From the Greek text they compiled in 1881 out of the corrupted 'Vaticanus' and the 'Sinaiticus', all New Testaments of modern English Bibles have been translated. The Revised Standard Version, the New International Version, the New American Standard Bible, the English Standard Version, the Message Bible, and even the New King James Version." He smiled, "Shall I go on?"

Kaci and Drew were stunned by what the professor had just said. Drew spoke softly with a raspy voice, "All...all of them?"

"Yes. *Every single one* of them!"

"How can that be?" Kaci blurted.

"Like I said before, most of it is blind ignorance." Alexander suddenly stood and almost in tears began to share the heaviness on his heart to his tender niece and nephew, "It greatly saddens me! It grieves me! A majority of Christians are *completely* oblivious to the perversion in their Bibles. They are being deceived with counterfeits. That is why I have dedicated my life to this kind of work...to linguistics...to archaeology. I want to help them see and understand! If we are able to find these scrolls, I am praying that we will be discovering the oldest manuscripts on the earth of some of the New Testament books. As a result, I believe that we will be able to prove once and for all that the *Textus Receptus is* the correct New Testament Greek source for translation. Ultimately then, we will discredit the heretical works of Westcott and Hort and the subsequent hundreds of Bible translations that have been produced from them. We need to find these scrolls. We *must* find them!"

Drew and Kaci stared at him in silence, blown away by the profound impact their discovery would make and, furthermore, the fact that God had uniquely bestowed this task upon them to hunt for it in the first place. Kaci whispered, "I don't know what to say."

Drew cleared his throat and added, "Now I see why we have met so much opposition along the way. Satan and his henchmen want to keep people blinded from the truth."

"Absolutely," Alexander agreed, slowly pacing back and forth with his arms crossed and his hand raised up to his chin. "Satan is the mastermind of evil. He hates the Bible more than anyone else. It is no surprise to me that he has empowered a radical group like the Demeons to try to stop us. But," he stopped and turned back toward his niece and nephew, a slow grin spreading across his face, "we cannot forget, *'Greater is he that is in you, than he that is in the world.'*"

Drew smiled as well, "I John 4:4. I love that verse."

"Yes, and Romans 8:37 tells us that *'we are more than conquerors through him that loved us.'*"

"Mom's favorite verse," Kaci piped up, "is Philippians 4:13, *'I can do all things through Christ which strengtheneth me.'*"

Alexander settled back down into his chair, "Unquestionably! God has guided us every single step of the way. It is incredible when you think about it. He has protected us thus far; He will not abandon us now. I personally believe that we are on a Heavenly mission to find these scrolls!"

"But I wonder why the Demeons, specifically, are after us? What is their hand in all of this?" Drew asked aloud as his mind drifted to the different villainous faces of the men hunting them.

"I don't know," Alexander slowly responded. "They appear to be an ancient society cloaked in mystery...I actually have been conducting my own research on them these past couple of days, speaking with some of my associates across the world during the midnight hours."

"Oh, really?" Kaci asked. "What have you found out?"

"Not much of anything. But from the little I have gathered, it seems that they are a part of a secretive plot to undermine the church, like the Inquisition during the Dark Ages," the professor took off his glasses, sighed, and rubbed his tired eyes. "I don't know for sure. But we must avoid them at all costs." Putting his glasses back on, he continued, "I *do* know that if they are able to stop us, then sadly, they will successfully keep the rest of the world in confusion about what manuscripts to use for Bible translation!"

"Yes," Drew replied, his eyes filled with resolve and his jaw clenched. "Although if people just did their homework, there would be no question!"

"Exactly. But an archaeological discovery of this magnitude will forever settle the question."

Kaci stood from the couch and went to grab her cell phone and the tile fragment from her knapsack. "Then I guess we should form a game plan for tomorrow so we can be quick and efficient, and get out fast before they catch up with us again."

She laid the tile gently on the coffee table and pulled up the picture she took of the plaque so they could read through the riddle again. She read over the words aloud.

> *'The guardians of truth the flames fled,*
> *With holy treasures laid the dead,*
> *Upon a hill six sentinels stand by,*
> *North of the lady doth he reside,*
> *Five and twenty stretch far and wide,*
> *While forty and ten the lines entwine,*
> *Two hands together to seek and find,*
> *The man who bears the secrets twined.'*
> *L XXV X XXV L*

They sat back to ponder them. Kaci spoke first, "Based on the mosaics we saw in Rome, the guardians of truth fleeing the flames were the ones who rescued the scrolls out of the city before it burned. They buried the holy treasures, or scrolls, with Timothy."

"We know that from the parchment we found in the sarcophagus in Spain," Alexander reminded them.

"North of the lady doth he reside," Drew quoted. "Could this be where he was buried?"

"Sounds like it, but what is this 'lady' the clue refers to?" Kaci mused.

"Assuming 'the lady' means Diana or, more likely, the *temple* of Diana, it should mean that Timothy is buried north of the temple ruins!" Alexander started to get excited, and then remembered there was still much more to the clue. "The six sentinels, they could be statues, columns? Something else?"

"Are there more statues there?" Drew asked.

"At one time there might have been."

They spent the next hour or so running through the riddle, but gleaned nothing new from the clues. As Kaci yawned and her eyes drooped, Alexander decided to call it a night. They would figure it out tomorrow. The kids protested, but he told them to get some sleep. They wouldn't get any further with this puzzle if they were exhausted. They traipsed off to their room leaving Alexander to stare at the riddle one final time, along with the curious tile, and wonder what tomorrow would bring. They stood at the very end of this path, ready to make a phenomenal discovery.

He prayed they would remain safe long enough to see it through.

CHAPTER XIV

A lexander rented an open-air Jeep first thing in the morning and the three left the hotel behind as they drove toward the Temple of Diana. The day was overcast, a foreboding sign Kaci didn't like as she watched the rolling hills of the countryside fly by. They didn't go too far away from the ancient city center of Ephesus before she saw signs for the temple and Alexander turned off the main road. The road turned to dirt and he slowed down, taking them around the white marble ruins until they were north of the structure. He parked off the road and they stepped out, glancing around to see if they'd been followed. Thankfully, they were alone.

As they walked into the faint looming shadow of the structure, Drew threw his arms up wide and said, "Alright, we're north of the lady! What's around here that has six?"

"Look for anything," Alexander mentioned, his eyes scanning the walls in deep concentration. "Could be anything."

"Maybe pillars? I don't know..." Drew's voice trailed off.

Then Kaci turned around and faced north, studying the distant hills that lay beyond them. "What about...trees?" she said quietly, then louder as she counted six trees atop one hill in particular. "Look, there! Six sentinels!"

The other two spun around and looked in the direction she was eagerly pointing. There were a few hills out of the many surrounding them that had trees on them. But only one appeared to have six uniquely tall and ancient-looking trees standing above the rest of the foliage. "Cypress trees," Alexander told them and gave a lop-sided grin. "I think we're on the right track. Let's go!"

Jumping back into their jeep, Alexander left quickly, spitting pebbles with the vehicle's rear tires as they left the temple ruins behind. Drew smiled, "I feel like we're so close!"

"Indeed! If we are able to find the scrolls," Alexander wryly replied, "like I have said before, it will be the most important discovery of Bible texts in history. Be in continual prayer, both of you. We really need God's help!"

They drove on in silence, each of them praying in their hearts for God to lead them as they sought to follow what they believed to be the last in a series of clues cryptically given to them from centuries past. The dirt road was filled with potholes and bumps, making the ride an exhilarating one as Alexander did his best to avoid as many of them as he could. As they came closer to the range of hills, the professor peered around to see if anyone had followed them. With no one in sight, he veered off the road and began to drive down into the thick weeds toward the hill where the thin, tall cypress trees stood.

"This is as far as we can go," Alexander said, as he put the parking brake on, once they had reached the bottom of the hill. It was a bit of a hike to reach the top, but they were too pumped up after figuring out another part of the riddle to be deterred by a climb. When they reached the six cypress trees, Kaci leaned back, and then leaned back even further to try and see the tops of them.

"These trees are huge! Can they really be *that* old?" she asked in awe.

"Indeed," Alexander nodded, gazing up in wonder. "Cypress trees are among the oldest living trees in the world. They can live for hundreds, even thousands of years. Many of the trees in this part of the world have stood strong as they watched the ages of mankind pass." He rested his hands on the closely clumped branches that wrapped themselves around the trunk, spiraling upward toward the sky, over sixty feet in the air. As he looked up, his heart lightened. "This is it!" He stepped back, walking among them, and continued, "This *has* to be the place. These trees are not randomly growing up in a forest but they stand here, in a row, too perfectly to be accidental. Look how straight a line they make and how evenly spread apart they are by several meters. They had to have been planted by someone!"

"What did the riddle say again?" Drew asked and Kaci brought it up on her phone.

"We're already north, so it says, *'Five and twenty stretch far and wide.'* That's the next line."

"Five and twenty?" the professor muttered to himself. Scratching the stubble on his jaw, he hesitantly mentioned, "Twenty-five...the only thing that makes sense to me would be twenty-five paces, maybe?"

"Far and wide," Drew mused with Alexander. "The outside trees! Twenty-five paces from the outside trees in opposite directions, right?"

"Worth a shot! Go to the right and I'll take the left. Kaci? You stand here in the middle and direct us."

"But Uncle James," Alexander heard Drew call out after him. "How far of a stride are we supposed to make to try and get this right?"

The man thought for a moment and then loudly spoke in return, "Well, the average Roman was roughly five and a half feet tall. It's an estimate, but we would need to walk a little over two feet per step." Drew nodded and signaled back with a thumbs up.

"Here we go!" Kaci exclaimed.

Alexander was a tall man. Walking only two feet a step was abnormal for him, but he tried his best and he and Drew counted out twenty-five steps from the farthest trees. He wasn't sure what they would find, but when he came to a stop and stared down, his heart leapt in his chest with what he saw peeking through the overgrowth a few feet beyond him. "Drew! What do you see? Look down!"

He crouched, pushed back the shrubs, and brushed away the dirt from a bright, white chunk of stone with a torch and flame engraved upon it. The years had weathered the image, but it was there, carved deep so it could withstand the ages.

After a few seconds of silence, "A marker! There's a stone marker here!" Drew yelled back, excited.

Alexander stood, knocking off the dust from the knees of his trousers. "Kaci? Next line please," he requested.

"Right, here goes. *'While forty and ten the lines entwine.'*"

"Could mean fifty paces..."

"But, which direction?" Drew asked looking around from where he stood. "Entwine?"

"Inwards maybe?" the professor assumed. His eyes lit up suddenly, "But at an angle! Drew, try to walk about forty-five degrees from your position." If they were wrong, the professor figured they could head back to the markers and try a different direction. "Let's do it!" He counted out fifty more paces, going down the slope of the hill diagonally. At that distance, they began to search the ground. Another white stone appeared in the weeds at his feet and Drew waved his hand over his head signifying he found one, too. "What's next?"

"Just one more line," Kaci told them. "*'Two hands together to seek and find.'*"

"Two hands together?" Drew glanced around confused. "What does that mean?"

Alexander frowned, unsure himself, but then he had an idea. "Wait...the Roman numerals, what were the numerals at the bottom of the poem?"

"Fifty twice, twenty-five twice, and ten," Kaci said then brightened. "Yes, ten! It's ten paces, like the ten fingers combined on your two hands!"

"And maybe *'together'* means that we need to walk toward each other!" Drew interjected.

Alexander and Drew laughed with excitement. They faced one another; and in unison aloud, they counted out ten steps. When they stopped, they both bent down to shove aside the tall blades of grass and weeds covering the ground. Silence hung in the air except for their rustling and the buzzing of insects in the sloping grassy field. Alexander was worried they weren't going to find anything, but then his hand brushed against something cold and hard. He tugged the grass and revealed a much larger white stone. Drew uncovered the other half of it and between the two of them, they managed to find the entire outline of a rectangular slab of white stone, sunken into the ground over the centuries. A layer of dirt and grass had filled over it, but after some initial hard yanking it was easy to peel back strips a little at a time.

"And resting in the shadow of the sentinels..." Kaci whispered as she joined them. "We found it!"

Alexander was ready to agree with her when he spied the torch symbol etched into the very center of the stone. "He's here, he's right here."

"How do we get in?" Drew ran his hands along the sides, searching for a way to pull the stone up. "There's no way to get inside unless we bust through."

But busting through could ruin whatever was inside, and Alexander wasn't about to potentially destroy this incredible find in his hurry to see what lay beneath his feet. He searched along the other edge again for any hint at what they were supposed to do, but it was Kaci who found it as she was pulling back dirt and weeds. Frowning, she sank to the ground and blew the residual dirt away.

"Uh, guys? I think I found something," she whispered. "It's weird."

Alexander moved to peer over her shoulder. "Do those move?" he asked, pointing to the glass tiles aligned vertically in six columns. There was a slit carved in the stone next to each tile, as if they were on individual tracks. Kaci reached out and tried to slide one over to the right a couple inches. "I think so," she replied. She used both of her hands. The dirt that had accumulated over the years had caused some of the tiles to stick in place. "I think it's some sort of locking mechanism."

"From that long ago?" Drew asked skeptically.

"You'd be surprised what men of the old days were able to do. Hold on a moment," Alexander reached for a bottle of water from Drew's backpack and, after blowing as much of the dirt out of the sliders as possible, he poured some water in them to act as a basic lubricant against any remaining grit.

"You think it opens the tomb?" Kaci leaned closer. "These tiles, they have pictures on them. An anchor, a scroll, a house, some sort of tomb...another tomb, a ship, and a temple."

"Those were our clues," Alexander whispered. "The path to finding this place. Perhaps we must move them in the right order to open the lock." He chuckled at his next realization. "Seven clues." He glanced up at his niece and nephew, "Do you know what the number seven represents in the Bible?" Both of them shook their heads no. He grinned, "It signifies completion."

Kaci looked to her brother with her mouth open, and Drew's eyes widened, responding in a whisper, "We are really here. No more clues. This is our final destination!"

Alexander shifted the first tile with a tomb picture over until it was as far right as it could move along the track. When nothing happened, he moved it back and tried the other tomb tile instead. As soon as it hit the end of its track, a loud clang echoed beneath them. "I think that's right," he smiled.

"Next was the library," Drew said, and Alexander moved the tile with the image of lines of text on it over as far right as possible. Another loud clang followed. "And after that was the other tomb at the necropolis of Myra."

"Then the ship and the anchor," Kaci said, bouncing with excitement. "And Rome!"

"And lastly," Alexander said as his hand hovered over the final lock, "the temple."

As the final tile slid into place, the stone slab shuddered and a loud grinding sound issued out, causing dust to explode outward from the seal. The slab separated in the middle and collapsed inwards. Bits of it fell away, but for the most part the ancient doors sealing the tomb remained intact.

"This is it," Drew said and hurried to his feet, shining his light down into the depths below. "There are steps, but I can't see anything else."

Alexander went first, taking a light from Drew and slowly descending into the chilly cavernous space. There were maybe twenty or so steps before his boots hit bottom and he stared into the corridor in front of him, so vast it seemed to swallow the light. Along the wall beside the bottom of the steps he saw old iron brackets holding torches just waiting to be lit. As Drew and Kaci came up behind him, they noticed the torches and quickly pulled matches from Drew's bag. They lit the two torches, instantly illuminating the darkness. Alexander wondered if this would be like the maze they found back in Rome, but after only walking for a few moments, the air grew colder around them and the corridor spilled out into a rounded room with a ceiling that reached far above their heads with no outside light filtering in.

"Uncle James," Kaci whispered. "Look."

He shifted his gaze and there at the far end of the room, built out of stone and set into the wall, was a coffin. Steps were carved leading up to it and together they rushed over and began brushing away centuries of dust and grime from the surface. Greek words were there, still in nearly perfect condition. Alexander's heart pounded in his chest as he translated the words and stared reverently at the casket.

"What does it say?" Drew asked.

It took a moment for the words to form, but when he finally read them, he could only whisper them, reverently. "'Here lies our beloved pastor and friend, Timotheus.' This…this is Timothy's grave! We found it!"

They hugged each other, rejoicing as they realized they were here…finally here. They had put their lives on the line many times in order to make it to this moment. But it would be worth every danger, for they were about to gaze upon scrolls that had once been in the hands of the apostle Paul himself. All that was left was to open the casket and find them, take them back to safety, and end this once and for all. They pressed their hands against the lid, shoving it as hard as they could. All three breathed with relief when it shifted, slowly but surely giving them a view of the inside.

"Wait, what?" Drew reached in and felt around, but there were no scrolls, no bag, nothing but old bones. "Where are the scrolls? I thought they were supposed to be here?"

Alexander stared over his shoulder. "I don't understand."

"This is his tomb though, right?" Kaci picked up her torch from where they rested them on a nearby rock ledge and walked around the room. "Did we miss something?"

"Maybe someone else got here before we did and took them already," Drew worried.

"The stone slab covering the entrance was still intact when we got here, so unless they found another entrance, no one's been in here in a very long time. Alexander picked up the other torch and the three spread out around the room. "This can't be a dead end," he mumbled under his breath, his chest tight with disappointment, wondering if, after all they'd been through, they had failed. "There has to be more...there *must* be more."

"Here!" Kaci yelled. "There's a mosaic over here!"

Alexander and Drew rushed to join her, the firelight reflecting off the mosaic covering half the wall before them. They'd been so intent on the casket when they arrived, they hadn't bothered to look at anything else. There was a crowd of men near the lower portion of the mosaic and farther up the wall, standing before them was another man. Scrolls were held in one hand, but the tile that held the image of what was held in the other hand was missing.

"The tile from Rome," Alexander said to Kaci. "Do you still have it?"

She dug through her bag until she found the small piece of glass with the torch on it and handed it to her uncle. Holding his breath as he stared at what he assumed was an image of Timothy standing before his congregation at Ephesus, he pressed the tile into the empty space. The torch fit perfectly in Timothy's hand, and going on pure instinct, Alexander pressed it into the wall like a button. Instantly, a heavy rumbling and shaking of the wall had all three scrambling backwards. Rocks shifted and dust and dirt fell over them as the mosaic slid back into the wall and with a horribly loud grinding sound, moved toward the right, disappearing into the other wall.

When the rumbling stopped, Alexander waved the dust from his face, coughing as he squinted into what appeared to be a secret room. Torch light to guide them, they slowly stepped inside to find a much smaller room with a four-foot high marble slab standing in the center. There was Greek writing on it and as Alexander whispered the words to himself, translating it, Drew walked around the perimeter of the room, lighting the ancient torches that lined it.

"This talks about Timotheus, or Timothy, and Stephanus," Alexander explained after he translated the first section. "How they smuggled the scrolls out of Paul's prison cell during the Great Fire of Rome."

"Timothy was one of them? Wow!" Kaci exclaimed.

"The other name, Stephanus, sounds familiar" Drew said as he lit another torch. "Isn't he mentioned in the New Testament?"

"Yeah, I remember," Kaci chimed in. "He was that guy addicted to the ministry or something."

"Correct. And throughout history, many theorized that Stephanus was actually the Philippian jailor." Kaci and Drew exchanged surprised glances as Alexander turned back to the slab. "It seems Timotheus was able to safely get the scrolls out of Rome due to the brave sacrifice made by Stephanus. He gave his life that night, letting Timotheus escape with the scrolls intact and safe, to be preserved throughout time." His fingers slid farther down and he paused. "These scrolls are copies of the originals by the author's own hand!"

Drew was still walking around the room when he neared the back wall to light the final torch. Paintings covered the wall, depicting scenes he assumed were from Timothy's life, but it was the final image on the wall that had him curious. Brushing his hand over it, he squinted at it then turned back around to the slab his uncle translated the story from. An iron lever protruded out of the back of the slab and Drew curiously reached out to pull it. With a hard tug, it gave way and three stones on the floor rose up, each with an opening in their center.

"Drew! What did you do?" Kaci rushed around the other side with Alexander close behind. As the pedestals finished ascending, she gasped when she saw what was inside the openings of each of the 4-foot-high pillars. "Are those...are those the scrolls?"

Alexander crept closer and read over the words etched in Greek on each pedestal. "Names, they're names. Matthew, Luke, and Colossians. This is it." He bent closer and stared at the scroll within the pillar that read 'Colossians'. He reached in and ever so carefully, picked the parchment up. A rush of exhilaration ran through him and he laughed in amazement.

He was holding a scroll that, at one time, Paul had possibly written on. Kaci took his torch so he could use both hands to gingerly open the scroll and lay it across the pedestal. Then he pulled out his Bible, with the Greek/English passages, and compared what was on the scroll to what he held in his hands.

"Well?" Drew asked anxiously. "Do they match?"

Alexander sighed with relief and grinned widely. "Unbelievable. They're a perfect match! We found them!!" Drew jumped with excitement and raised his hands in the air, giving God the glory.

In the midst of their rejoicing, Kaci, who was closest to the doorway, heard something bounce along the stone floor into their room. She began to cough as smoke poured out of a canister. With one hand she attempted to motion to her uncle and brother of the danger while trying to cover her nose and mouth with the other, but it was too late. The smoke filled her lungs and made her dizzy. She sank to her knees as her vision blurred. Alexander and Drew called out to her, but they soon began coughing harshly as they collapsed beside her. The last thing she saw were silhouettes of cloaked men standing in the doorway, breathing masks over their faces. Then her world went dark.

◊ ◊ ◊

When the smoke cleared, the men removed their masks and stepped into the inner chamber.

"Get them to Kadir and bring the scrolls. Don't leave anything behind." The man watched as the professor and the teenagers were dragged out of the chamber and taken back up to the surface, where a storm was brewing. Thunder rumbled as the man grinned and admired his handiwork. He would be well rewarded for his efforts now that the troublemakers could finally be brought to justice.

"To think we were so close to it this entire time," another man mentioned. "Strange coincidence."

"No coincidence," he argued. "It is our beloved goddess at work. Hurry, Kadir is impatient."

Later, they would come back and destroy this place. For now, their priority was to get Kadir what he needed so they could put this matter behind them – once and for all.

CHAPTER XV

Alexander's head throbbed, and he heard unrecognizable voices all around him. His arms were bound and something hard pressed against his back, rounded like a column. Light flickered around him, torches? Candles, maybe. He couldn't focus well enough to tell. He had to cough, but didn't want to make a sound and alert anyone near him that he had awakened.

Keeping his eyes squinted shut, he stared around the room. His vision slowly began to clear. An altar of some sort sat before him and beyond that, a throne with a man seated on it. Two more robed men flanked the throne as others spread out in a circle around the room. It was strangely shaped, though, and the men's voices echoed off the stone. There was a chill to the air that made him feel as if they were underground, but this was definitely not the tomb of Timothy. They'd been taken somewhere else and his heart sank as he realized where. Along the walls were head busts raised on pedestals. Some Alexander recognized and it made his blood run cold to see the faces of Nero, Hitler, Westcott, and Hort. There were more, but he would have to fully open his eyes to see them clearly.

He fiddled with what bound his wrists – it felt like rope – tugging to see how loose it was. Not loose enough to pull free.

He turned his head to see Drew tied to a column to his right and Kaci tied to one on his left.

"Ah, you're awake."

Alexander gave up his act and opened his eyes, straightening as tall as he could with his arms bound the way they were. The man who sat on the throne stood, his hood thrown back to reveal the symbol of Diana tattooed on his skull. "Where are we?" the professor demanded.

"I am Kadir and you are in my home, but I'm afraid you aren't guests."

The men that had been moving around came to a stop, encircling the giant stone slab that Alexander quickly realized was raised and only attached by the walkways behind him.

"You had to make things difficult, Professor," Kadir shook his head, looking down at Alexander as if he were scolding a naughty child. "Now look where you are and with your family being dragged down with you. For shame." He clicked his tongue as he walked closer. The robed men sank to their knees and an eerie chant started, flowing out of their mouths, a deep sound that reverberated around the room and made Alexander's ears itch.

"You could have left us alone," Alexander said.

"Why, in the name of the Goddess, would I do that? You found the scrolls for me." He waved his arm backward and Alexander sagged against his bonds. There on the altar lay the scrolls, carelessly heaped in a pile. "Now, thanks to you, no one will ever know these even existed."

"Uncle James?" Drew whispered beside him. "What's...what's going on? Kaci? Where's Kaci!"

"She's here," Kadir said and approached the still-unconscious Kaci, softly placing his fingers upon her chin. "I'm afraid she has not yet awakened."

"Don't you dare touch her!" Drew snarled, struggling. "Kaci! Come on, Kaci, wake up!"

As Drew continued to yell, Kadir stomped over to him and smacked him hard across the face, causing the boy to quiet down instantly.

"Stop! He's just a boy! Leave him alone" Alexander bellowed, pulling harder at the ropes, but it was Kaci's voice that made Drew finally calm down.

"Drew?"

"Kaci! I'm right here! It's...it's gonna be okay."

Kadir smirked darkly. "Good, I'm glad you're all conscious so we can finally begin."

"Begin what?" Alexander seethed, though he had a feeling he really didn't want to know.

Kadir stopped in front of him and his grin darkened even more. "The burning ceremony, of course." He turned his back on them and raised his arms high. "We are the Demeons, worshippers of the great goddess Diana, followers of her prophet and our leader from ancient times, Demetrius!"

The chanting grew louder and the men stood as Kadir stalked toward the altar.

"You won't get away with this! We *will* stop you!" Alexander yelled.

Kadir whipped around glaring at them. "Silence, you insolent fools! There is nothing you can do now. You are powerless. We are the Demeons—"

"I think you mean *demons*," Drew said with a loud laugh. "You know, the ugly guys with the big horns and no brains whatsoever? Yeah, that's what I think you mean."

Kaci snickered along with her brother as Alexander tugged at the ropes again.

"Oh you simple-minded children. You know not of what you speak. Our name is based upon the ever-holy Demetrius. He was one of three silversmiths that spread our Diana's fame across the lands. And we will live on for centuries to come! Long live Diana!"

The chant was taken up by all men present, the sound sending shivers down the three prisoners' spines. The chanting fell deeper and the men swayed as if they were in a trance as Kadir circled the altar. Alexander had never felt more powerless as he realized that any second, this pawn of Satan would light those scrolls on fire. He had to stop him. There had to be way to end this!

"Demetrius," Alexander mused aloud in a conversational tone, causing Kadir to sharply look toward the professor, "I remember reading about him in the Bible."

"You will NOT speak of that vile book here in our holy sanctuary!" Kadir screamed, spitting in his face.

"Excuse you," Alexander chuckled as he shook his head in attempts to get the spittle off his cheek. "I was just trying to connect the dots for my niece and nephew here who were wondering who you all were." Looking toward the teenagers and completely ignoring Kadir who hovered above him, he nonchalantly related, "Paul was a sort of nemesis of Demetrius. As a result of the evangelistic crusade that took place in Ephesus on one of the Apostle's missionary journeys, the city was in an uproar. People were getting saved, lives were being changed, and the church was grow—*Oomph!*"

Kadir clobbered the professor hard in the gut with his ring-studded hand.

"Yes," he hissed. "Paul ultimately ruined everything! And how fitting that we will destroy *his* most cherished parchments!" He erupted for a moment with a sinister laugh that blended in with the repetitious chant of his men, and then suddenly changed his composure to an air of tranquility, "We will destroy his parchments upon the very altar that was used to sacrifice to the goddess Diana."

He strolled around to the front of the ominous marble platform and rested his hands in reverence upon it. "We were not always called 'Demeons,' but we were first known as 'Dianites,' a peaceful sect of believers who provided life, wealth, and pleasure to all people. For you see, the worship of Diana was the foremost religion in the world until the rise of Jesus Christ. We had control of the minds and hearts of every race. They were ours, and you…your people stole them away from us!" He slammed his palms on the altar. "The hearts of the emperors were within the palms of our hands! We had control of the world."

He spun around as he spoke, his arms encompassing the room and the historical figures that surrounded them, their glaring eyes all aimed at the altar.

"And then *Jesus* was born. Christianity spread like wildfire," he spat furiously. "But especially Paul…he was converting everyone everywhere across the most vital parts of our domain. He even had the audacity to start a church *here* in Ephesus where the temple of Diana stood as one of the seven wonders of the ancient world!

"Demetrius understood that our ceremonial priests had to do everything in their power to preserve the legacy and continue the worship of our great Goddess." Kadir viciously continued with a wild look in his eye, "Even if it meant to begin to *kill*. We subtly influenced the Roman world to start slaughtering your men, women, and children. Nero was already one of our followers and he was easy to sway. The great fire of Rome was started by our very own to turn his heart against those heathen God-followers and to begin the global mass slaughter of the thousands of blinded worshippers of the 'Messiah,'" he said using air quotes as he mocked Christianity in his rant.

With a sacred calm, he declared, "And from that day, the *'Demeons'* were born, forged by blood and fire, and we will never rest until all the church is extinguished!"

Kaci and Drew now tugged and pulled at their bonds, but the ropes held fast. There was no easy way to get out of this mess. To their horror, Kadir turned around to face the altar again and with a wave of his hand, a circle of flames burst to life along the perimeter. Kaci blinked, wondering how he'd been able to do that. A trick, it had to be a trick.

"He's going to burn them!" Drew yelled and thrashed even harder, but it was no use.

Alexander wasn't ready to give up and closed his eyes to pray, letting his faith guide him and show him the way to get out of this mess. "Greater is He that is in us than he that is in the world," Alexander whispered to himself. His faith lifted his spirits once again and he began to stare down the mad man before him.

"Praying will not save you, Professor, not this time."

"We shall see," Alexander replied.

"Look around you! No help is coming. We hold the power, the true power and we will never stop in our war until all of Christianity is eliminated. And..." he paused for dramatic effect, "we are everywhere," he whispered as he marched toward Alexander. "We are in the Catholic church and the governments of the world powers. We are imbedded within every culture. I'm sure you are well-familiar with the Inquisition during the Dark Ages and the Holocaust with Hitler?" He bowed mockingly, "That was all us."

"But you haven't destroyed anything," Kaci argued. "Christianity is still alive and well."

He glared at her, but she held his gaze just as strongly. "It is true," Kadir replied reluctantly, "the Protestant Reformation, the Renaissance, the birth of America, and the rise of the free world crushed our intentions of being able to carry on our persecution of the church. So," he said brightly as if they discussed the weather, "instead of killing Christians, we found that deceiving them worked better. Perverting their minds would eventually render them useless. Less work for us. Less…messy," he said, dusting off his hands and cringing.

The robed men in the circle began to walk around the edge of the huge platform, which appeared to drop off into pure blackness. They moved a few steps further before stopping, chanting and bowing their heads and waiting a moment before, in perfect unison, they moved again. All the while, the flames at the edge of the altar in the center of the platform crept closer to the scrolls, threatening to destroy them. Alexander tried to reach into his pocket, feeling for a knife or anything else that might help, when one of the robed men passing by him tilted his head enough for him to see beneath the hood.

Faith rewarded indeed, Alexander thought and hid a smile as he recognized the familiar face.

"Infiltrating Christianity with inaccurately-translated works became our new strategy to bring down the believers," Kadir went on, not noticing Alexander's brief glance with the robed man. He was too busy staring in reverence at two statues on the far side of the room. "Ah! Two men with such brilliant minds who wove so much destruction." He clasped his hands together and laughed fiendishly.

Kaci frowned. "You've got to be kidding me! Westcott and Hort?"

Kadir turned around with a curious grin that would have seemed friendly if not for the malicious glint in his eyes. "Oh, so you know of them. They were two of our greatest priests! Their work heralded in a new age of corruption for us, tainting Bibles for decades to come!" He glanced at the parchments on the altar and his face darkened. "If these original scrolls were ever made public, all our forefathers' work and sacrifice would be for naught. They would be labeled as frauds and I fear we would lose millions of people that have already been successfully blinded."

"Such a pity," Drew snapped, but Kadir ignored the jibe.

Alexander had kept his eye on the one familiar robed man as they continued moving worshipfully around the perimeter of the stone platform. Suddenly, and noticed only by the professor, the man slipped out of the circle and hid behind the column nearest Kaci. Alexander wanted to keep his eyes on him, but the flames on the altar suddenly sparked larger as if life was breathed into them. Kadir grinned, admiring his work.

"Soon, these scrolls will burn and the truth will forever burn with them. As will the three of you, '*truth seekers*,'" he spat. "I cannot allow you to run off and give away our secrets."

Kaci flinched when she suddenly noticed a robed man crouching down behind her out of the corner of her eye. She almost screamed, but then she felt movement on the ropes tying her wrists together and realized with astonishment that the man was cutting through them in an attempt to set her free! "I am sorry, my friend," a familiar voice whispered and, though she couldn't place the voice, she subtly bobbed her head in thanks, not moving her arms yet as the man slipped behind Alexander. Kadir was facing the altar still and thankfully, hadn't noticed anything amiss. But they knew time was very short; they had to stop those flames from spreading.

Alexander was cut free next. The second Drew's wrists were unbound, Alexander made eye contact with his niece and nephew, giving them a slight nod, and with one final prayer for help, he leaped up behind Kadir and tapped him on the shoulder.

"Funny thing about truth..." The man turned around confused to see Alexander standing before him with a wry smile. Before he could react, Alexander decked him. "Ye shall know the truth..." he punched again, "and the truth..." another punch, "shall make you free!" With all his strength, he dealt a final blow that sent the robed man flying back into the front of the altar.

"Stop him!" Kadir dizzily bellowed from the ground as the men stopped their chanting to go after Alexander.

"Kids! Get the scrolls!" the professor yelled as he was joined by the man who had helped cut them free. "Santiago...how can I ever repay you?"

"No time to discuss it now, my friend!" the Spaniard replied as he dealt blow after blow to the robed men coming toward them. Alexander kicked out hard and sent two of the men flying back toward the altar. Their arms flailed and the sleeves of their robes caught fire. Yelling in panic, they beat at their arms and legs, but forgot to pay attention to their surroundings. Their screams echoed as they tumbled over the edge of the elevated platform and down into the dark abyss beneath.

Kadir pulled a knife from his sleeve and pushed to his feet, glaring at Alexander. "You will pay for this! By the Goddess, you will not make it out of here alive!"

As Alexander stared down the crazy man with the knife, Kaci and Drew dodged the robed men, tripping up as many as they could on their way to the altar to save the scrolls. They were almost there when a man grabbed Drew around the neck and tried to strangle him. Just as Drew was starting to see stars, Kaci leapt on the man's back and he let go, allowing Drew to punch him hard in the gut. Kaci jumped off his back and together, they sent him somersaulting backwards with a hard kick. The two albinos who hadn't moved away from the throne yet stepped toward the edge of the dais, their arms raised high, and their eyes rolled back into their sockets.

"What are they doing?" Drew asked.

Rough words slipped from their lips and Kaci felt like the temperature in the room dropped as a gust of cold wind rushed past them and hit the altar, sending the flames shooting into the air as they took on a life of their own.

"No! We have to stop them!" Kaci yelled and without waiting for her brother, she took off to tackle both men to the floor. All she managed to accomplish, however, was to knock one into the other, as both were almost two feet taller than her.

"Child, you understand not what you do," they said in eerie unison as they loomed over her as if they were floating. "Soon, you will."

Kaci fell backwards as she tried to quickly scoot away from their pasty gnarly long fingers reaching closer and closer to her throat. Drew caught her gaze, and realized she wasn't really backing away out of fear, but to draw them away from the altar. The albinos were solely focused on Kaci, which gave Drew a chance to rescue the scrolls before they were burned and lost forever. He tore down a tapestry hanging from a brass pole and tried to put out the flames, but they wouldn't die. It was as if something was keeping them alive.

Or someone.

As he battled the flames, Kaci scrambled to her feet and found herself trapped between the albinos and the wall. They grinned at her with abnormally wide smiles and reached out again when her gaze shot over their shoulders and they paused. Then, as one, they turned and snarled in a strange tongue when they saw Drew batting out the fire. He nearly had it out, but the men's arms rose again and the chant brought it roaring back to life. Drew yelped as the flames clawed at him, but his cry wasn't the only one rippling across the walls of the cavern.

Alexander grunted as Kadir landed a kick to his chest and he flew backwards into one of the columns. The raging man charged at him with his knife, but Alexander ducked and the blade struck marble instead. He punched Kadir in the gut and ducked under his arm, trying to get back to the altar where Drew was fighting the flames and Santiago was decking any blue-robed man that came too close.

As he ran toward his nephew, suddenly Kadir's arm wrapped around his neck and yanked him back. They tussled on the ground before winding up with Kadir over Alexander, attempting to push the knife into his chest. Alexander held his wrists, using all his strength to try to hold him off. He sucked in a breath as the man cackled over him, pushing down even harder in an effort to end his life once and for all.

While Alexander battled with Kadir's blade, Kaci glanced around for anything she could use as a weapon as the flames leapt out and, almost as if they were alive, tried to lick Drew. She had to stop the tall robed men's chanting, but she couldn't just tackle them. Then it dawned on her. She had to knock them out. Her eyes landed on the bust of one of the men Kadir idolized. She hefted it into her arms, struggling not to drop it on her feet as chaos ensued around her. With a yell, she slammed it into the back of one of the men and he gasped as he collapsed to the floor.

She dropped the marble head, unable to keep holding it up, but the other man was still chanting. The bust crashed to the floor and she clasped her fists together to whack the other man in hopes of distracting him, if only for a few seconds.

But the albino didn't even budge and Kaci didn't bother trying to hit him again. Instead, she rushed to help Drew and Santiago before the scrolls caught fire.

"You're going to die," Kadir snarled in Alexander's face as the knife moved toward his chest again. "Right here, you and your family!"

"I think it's you who's going to die," Santiago yelled and thrust his fist into the air.

For a moment, Alexander wanted to yell at his friend to maybe come help get the knife away from Kadir, but then he heard a click and explosions sounded far below them, shooting up toward the platform and the walkways leading back to the stairs. Rocks crumbled from the ceiling and walls sending robed men fleeing for their lives, leaving Kadir all alone with the one albino still chanting away.

"No," Kadir cried in horrified confusion. "*NO!* What have you done?!?"

Alexander didn't waste time, but threw the man off him, kicking the knife out of his hand and sending it skittering over the edge and into the darkness below.

The second albino was thrown off balance when another explosion erupted beneath them, shattering two of the walkways from the platform. The ground shifted, causing the unconscious man to slide right off the edge and into the abyss as the other stared down in horror. Suddenly a large boulder fell loose from the ceiling and came crashing down on the second albino, knocking him, screaming, into the darkness along with his cohort.

Drew and Kaci fought to keep their balance as the flames finally died out on the altar and they grabbed the scrolls, pushing them into Kaci's bag as delicately yet quickly as they could.

Alexander wobbled and grabbed hold of the center column as he watched the two outer walkways fall away. "You had to go with explosives?" he asked Santiago.

"I had very little time to plan this," his friend yelled back. "You know how it goes!"

"Kids! Hurry up!" Alexander urged, holding out his arm for Kaci and Drew as they gingerly tiptoed toward their uncle. There were only two more pathways they could take in order to escape. With the way things were falling apart, the professor knew those stone walkways wouldn't last much longer. Kaci was almost within his reach when Kadir grabbed hold of her and threw her back. The bag with the scrolls inside nearly fell off her shoulder.

"No! You are not leaving here with those scrolls!" he bellowed, enraged. "Give them to me!"

"Kaci!" Drew yelled and grabbed for Kadir, trying to pry his hand off Kaci's arm. "Get off my sister!" He landed a kick to Kadir's face and the man let go with a groan of pain. Drew shoved his sister towards Santiago and safety, reaching for the knapsack that had fallen to the ground in the shuffle. Kadir, eyes like a laser on the scrolls, reached for Drew but didn't even have a chance to make contact before Alexander charged forward and decked Kadir in the face.

"Stay away from my family!" he yelled and turned to run after the kids, but another rumble of shifting stones beneath him sent him staggering toward the edge of the platform, its edges crumbling away, disappearing into the flames roaring beneath. His balance off, Alexander felt his body leaning toward the chasm as his arms flailed wildly. The rocks crumbled beneath his feet and in that split-second, his body suspended between life and death, all he could think about was how he'd failed. He'd failed God. He'd failed the mission. He'd failed Christianity. He'd failed his sister. And he'd failed those kids, who had never stopped trusting him, never stopped loving him. As he felt his body begin to fall, suddenly a big burly hand reached out and grabbed his shirt, pulling him back to safety. "Now you really owe me one!" Santiago laughed.

"I'll make it up to you, as soon as we save those scrolls!" He gave his friend a lop-sided grin as the cavern continued to collapse all around them. "Now let's get out of here!"

They were rushing toward the last two paths remaining, when stones from the ceiling fell free and landed on one of them, shattering it completely. Only one path remained now and Kaci led the way across, dodging falling stones and forcing her eyes straight ahead so she wouldn't think about how far down the drop truly was. More stones crashed onto the platform, shattering the throne and the statues, sending debris and dust everywhere, partially blinding them. The path was becoming less visible now, and as Drew brought up the rear, he felt the stones start to give way beneath his feet.

"Drew!" Kaci screamed, from the stairs at the end of the pathway, "Hurry!"

He could hear the rumble of the platform collapsing, pulling the pathway down with it. The stones became less stable with every second that passed. Out of nowhere, a yell sounded behind him and suddenly he was sliding down the collapsing stone path as Kadir tackled him, grabbing for the knapsack. The platform was lost in the flames below now, and the pathway had just minutes, if not seconds, left before it also crumbled completely. Drew, still in the grasp of Kadir, turned around and watched as the man's body threatened to slip off the edge. He was too busy trying to get the scrolls, a mad look on his face, to notice that they were in immediate danger of falling to their deaths.

"Give me the scrolls!" Kadir yelled, letting go of Drew and hanging onto just the bag.

"No! Let go or we'll both fall!" Drew tried to tug the bag free, but then the path gave way more and Kadir yelped as his body fell over the edge and the only thing holding him up was Drew. They both clung to the bag, but Drew began to feel his body slowly being pulled over the side from Kadir's sheer weight. Yet, he *knew* that he couldn't let go because if he did, they would lose the scrolls forever. Alexander had run back and began inching forward on the unstable ground, trying to reach him. "Drew, listen to me. Let go of the bag. Your life is worth far more than those scrolls." He spoke in an intensely hushed voice. Suddenly, more stones fell from the ceiling, breaking apart the pathway even more.

Drew yelled at him to stay back, "I can't, Uncle James. I won't give up, not after all we've been through!"

"You have no idea what forces you meddle with!" Kadir's eyes were wide with madness as he tugged harder at the bag, reaching up to grab Drew.

His uncle always told him to have faith and now, as he prayed, Drew felt that faith swell within him and fill him with what seemed to be an impossible strength, "Yeah, but *you* are no match for the power of God that is within *me*!" He bellowed as he gritted his teeth and pulled the bag up with all his might. Snap. The straps finally surrendered to the weight of the man holding onto them.

Kadir screamed as he plummeted into the flames of the abyss and Drew flew backwards, hitting the stones hard. He looked down in his arms. The bag. The scrolls were safe! He held them close and took a second to catch his breath before the others shouted for him to run. As he leapt to his feet and began to sprint toward them, a pile of stones suddenly dropped onto the end of the pathway, causing it to break apart right before the stairs. Drew never stopped running. When he was within a few feet, he took a flying leap as the rest of the path crumbled and collapsed behind him. Kaci covered her eyes with her hands, certain her brother could never jump that far and would surely fall to the depths below. She heard a grunt and peered through her fingers to see her uncle catch hold of Drew, dragging him to safety. She hugged her brother tightly.

"I love you, too, sis!" he grinned.

"Uh, guys, we're about to be buried alive here. Can we share hugs later?" their uncle nervously chuckled, as he pulled them down the stairs and away from danger.

Together, the group sprinted their way through the Demeons lair and up toward the surface.

They didn't pass any other men on their way out. *All of the guards here must have been at the ceremony,* Alexander's mind raced. Praying that the path they were on would lead them outside to safety, they pressed onward until they reached a door. Dust was beginning to fill the passageway quickly, along with thick smoke. Santiago snatched a torch from a sconce and held it high to illuminate the arched exit.

"On the count of three!" Alexander wheezed. *We've got to get out of here fast.* All of them were now coughing uncontrollably from the fumes and their strength was slipping away. He and Drew threw their shoulders against the hard wooden door twice, but nothing budged. Santiago dropped his torch, its sparks skidding across the ground, and barreled into the door as the other two gave one last push. It shredded on impact, and they spilled out onto a grassy slope, the night sky overhead filled with thousands of stars.

Collapsing on the grass, the group panted and grinned at each other in disbelief. They'd made it out, they'd defeated the leader of the Demeons, and they had the scrolls. It was a miracle!

Alexander rolled to his back and tilted his head as he stared up at the temple ruins. "You've got to be kidding me. Seriously? This whole time?" His laugh started slow at first and then grew into hysterics.

Kaci and Drew frowned, but Santiago burst out laughing with him, slapping his thigh and elbowing Alexander when he managed to sit upright. "Uh, what's so funny?" Drew asked.

"The ruins," Alexander gasped between bouts of laughter. "The Demeons were under the temple of Diana the whole time. And Timothy's tomb was right under their noses for centuries! But they never found it!"

Kaci grinned as she finally recognized the surrounding hillsides and the six sentinels standing tall in the distance, waving in the soft breeze as if they were greeting her. Drew joined her and put his arm around her shoulder. They let the cool night air rush over them, thanking God for getting them out of there safely and with one of the greatest treasures ever found in hand.

EPILOGUE

Kaci thanked Simmons for the hot chocolate as they sat in the comforts of Alexander's home once again. Drew sat beside her on the couch while their uncle and Simmons occupied the winged chairs in the study. Simmons was shaking his head, muttering under his breath about how crazy they were for risking their lives so.

"Extraordinary! But you all could have died. Numerous times!" he scolded them with a wry smile. "You *do* understand that, yes?"

"But we didn't and that's something to be proud of," Alexander replied and his assistant rolled his eyes.

"You are a horrible influence on these two youngsters, sir!" Simmons slapped the professor on the back. "But I suppose it is inevitable. Thrill-seeking runs in the Alexander blood."

"Believe it or not, these two *youngsters* saved my life more than once on this adventure. They took more risks than I did." He scooted closer and held out his mug in a toast. "To our family and our exciting lives."

"To having faith," Drew added and held his mug up to Alexander's.

"And to being back home safe and sound," Kaci added. Simmons added his mug and they grinned before taking long sips of the rich drink. "Uncle James? Santiago's back with his family, right? They're all safe? He took off so fast once we got back to the city, I didn't get a chance to ask him."

"Yes, he called this morning to let me know he and his family are back in Spain, safe. He wanted me to extend to both of you again his warmest expressions of gratitude for your forgiveness and understanding spirit." Alexander rubbed his stubbled jaw. "The poor man was in quite a predicament. I'm just glad he made the right decision in the end!"

"We'd all be dead if it weren't for him," Drew reminded them.

"It seems he had a choice. Be sent to prison and have no chance of helping us defeat the Demeons, or pretend to join them and hope that one day, his moment of escape would come."

"Boy, am I glad he chose to join them!" Kaci sighed in relief and Drew shared the sentiment.

Alexander stood and paced toward his desk where the ancient scrolls rested, waiting for tomorrow when they would be picked up and taken by the archaeology department. He wanted to study them further, but after spending so many hours tracking them down, he didn't want to tempt fate by keeping them any longer. They might have defeated the Demeons for now, but Kadir said it himself, there were many more out there.

"Did you have a chance to study them last night?" Simmons asked as he and the kids joined Alexander at the desk.

"For a few hours until I fell asleep. They are indeed first century manuscripts of the Holy Scriptures," he said in awe with a lop-sided grin. "They're an exact match, proving once and for all that the *Textus Receptus* is the correct Greek New Testament."

"Splendid, sir!" Simmons rejoiced.

"Wow," Drew mumbled with hushed excitement. "That's incredible."

Alexander nodded as he removed his glasses to clean them with his handkerchief. "It is. To God be the glory! This is going to change history *forever*."

He held his glasses up to the vintage light fixture hanging from the ceiling to check if he had wiped all the smudges. "It proves that all the modern English translations, such as the New King James Version, RSV, NIV, and ESV are all flawed." He paused for emphasis, taking that moment to put back on his glasses. "They are *not* the inerrant Word of God."

Drew shook his head, not believing how for so many years devious men had managed to taint God's precious Word for their own gain, deceiving millions and knowing full well the damage they inflicted. "I thought I treasured my Bible before, but after this, I think I'm going to read it in a whole new light for the rest of my life."

Alexander chuckled suddenly and the kids eyed him with curious glances. "I forgot, I received an e-mail from your mum this morning wondering how the trip was going. She wanted to know if you two were driving me insane yet."

Kaci and Drew exchanged a cringe, the color gone from their cheeks. "Do we tell her about everything?"

"You'll have to decide that between yourselves," the professor suggested, crossing his arms. "But I think for the moment you two have earned some genuine vacation time along with a dip in that pool! You can call your mum later; it's terribly late there anyway."

Kaci squealed joyfully and raced her brother out of the room to change and jump into the pool they had wanted to swim in for days. Simmons loudly and emphatically cleared his throat as they reached the doorway, causing both of them to turn their heads, eyes wide with youthful excitement.

"Your belongings have safely returned from Mama Selina's; you will find everything in order and laid out within your quarters. Be *careful* as you carry on."

In a mad dash, they were gone and Alexander laughed as he heard them running up the steps. Seconds later, they called him to the foyer, both grinning down at him from the railing. They might be teenagers, but to him they looked like little kids, eyes bright and ready for their next adventure.

"Afterwards, can we go get some more fish and chips?" Kaci asked as Drew nodded enthusiastically beside her.

"Most definitely, my little monsters," he said with a grin. "Most definitely."

A NOTE FROM THE AUTHORS

We pray you have enjoyed reading this book as much as we enjoyed writing it – our very first work of fiction. While the majority of characters and storyline is completely fictional, we wanted to make it clear that some aspects of this story are, in fact, very true.

While the Demeons and Kadir were birthed out of our imaginations, men like Westcott and Hort truly lived and were indeed a detriment to the translation of the Word of God. All the explanations Alexander gave Kaci and Drew about the inspiration, preservation and translation of the King James Version of the Bible have been researched fully and are proven documented findings.

If you would like to study this topic further, you may be interested in reading Caleb's book, Our Blessed Book, *which can be found on our website: **www.remnantministriesonline.com**.*

ABOUT THE AUTHORS

Caleb Garraway was born into a Christian home on July 20, 1986, and was born into the family of God on November 9, 1994. At the age of 11, he was called to preach through the preaching of Dr. Jack Hyles at Pastor's School in Hammond, IN. When he was 16, God called him to enter the field of evangelism. While attending Oklahoma Baptist College, Caleb traveled with the men's singing group for four years and also worked at the Windsor Hills Baptist Church for two years. He entered full-time evangelism in the beginning of 2009.

Katie was born on November 9, 1985, and was blessed to be able to grow up in a Christian home as a Pastor's daughter. She accepted the Lord as her Savior in 1991 and surrendered her life to the Lord's work in 1997. Through the years, God has allowed Katie to use her musical gifts in the local church as pianist, singer, children's choir director, and teacher. She has written many songs and arranged many hymns and hopes to continue this much needed ministry as the Lord allows.

Caleb and Katie were married on March 20, 2010. They traveled out of Oklahoma City until God providentially led them to Marion Avenue Baptist Church of Washington, Iowa, in May 2012. After much prayer with Pastor Joseph Brown, Caleb launched *Remnant Ministries*, a God-and-Country ministry with a strong three-fold thrust: Redemption to the lost, Revival to the church, and Restoration to the country. To God be the glory, thousands have been saved, and many have been reignited with a sacred fire to rise up and serve God while there is still time.

Caleb and Katie have written a number of other books including: *A Biblical Approach to Music, America: A Journey of Faith & Freedom, Baptists and the American Revolution, Found Fully Faithful, Her Knight in Shining Armor, Let God Write Your Love Story, Men on Fire, Modesty: An Issue of the Heart, Not I But Christ,* and *Our Blessed Book* – a practical study on the inspiration, preservation, and translation of Scripture into the English language.

The Garraways have been blessed with three children, David, Jonathan, and Alyssa.

For questions, comments, or additional copies of this book, please contact us:

✉	**WRITE**	Remnant Ministries c/o Caleb Garraway 215 S. Marion Avenue Washington, IA 52353
☎	**CALL**	917.412.0059
⌨	**EMAIL**	remnantministriesonline@gmail.com
🖱	**GO ONLINE**	www.remnantministriesonline.com